WALK
BETWEEN
WORLDS

Samara Breger

Ann Arbor
2021

Bywater Books

Copyright © 2021 Samara Breger

Bywater Books First Edition: August 2021

Print ISBN: 978-1-61294-225-4

Cover Design by TreeHouse Studio

Bywater Books
PO Box 3671
Ann Arbor MI 48106-3671
www.bywaterbooks.com

This novel is a work of fiction. Names, characters, places, and incidents are the product of the author's imagination.

Printed in the United States of America.

For Kelsey

West, west, west to the ocean
Onward to the sea
The steps we take, so in our wake
Our subjects can live free
A strong and watched o'er people
Under our banner high
West, west, west to the ocean
Further, to the sky

Chapter One

When Scratch had envisioned this day, she hadn't anticipated that her pants would be so tight.

"Would you stop fidgeting?" James poked her with the back of his fork. "You look gassy."

"I'm not gassy. It's the pants."

He scrunched his forehead, his robust eyebrows merging into one dense hedge. "The pants are gassy?"

She frowned at him. "I know what you're doing."

"What am I doing?" he asked, blinking his wide green eyes with an air of well-practiced innocence.

"Trying to make me less nervous."

"Is it working?"

"No."

Beneath the uncompromising waistband of the damned pants, her stomach churned. Her skin itched, hidden under three layers of military pomp. Around her, the sounds of feasting and revelry blurred to an unfocused din, like the hum of some monstrously large, drunk bumblebee. The banquet hall was massive, with its tall beams, vast tapestries, and wrought-iron torches casting shifting shadows against the ancient stone walls. Still, it seemed too full, too many soldiers packing the place with their ale-soaked cheers and slurred song. On a metal plate before her, a chunk of ham and a few wedges of potato sweat uninvitingly. She hadn't taken a bite.

"Eat something," James urged, apparently reading her mind. "You look ill."

"Maybe I *am* ill."

"You aren't ill."

"Maybe I'm dying."

"Scratch, darling." He set a comforting hand on her shoulder. "We're all dying."

She diligently cut herself a square of ham, chewing it for what felt an appropriate length of time, and swallowed it down, choking. It tasted like dirt.

"Feel better?"

"Oh yes, Jamie." She chased the ham with a rictus grin. "Splendid."

"Come on now." He smiled, flashing a retaining wall of perfectly white teeth. "It's your special day, My Lady."

So it was, though very little felt special about it. She and James sat at their usual table, eating the usual fare, to the familiar off-key tune of the same-as-always minstrels. On the dais just ahead, the king and his court dined before a backdrop of stained-glass gods, reflective effigies flickering in the torchlight. The king was shouting, his face cheerful and ruddy with drink. His crown listed dangerously over his mane of yellowy-white hair, nearly the same shade as Scratch's own.

Come on, she thought in his general direction. *Do it now.*

Predictably, the man did nothing.

A drunken band of foot soldiers strolled by, bumping into her back, bonking her ribs against the table.

"Evening, Bowstring!" they slurred in slippery chorus.

"Evening, boys," James replied, lifting his tankard to them. "Stay upright, yeah? Long night ahead."

Scratch scowled, watching them go. "Pleased, Bowstring?"

"Oh, immeasurably." He licked a droplet of amber from his weak attempt of a mustache. The God of Hair had wasted all the good strands on his eyebrows. "A good nickname, Scratch, is a story of its own. It's a ballad."

"It's a word."

"Two, you'll find." He wriggled his nose. "Or a compound word, at least."

"It's cheating. You gave it to yourself."

"Did I?" He arched an eyebrow. "Or did Burnfen think of it on his own?"

"No, you did. Remember, darling, we were out at the pub—"

"Thank you, Scratch. If you could lower your voice a touch, that would be lovely; there's a dear."

"And you said to Burnfen—after several pints of course, 'I do love your new name for me.' To which he replied, 'What name's that?' And you said—"

"Scratch, I will poke your eyes out I swear to the God of Threats."

"'Bowstring, of course, because I'm tall and lean and I can use a—'"

"If you're picking on me to assuage your nerves, it's very mean and small," he sniffed, pointedly shifting away. "Go ahead, then. Be nervous. Big night for you. Are you really sure about those pants?"

That popped her bubble. She speared a potato, squeezing her fork so hard the blue veins on the back of her hand popped out. "*Lake veins,*" her mother had called them. *The water of the Tangled Lakes flows through you.* Purpose Keyes had been wrong, of course: Scratch was filled with blood, just like everyone else. Blood and bone and viscera, all turning to sausage within the casing of these ridiculous pants. If she hadn't been wearing undergarments, they would likely have made their way up to her throat by now.

"At least someone else looks as miserable as you do right now."

Scratch lifted her head. "Hmm?"

James jerked his thumb towards the dais. Beside the king, the princess poked forlornly at her meal, nodding diligently as the king's wizard whispered in her ear, his long, oily hair trailing on the wooden table.

Scratch shivered. "I'd be miserable too if I had to sit next to Gorn."

"Nah. She likes Gorn."

"She likes *Gorn*?"

He nodded. "Ferrin is guarding her now. He says she likes Gorn."

"Which Ferrin?"

"Ginger Ferrin."

She scoffed. "Gossip."

"Sure," he conceded. "But an honest gossip."

"Oh yes, a model gossip."

"The gods' own gossip. Anyway, Ginger Ferrin says the princess likes Gorn and hates Levon."

Levon. Scratch spared a glance for the King's Hand as he sucked on a bit of hambone, his craggy lips glistening with pork fat and the sticky remnants of ale. Heavy rings loaded his thick hands, the largest sitting atop his pinky like a silvery fortress.

"Well, if given a choice between the two . . ."

"And, if you please," James leaned in close, batting his overlarge eyelashes, "Ginger Ferrin says the princess has a lover."

"What?" Scratch yelped, causing a few heads to turn their way. She grinned tightly back at them until her audience was properly convinced there was nothing to see. "How? She's more protected than a holy relic."

"She's had nearly eighteen years to figure out how to lose the guards, Scratch. What did you think she was doing all that time? Needlepoint?"

Luckily she was spared having to admit that, yes, needlepoint sounded about right, by the scrape of a chair on flagstone commanding their attention. The king rose.

"Oh shit, it's happening," she hissed. "James, shut up."

"I'm not saying any—"

"Shh. Shut up."

"People of Ivinscont." King Ingomar raised his arms. Under

4

the flames of torches, his crimson garments glowed like lizard eyes in moonlight. "Tonight, we celebrate victory!"

A hundred flagons slammed on wood tabletops, the racket nearly as loud as the pounding of Scratch's heartbeat in her own ears.

"Every inch of land we gain, our country grows stronger," he continued. "Our nation grows prouder. The colors of our flag become known far and wide as a symbol of unshakable might! Only five years ago, we were a small country. A modest country. And now, thanks to the valiant efforts of our armies, we have grown ever larger, ever stronger!"

Again, the flagons beat a rhythmless tattoo on the oak boards while a storm of voices shook the rafters with cheers. Scratch gave a halfhearted "Woo!" James gave a wholehearted "Fuck yeah!"

"And to whom do we owe this victory?"

Flagons, tables, cheers. Scratch trembled like a baby chick fallen from the hen house, peeping into the cold night. It was now. Around her waist, the pants tightened nearly unbearably, her stomach roiling underneath. Now. *Now.*

"To Lord High Commander Elwyn, of course!" King Ingomar grinned, cheeks turned to orbs of splotches and veins. He raised a meaty hand in acknowledgment of the Lord High Commander, who lifted a skeletal, shaking digit in return. "His planning is the reason that we have returned from the Western Wilds without any losses! His implementation of the great octagon, the clever maneuver that trapped the fighters in their own clearing, allowed for the most decisive victory in the history of our land. West, west, west to the ocean, Ivinscont! Further to the sky."

Her stomach sank. Okay. It hadn't been then. But there was still time. It wasn't over. Still, he could still say something . . .

"Thirty years ago, the Koravians tried to claim our lands. They burned up half our nation before we beat those brutes back. Well, look at us now, eh? Larger and greater than ever before. If the Koravians come again, we'll send them back weeping. Now, be merry. Long live Ivinscont!" the king declared, and sat.

The room fell silent.

No. It couldn't have, because there were the flagons, there were the tables, there were the open mouths wailing to the ceiling with jubilation. But Scratch couldn't hear a damned thing, save for a distant ringing and something that thrummed like a heartbeat, but too quick. Maybe a hummingbird's heart, tiny and faint and too fast, too *fast*.

She regretted that one bite of ham. It was now charting a speedy course back up her throat—with ice picks, by the feel of it. Her palms sweat and her cheeks burned and the pants, the fucking pants, gripped her so tightly she thought her eyes might pop out of her head.

"I have to get out of here."

James clamped his hand over hers, green eyes dark. "I know. I know, I'm sorry. But you can't leave so soon. People will know."

"I'm gonna—"

She was ready to say "be sick" but that wasn't it. It was terribly, horrifically worse.

She was going to cry.

She felt eyes on her like finger pads, peeling back her clothes to peek at the skin underneath. Everyone was looking, or else her imagination had run wild and nobody was looking and, gods, which was worse?

"Just a minute, Scratch," James murmured. He was so rarely gentle, but when he turned it on, the man could be a blanket. Somehow, that made it worse. "Just a few moments. It's all right. Just plaster on a happy face. You're fine. You're *fine*."

She wasn't fine, but that was hardly the point. The point was getting through the rest of this meal without bursting into flames. The point was her ten years of service, of good service, without a damned scrap of respect. The point was becoming a godsdamned knight.

"I'm leaving."

"Scratch, where are you—?"

But she wasn't listening anymore. She was barely seeing. She moved as if in a trance, boots slapping against stone floor as she burst from the hall and into the moonlit night. It was gentle weather, chilly and starlit late springtime, but it slapped her in the face like winter winds. She gasped, choking down the freshness, wishing away the soupy rage that clotted her throat.

She kept moving. She wasn't entirely aware of where her body was taking her, but when she finally arrived, she wasn't surprised. There was a corner of the palace grounds, a strip of garden between two hedges, that housed only a stone bench and a patch of weedy grass. A place the gardeners forgot, where a soldier could breathe, unnoticed and unbothered, for hours at a time. Few people knew of it—at least she assumed so because nobody ever bothered her here. Not in this little spot outside of time.

She stood rigid, waiting for the pain to pass. It didn't. Instead, it morphed, hot anger and wet shame melding into a many-toothed chimera, canines splitting her skin while molars ground her to pulp. She deserved the pain. She had known that there were no guarantees, that this disappointment was always a possibility. Hoping for anything different was entirely her own fault.

Hope wasn't one of her usual vices. It was bad strategy. When she planned, she did so with all possible outcomes in mind, none weighted more heavily than the next. It was a rule: prepare yourself for every eventuality and you will never be caught off guard. But today, as she had tied her hair back with meticulous care, rolling all possibilities in her callused palm like marbles, she couldn't help but notice that the shiniest path was also the likeliest. As long as the king knew that Scratch had orchestrated the octagon, she would leave the feast as Lady Commander.

She balled her fist and slammed it against her thigh. It hurt, and it felt like justice. Someone had to pay; who else could she blame?

She could blame James. "You rewrote the books," he had said. "This is history." She should have known better. James only read fiction.

"Odd place for a bench, isn't it?"

If she hadn't been a trained fighter, Scratch might have shrieked and launched herself in the air. Thank the gods for the Academy. Instead of wailing, she managed to turn slowly around, her deft hand coming to rest on her sheathed sword.

"Who's there?"

"Relax, Sergeant Major." A crimson-clad figure materialized from the dark, tall and slender, a wiry golden crown perched atop her head. "I'm peaceful."

Scratch dropped so quickly her knee made a divot in the earth. "Princess Frances. My apologies."

"Rise." The princess waved a lazy hand and plopped on the bench. "Join me."

Scratch peered toward the boundary of her little nook. No guards, just a princess walking the palace grounds alone at night. If someone found them here, they'd both be in trouble.

Frances tapped the bench. "Come sit. I'm having a smoke."

Scratch watched in stunned silence as the princess pulled out a pipe and a small hempen bag of pinkish flowers. Wait, if they were pink—

Frances held out the pipe. "You?"

"I, uh . . ." Reason dictated she say no. Aside from ale, it was forbidden for members of the King's Guard to alter themselves. Besides, it was the truth. Scratch never touched the stuff. She had the sudden urge to laugh. All of that tedious rule-following had been in service of becoming the best little soldier she could be. And what had that led to?

"Um, sure." She slithered from ground to bench (the waist-band of her pants wailing its disapproval) as Frances packed and lit the Roselap pipe. The orange flame flickered over the Princess's dark, wily eyes and piebald hair, streaked black and white, spilt ink on parchment. Maybe it was that Scratch had never been this close to the girl, or that she had only seen the composed image of "Princess," but, in this moment, she wondered why she had never realized how deeply Frances resembled a badger.

"Thanks." Scratch took the pipe—a slender, elegant thing—and inhaled. The smoke was sweet and earthy, and filled her lungs like sunshine. And then she coughed.

"Oh, shit." Frances took the pipe back. "That was a lot. Don't worry about the coughing; it'll pass."

Scratch managed a watery nod of thanks as she sputtered out her innards, sopping the leaky bits of her face with her handkerchief. This took a minute or so, as all the bits of her face had suddenly become leaky bits.

"That's better," the princess declared when Scratch was through. "How do you feel?"

"Uh." She stretched her fingers and toes. "Warm."

"That's the intended effect." Frances grinned through the curling smoke and took a drag. She didn't cough at all as she released a rosy plume into the night. "Strange to have a bench here, don't you think? Not much of a view."

"No, but the privacy is nice." She froze, the blood rushing to her face. "Not that I mind, I mean—"

"It's all right. I followed you here."

Her mouth went dry. She had heard this was a side effect of the Roselap, but this dry mouth felt organic. No, organic wasn't the word. What was it again? Oh, yes: *Panic.*

"You did?"

Frances nodded, lighting the pipe again and inhaling deeply. Thankfully, she didn't offer any more to Scratch.

"I hoped he'd give you a command, too."

Scratch didn't speak. She must have misunderstood, or maybe she hadn't heard clearly. Perhaps her desire was so desperate, so totally consuming, that she had unwittingly immersed herself in a hallucinogenic daze on the wings of one puff of Roselap.

Then again, if this were a pleasant hallucination, Scratch would probably have found herself in more comfortable pants.

The princess dumped out the burnt petals and hid the pipe away in the folds of her dress, a secret pocket just for pipes and drugs.

"I know you planned the octagon."

Scratch swallowed sourly over a throat like an open wound. "It was a team effort."

"Don't lie. I know it wasn't." Frances stared at the hedge as though it were a vista overlooking the Royal City and not clumps of leaves in darkness—as though she could see past the castle hill straight to the city limits, the new mills and factories sloshing and burping out paper and logs. "And I know you kept Sir Yunnum's regiment together. That kid is a mess."

"That kid" had five years on the princess, but he was younger than Scratch and had already been leading his own regiment for six months. Then again, his father was some sort of duke. So what if he couldn't fight his way out of a box of kittens? In the eyes of the kingdom, he was born to be great.

Scratch hated that kid.

"Thanks." She coughed into her hand. "Thanks for noticing, I mean."

Frances waved her away. "Oh, it's not about noticing. Everyone noticed."

"Everyone?"

"Sure. All the regiment commanders, obviously. You presenting them the plan all at once, that was clever. That way Yunnum couldn't take credit."

"Thanks."

"Stop thanking me. And then Sir Onbriars told Lord High Commander Elwyn and he told the king."

"He told the king?"

She had walked into the feast hoping—that blasted hope—that King Ingomar knew what she had done. That she, a command-less commander, was the strategist who had snatched the land he had so cavalierly claimed before even a whisper of an attack had been planned. He would have had to know, and if he knew he would have had to honor such an asset with a command. He hadn't. Instead, he had congratulated Elwyn and sat back down and tucked into his ham and potatoes, not even acknowledging the great gift of Scratch, just a table away, slowly asphyxiating under lungfuls of disappointment and an overzealous waistband.

"But if he knew that I had planned the octagon . . ."

Frances faced her. The princess had a feral sort of beauty, more woodland imp than fairy, with short, stubby eyelashes and brows that arched mischievously, even through an otherwise blank expression.

"Come, now. You had to know this would happen."

"I had to know what?"

There was pity on Frances's face, strange and discomfiting, and Scratch remembered with startling clarity that she was talking to a princess. Moreover, she was freshly aware of her own body, that of a shrimpy, blue-veined Tangled Lakes girl. She was entirely out of her depth.

"You had to know," said Frances, voice soft with gentle patience, "that he would never give you a command."

She blinked. The leaves in the hedge began to form swirling pictures, the darkness revealing wavering images of menacing faces, garish, tonsil-bearing laughter, her mother's raised hand. She blinked and blinked and they changed, kaleidoscopic mockery and dirt-dizzy fallen soldiers, mouths biting the wet, maggoty earth.

Oh. She was high.

"You're from the Tangled Lakes," Frances murmured, with the tone of an apology. "You have no breeding. No lineage. You don't look like anyone in charge. You're, pardon me for saying so, very small. And," she chuckled darkly, "you're a woman."

"There are women in charge," Scratch countered, though that was hardly the point. What was the point? Perhaps she had lost the point entirely. No, no, this was the point the princess was making—that there was no point. No point in trying, no point in striving. Because Scratch had made the mistake of being born to a penniless Tangled Lakes woman in the Royal City slums and, thusly, had no point at all.

"The women in charge are well-bred. They're the exceptions. The commanders without breeding are men. And they're all

11

exceptional. Have you seen Julaine throwing a spear without his shirt? So what if he's from the Southern Reaches? The man is a side of beef."

"Of course I've seen Julaine throwing a spear," Scratch spat, and instantly regretted it. "I'm sorry, Your Highness."

"Don't think on it." She smiled tightly, her wicked eyebrows dimmed by discomfort. "Maybe if it was just 'commander.' But it's 'lord commander.' Or, I suppose, 'lady commander.'"

"Yeah. Lady." She was ambivalent about being a "lady"—different than "woman," which, come to think of it, had its own baggage—but the knighting? That was uncomplicated.

Lady Scratch Keyes, Lady Commander in the King's Guard. She had imagined it so many times: the weight of the sword on her shoulders. The feel of the rug pile beneath her knee. Rising before her king as a knight of the realm.

"You ought to know, Keyes," Frances murmured. "My father will take everything from you. He'll keep you just comfortable enough to keep thinking you can reach for more." She met Scratch head-on, those dark eyes unblinking. "He'll never give it to you."

She felt impossibly heavy, as if she and the bench were both sinking into the mulch below. She tasted soil.

"Why are you telling me this?"

"Because it's not too late to do something else."

She fingered the white raised scar on her face, a line drawn by sword point from forehead to cheek.

"Something else . . ."

Frances shrugged. "Something other than being in the King's Guard. He won't knight you. You've reached your ceiling there. Maybe you could be appreciated elsewhere, doing something else."

"Like what?" She didn't care that she sounded desperate. She *was* desperate, because there was nothing else. There had been nothing else since the day the Academy recruiter plucked her from the streets—a stringy ten-year-old, her pockets heavy with stolen fruit—and told her she would be a soldier. There was nothing else she was good at. There was nothing else she liked. Without the King's Guard, Scratch Keyes was nothing at all.

"You'll think of something," said the princess, and she strolled off into the darkness, leaving Scratch entirely, achingly alone.

Chapter Two

Scratch had lost track of time. Maybe it was the Roselap. Maybe it was the grief. Maybe it was the pants. Whatever the cause, the night was silent and still when she made her way back to the barracks.

The guard at the door nodded in greeting. "Bowstring was looking for you."

She grunted acknowledgment as she slipped indoors and found her quarters. Of course James had been looking. He had probably been worried. She knew a spike of guilt, quickly blotted out by a petty slash of rage. James Ursus, that green-eyed aristocrat, would never have had this problem. If he had been born with a tenth of her drive, he would have been a knighted commander by now.

But James didn't have any desire to take command. He had chosen to support her instead. Oh fantastic, now she felt guilty again.

She released herself from her pants, not bothering with any of the pre-bed grooming rituals James had foisted upon her, and stubbornly closed her eyes.

Scratch didn't have sleepless nights. After her first few weeks at the Academy, when she had realized that her name and appearance were, as her peers so helpfully informed her, lacking, she had trained herself to sleep on command and wake early. Her secret tools were two cups of hot water, which she procured from a motherly kitchen maid who had loved to fuss over her runty, underfed form. She would down the water at lights out, allowing the heat to soothe her to sleep. In the morning, when the urgency of her bladder woke her in the predawn hours, she rose quickly and quietly, with enough time to ensure her cot was neat, her fair hair tightly restrained, and her demeanor cheerful before any of her peers had even opened their eyes. Soon, she didn't need the water to fall asleep instantly or to wake before the sun. Her body, like Scratch herself, had learned to adjust.

So she slept, against all odds. And it was a peaceful sleep. All two hours of it.

"Up, Keyes!"

She jolted awake, blinking away the afterimages of closely held torchlight.

"Branch?" She peered at the three men surrounding her: one with fire, two bearing swords. "Hester? Gultin?"

"I said up! And put on some clothes."

She scrambled out of bed and fell directly onto a pair of pants, which she promptly wriggled into.

"Can I do my boots, or—"

"Do your boots!"

Her fingers skipped over the laces, tangling them into knots. She could barely piece together a coherent thought. Was she going to be killed? These three men—they were her peers in the Kings Guard. They hadn't particularly liked her (the feeling was rather mutual) but there certainly wasn't enough hatred to garner a midnight murder. And they were all sergeants; she outranked them.

"Where are you taking me?"

"You don't get to ask questions."

She needed to stall. Her sword and dagger were sheathed across the room. Maybe, if she scrambled over, she could—

"Time's up." Hester, the largest of the bunch, revealed a length of rope and bound her arms. Her bootlaces trailed like

16

tripwires under her toes as he yanked her upward, her shoulders jamming into the back of her neck.

"Ow," she said.

"Sorry," he murmured. "King's orders."

"King's . . ."

Her mind went panicky-white. The moisture left her mouth so quickly her teeth ached.

"Why does the king—"

"I said no questions!"

She diligently clamped her mouth as her captors dragged her out of the barracks and into the night, holding her just-too-high to walk for herself. Her toes scrambled for purchase on the packed earth of the palace grounds. They reached the hall, where the remnants of dinner lay like untouched murder evidence, then through to dank palace corridors. And farther, to where bare stone shifted to rugs, blank walls to tapestry. Then, an oak door, oiled so recently it reeked of linseed and pine tar. It opened.

Her knees slammed against the floor before her mind had a chance to catch up. *Oh, I've been shoved.*

"You look well," a familiar voice slurred beside her.

She bit back a gasp. James's lips puffed like a seedpod ready to burst, a pinkish sap of drool and blood seeping from the corner of his mouth. One of his vibrant green eyes was swollen shut.

"And you," she whispered, attempting to breathe. He looked at her like he knew what she meant: *You're my best friend. I love you.*

She glanced around her new prison. Three thrones sat at the edge of the room—the throne room, apparently, though she had never seen it before. Thick pennants hung from bronze flagpoles jutting from stone walls striped with arched stained glass depicting the major gods. The Mother, god of hearth and home. The Sister, god of poetry and piety. The Brother, god of war and music. The Twice-Buried, god of sex and death. And, behind the thrones, the largest window of them all: The Father, the etheric god that built all on the first day and would destroy all on the last.

17

It seemed unlikely that any of those gods would come to her aid. The last time she had prayed, it was to The Cheesemonger, god of cheese, and it was on a dare.

"Sergeant Major Keyes." Sir Levon, Hand to the King, leaned back in his throne. The leather of his black jerkin creaked over his stomach like a beetle's carapace. "So glad you could join us."

"Pleasure." Her teeth chattered. She clamped her jaw, twitches jolting down the muscles of her throat.

Levon raised an eyebrow. "Of course. In a moment, King Ingomar and his wizard will arrive. It would behoove you to give me any information you have before they do."

"Information?"

"On the girl."

"What girl?"

In a moment he was before her, raising his craggy hand. The slap stung worse than she could have anticipated. No one had slapped her in years, and the indignity burned even more than the act. For a moment, she was back in her mother's shack, on the wrong end of Purpose Keyes's long-nailed claw. It was enough to send her heart speeding, her eyes blinking away shameful moisture.

She breathed herself back into her body as Levon glared down at her, his teeth bared.

"I'm sorry, Sir Levon," she tried once more. "But I don't know what girl—"

Another slap, this time to the other cheek, and she hit the floor. It would have been better to be punched. She could take a punch. She did, regularly. But there was something about a slap—like Levon didn't respect her enough to close his fist. Like he was scolding her.

She generally didn't mind being a woman, but there was something jagged and painful at the juncture of woman and slap and it tore at her, uncomfortably deep.

"Ah," said Levon. "Your Highness."

She struggled back to her knees. Behind the wobbly wetness

obscuring her vision, she watched King Ingomar and Sir Gorn take their thrones. The king still wore the celebratory crimson he had worn at dinner, thick ropes of golden brocade lining every seam. The red of his cheeks, usually a sign of joviality, glowed with barely-contained rage.

The wizard was watching her with narrowed lavender eyes, made all the more vivid by the purple cloaks he was never seen without.

"Keyes. Ursus." Gorn sneered down his sharp-edged nose. "You stand accused of aiding in the abduction of Princess Frances. How do you plead?"

"This isn't a damned trial, Gorn." King Ingomar vibrated in his throne. "We know they're guilty. They have taken my daughter and I demand to know where!"

Scratch's skin turned to icy gooseflesh. Her stomach sank down past aching ribs to throbbing knees. Beside her, James let out a whimper.

What was the word? *Panic.*

"You heard your king, girl," Levon hissed. "Tell us where the princess is and we might spare your life."

A lie. She'd be killed no matter what she said. It didn't help, of course, that she had nothing at all to say.

Behind her eyes, she saw a vision of Frances blowing a plume of rosy smoke into the dark night, then slipping into the billowy stream and melting into starlight. She shivered.

"There's no point in denying it." Gorn drummed his long nails on the carved armrest of his throne. "Ferrin. Report."

A freckle-faced soldier approached, ginger curls frothing over his scalp like spiced cream.

"Sir Levon." He bowed his head. "Sir Gorn. Your Highness. My peers reported losing track of the princess's whereabouts—" King Ingomar let out a tight hiss "—at ten minutes to eight bells, two minutes before Keyes was seen leaving the feast. Ursus followed a minute after. Neither was seen again until ten bells, when Ursus returned to the barracks. Keyes returned at a quarter to midnight. The princess was not seen again."

19

James ran his tongue over his swollen lip. "H-how do you know she's missing?"

"Because we can't find her, you fool!" Levon bared his teeth like a wild animal, gray whiskers trembling. "Her chambers have been ransacked. The castle has been searched. Two horses are missing, including her own. She has been abducted!"

Scratch could barely breathe. There was no air in the room, the atmosphere ragged-thin, too hot and too cold all at once. She greedily sucked in air, but there was no space inside her for it. Why were her lungs suddenly so small?

Oh. The pants she had hastily grabbed as three unnecessarily large soldiers dragged her from her room were the too-tight pants that she had selected so she might look like a commander when she accepted her first command. Slim-fit and tailored, a gleaming maroon silk that veered toward crimson, her nation's bloody hue. She had squeezed herself into them, the curves of her body remolding to a new, more desirable shape.

She was going to die in these pants.

The world came to her through a fog of noiseless sound. Someone, maybe Levon, may have said, "Throw them in the dungeons. That'll motivate them." And she was up, wrists rubbing, knees throbbing, face still aching from a humiliating pair of slaps that had told her, wordlessly, exactly who she was.

"You have until morning light," Levon growled. "If we don't know where Princess Frances is by dawn, you will die." He scowled, smoothing his mustache with fingers weighed down by rings. "Sleep well."

Chapter Three

By the time the party reached the dungeons, Scratch was certain she would have finger-shaped bruises all over her arms.

Unfortunately, that was the least of her concerns.

"Your new home." The same trio of King's Guards that had yanked her out of bed had the honor of throwing her and James into their dank cell. With her arms bound, she had no choice but to land on her shoulder—more bruises. "Oi, Bowstring. You do look like shit, you know?"

James sucked up some spittle. "You should see the other guy."

"I *was* the other guy."

"And you do look awful." If he were capable, James might have winked. "Really, Gultin. You're a gods-crafted disaster."

The soldier only smiled. "I'd hit you again if I didn't think it'd kill you." He spit into the cell for good measure. "Ponce." And the men closed the gate, leaving Scratch and James alone in the darkness.

Scratch lay, the cool filth of the dungeon soothing her aching skin. Overhead, something drip, drip, dripped onto the clammy floor. Errant scraps of hay littered the cell, the moonlight from the tiny barred window illuminating their jagged edges. On the walls, rusted manacles hung like open mouths.

"Scratch?" James's bravado was gone. All that remained was threadbare, a tiny voice through busted lips. "What . . . what happened?"

"Jamie." She wriggled over to him. She couldn't do much with her hands tied, but she managed to press their bodies together—a filthy, pathetic cuddle. "Oh, hells. This is it, isn't it?"

"It appears to be." He sniffled. "I never regretted being dis-owned before, but now . . ."

"I don't even think your father could get you out of this one, darling." She smooshed her face into his shoulder. "I wish he could."

"It would have to be both of us," he whispered. "Where you go, I go. Remember?"

"Yes. It seems—" She choked on one sandpaper sob. "It seems that's the case."

She had long ago decided that James was the love of her life. If he had liked women and she had liked men, perhaps they could have had the happiest marriage in creation. Then again, maybe their utter lack of desire was what made their love so strong; like without sex all that was left was pure, unadulterated affection.

"What do you think happened to her?" he asked.

She didn't want to think about Frances, especially after last night. Imagining that piebald girl swept away by villains stung Scratch's throat like bile. Those keen, wily eyes were too bright for fear, those wicked eyebrows too confident.

Princess Frances was a forest fae in reverse: she didn't trap you with magic; she cleared the magic from your vision. To step into her realm was to see the world as it was.

She would have been a very good queen.

"I don't know, Jamie."

"Were we really the only ones out after curfew? D-do you think we were set up?"

"I hadn't thought about it." But she had a different thought. It pressed on the inside of her skull like a gnat caught in a lan-tern. "Jamie, I met Frances today."

She told him about her unexpected smoke break with the princess. How Frances had, calmly and without cruelty, told Scratch that there was no hope for her. That it wasn't too late to figure out something else to do with the rest of her life.

"I don't believe her." James carefully wiped his weeping lip against his shoulder. "You're too special to not become a knight. I just thought . . ."

"You thought that if you believed I could do it, everyone would. You wanted me to have a command, and you always get your way." She attempted to pat his head with her cheek. "My poor little nobleman. But that's not the point I was making."

"I've been beaten nearly to a pulp, darling. Forgive me for missing a point or two."

"I think she might have left, Jamie." Frances had spoken like a woman who knew more than she let on, who understood that there was no hope for a future where she was. Like someone who had made alternate plans. "Two horses were gone, hers included. She could have ransacked her room as a decoy."

"Why would she have done that?"

"Well, I don't know." She had roughly a dozen theories. "But think about it: Levon barely asked us where Frances had gone. He and the King weren't demanding answers, they were looking for someone to blame." The ideas were sparking, making her nose itch. "It's far easier for them to pin it on us than to admit that Frances ran off. And if they really thought we had spirited her away, we would be in a torture chamber right now getting our eyelashes plucked out."

"Well, thank the gods for small mercies." He spread out on the floor and sighed. "Scratch, I understand that you're looking for answers. I wouldn't mind a few myself. But if the king has decided we're guilty, we're guilty."

"You aren't allowed to be right." She felt heavy, the thick dungeon atmosphere pinning her to the ground. "Gods, Jamie. Nothing's been going my way today."

"Poor babe." He chuckled, wet and throaty. "You know, I have a book in my pocket."

She couldn't help the smile that dragged her cracked, painful lips across filmy teeth. "You what?"

"I fell asleep reading. I just put it in my pocket. They didn't seem to care." His voice broke. "Nobody cares. They didn't care. They didn't—"

"Shh, Jamie." She shifted closer, stemming his tears with her hair. She wished she could open her mouth and swallow the tears and, with them, the pain. He was a soldier, but he was soft. Not like Scratch. She had built her armor early, stealing through the slums with an empty belly, reaching her grubby hand into strangers' pockets for a few coppers. James had the privilege of softness, and it suited him beautifully. Gods, if she could only take this from him. "I care. We have each other, all right? We're okay. If we're together, we're okay."

She whispered nonsense until his sobs faded to the deep breathing of sleep. Then, she was alone.

She tried to close her eyes, but her mother was waiting behind her eyelids. If Scratch was to be publicly executed, would Purpose Keyes be brought out to watch her daughter drop? To see her only child's blond head take leave of her body? Would she weep, or would she stare in that blank way of hers, a closed door shaped like watery blue eyes in a face too miserable for sadness?

The Academy had been Scratch's freedom, her escape and her promise. God of Days Ahead, she was an idiot. She had thought that if she just kept being exceptional—fighting harder, running faster, strategizing beyond what those useless commanders could dream—the rest wouldn't matter. Her family, her gender, her size: Scratch could build herself greater than the bricks of her birth.

It was all for nothing in the end.

And this particular end was the real elderflower drizzle on the shit cake: no one could craft a crueler death for Scratch than one she didn't understand. Were she and James truly the only ones who hadn't been accounted for last night? Were other members of the Guard out looking for the princess, or would her disappearance be swept away, left to ossify into the brittleness of national tragedy? And if that were the case, who benefitted? At the center of every tangle was the person who had something to gain. If only she could map her way toward who, pull the thread from the snarl until someone with a story popped out.

What she wouldn't give for a piece of parchment.

James stirred. "There's someone here."

"It's too early, darling. Go back to sleep."

"No. Scratch." She could see the deep green of his wide eyes in the scant light. "Listen."

She listened. Sure enough, the sound of footsteps interrupted the drips of the mysterious dungeon moisture. Not a guard to bring her to the block—a quick, confirming glance at the tiny window exposed a sky not yet touched by the cool light of dawn. There was a jangling—keys, maybe? And then—

"Get up," the intruder hissed. "Which key, which key. . . aha!" Metal scraped against metal, the gate screaming as it swung open. "Come on, we don't have a lot of time."

Scratch and James scrambled up, using each other's bodies as leverage. Hells, she was exhausted. Her ribs ached.

"Our hands are still bound." Scratch turned, exposing the rope at her back that rubbed her wrists raw. "Could you . . ."

"Oh, yes." The stranger—a woman, from the sound of her voice—pulled a knife from the folds of her skirts and quickly slashed through the ropes. "Not much time. Follow me."

Scratch met James's eyes for a brief, silent conversation. A raised eyebrow. *Who do you think . . . ?* A shrug. *Does it matter?*

One last risk wouldn't kill them. And if it did, what difference did it make?

It hurts to hope, she reminded herself. *Don't let yourself hope.*

Still, they followed. The woman didn't lead them down the hall to freedom. Instead, she brought them to a neighboring cell. There was a quick dance with the keys. "Which one, come on?" And they were in. The woman closed the gate behind her.

And now they were trapped in a new, smaller cell. This one, if possible, was even damper.

Scratch tugged on her waistband. "Um . . ."

"Quiet." The woman hunched down in a corner, frantically pawing at the wall. "Ah!" A little exhale of triumph as her fingers found a loose rock. She pushed it to the side, opening a slender hole in the wall, just big enough for a moderately sized human to crawl through.

"Ursus first, please. If you get stuck, I want Keyes behind you to push." It was dark in the dungeon, but Scratch was still able to detect a smirk on the woman's face. "If you please."

James hesitated. "Could you tell us who—"

"No time." The woman pushed him towards the hole. "Stay here and be executed, if you please. No skin off my feet." The way she manhandled James cut a few holes in her nonchalant veneer, but he was swayed. With a shrug and a wince, he crouched into the darkness.

"Now you, Keyes. I'll be right behind you. Just have to close it up after us."

Scratch swallowed thickly, obediently making her way into the tunnel. She had known the advantages of her size—counted them, wrote them out, internalized them so that no one could tell her being small wasn't worth something—but she had never considered within those advantages the ease of escaping the castle dungeon on the eve of her own execution. The passage was downright roomy. For her at least.

"Ugh," James groaned. "How much longer?"

"Not much." Their savior (or captor—there was really no way of knowing) was also having a bit of trouble getting through. Scratch bit back a surge of wild laughter. This was ridiculous. She had been preparing to die only a moment ago, and now, upon the instruction of a nameless stranger, she was wiggling through a secret passage to nowhere. The only thing that would make this more absurd was if the whole tunnel collapsed and the last thing she ever saw was James's ass as he shuffled a foot ahead.

A short, percussive noise rent the close, warm air.

James stopped short. "Scratch, was that your pants?"

26

"No," she hissed, though she couldn't deny her sudden ability to take full breaths, nor the tiny breeze at her backside. Of course her pants would rip. Whatever god had it in for her must be having quite the giggle. Her face burned.

"No time for ripped pants," the woman whispered, a barely concealed hitch of laughter in her voice. "We're nearly there. Ursus, push up when you see the iron bar."

He did, leading them out into what was most certainly an alehouse basement. Barrels lined the walls, and the sharp smell of fermentation prickled in Scratch's nostrils.

The woman emerged from the tunnel, closing the trapdoor behind her.

"Through the window now."

They slipped through a high-set window (Scratch insisted on going last) and rolled out into a dingy alley. The stranger pressed a finger to her lips, gesturing them to follow. She led them through small streets, quickly darting behind buildings and carts when anyone came near. They didn't need to worry. It must have been close to four in the morning and the streets were nearly deserted. Scratch didn't recognize the area, but the sickly, heady smell and general filth had the feel of the slums where she was raised. It gave her the sensation of jolting through time, running from the neighborhood children whose greatest joy was to corner and pummel her. Her lungs felt tight, and she could taste her own breathing, rough iron on her tongue.

Finally, the stranger opened a warped wooden door and shooed them inside. It was a living room. Dingy paint cracked from wainscoting to baseboards, and the floor beams listed like a ship carried by sea wind. A hearth crackled with the last gasps of tired-out logs, spitting ash and dust onto a balding rug.

"We're here," the stranger announced.

From the dimness, a man and a woman approached. They looked to be siblings, both thick and broad-shouldered, as if they had been well fed on milk and eggs since birth. They had nearly identical ropy arms, russet skin dappled with scattered-spice explosions of freckles. Their hair was the medium

27

brown of burnished bronze, hints of gold peeking from the man's cropped curls, the woman's twin thick braids. Their lips were plump and rosy-brown and, like the rest of their bodies, so startlingly healthy. Scratch could see the definition of their muscles through the soft linen of their garments, the dips and divots of biceps hiding under the man's open-necked tunic, the woman's simple, pale-blue shirt. Oddly, even though she wore trousers, the woman had tied an embroidered apron around her waist.

"You got them," the man said by way of greeting. His voice was low and rich, a bass that rumbled through her toes. "Good."

The new woman said nothing, the lines of her mouth tense and downturned. Her eyes burned a dark topaz verging on amber, ancient sap grown hard, long dormant insects trapped between the threads of iris.

James drummed his fingers on his thighs. "Hello." He wiped the drool from his swollen lip. "I'm terribly sorry to report that I'm not at my prettiest." He eyed the man. "You, on the other hand—ow, Scratch, o-kay. I'm James."

The man bowed his head in greeting. "Vel Shae. This is my sister Brella."

"Lovely to make your acquaintance," James replied, with a bravado Scratch knew sheltered a trembling unease. "And—not that I'm complaining, of course—but may I ask: why have you sprung us from the dungeons?"

Brella glared at their rescuer. "Iris. You didn't tell them?"

"We didn't have time." In the glowing light of the room, Scratch could see that their escort—Iris—was wearing the dress and apron of a palace maid. She ripped off her bonnet, exposing a head of bedraggled bronze hair.

"They don't know where we're going," Brella spat as Iris flopped onto a moldering sofa. "They haven't agreed to anything. Damn it, Iris."

Iris closed her eyes and began to rub the bridge of her nose. "What do they need to agree to? They were going to die, and now they're not. Now, please, go rescue Frances."

Scratch choked. "Rescue . . ."

"Listen." Vel's voice was calm, but his eyes kept darting to the door and his hands were in fists. "Iris works in the castle. She and Frances are . . ." He bit his lip. "Close. She and the princess overheard some details about an abduction. Frances brought it to Gorn. He didn't do anything. It seemed like . . ."

"Like he was in on it." Brella's jaw was set, her rust-toned eyes fierce. "There was no one the princess could trust in the castle. No one but you two."

James raked a hand through his hair. "Us?"

Vel nodded. "Unless we get Frances back, you'll die for this. You didn't do it."

"We could have," James reasoned. "I mean, maybe we knew too much. Maybe they had to kill us to get us out of the—ow!"

Scratch rolled her heel over James's toes. "We're not in on it," she assured the Shaes, tethering herself to reality through the sensation of James foot underneath hers. Plots? Abductions? Conspiracies? When she finally got the chance to pick this all apart, she would need a very large piece of parchment.

"Yeah," Brella said. "We know."

Scratch took a deep breath and let it out through her nose. "So where is she?"

The Shaes locked eyes for a moment.

"Koravia," Vel said, and it was all Scratch could do not to crumble to the floor.

To fight for Ivinscont was to fight against Koravia. That had been the whole point of her recruitment—hells, it was the point of every recruitment. Even if Koravia was not the enemy of the moment, every fighter Scratch felled, every horse she hobbled, was in the name of destroying that nearby nation, those aggressors who had nearly brought Ivinscont to its knees only thirty years before.

They had invaded on black horses, spears dipped in wizard-wrought potions to make each death quick, to turn each nonlethal stab into inevitable destruction. They had claimed nearly all of the Eastern Steppes before they had met Ivinscont's army, stronger and cleverer than they had anticipated. There had been death on both sides, violent, ugly death, each soldier facing their end with cold certainty. It had been the sort of war that could have no victor.

Seeing no end to the bloodshed, two kings signed a treaty for peace. They were the fathers of the men who now sat upon their thrones. The late kings had kept to the treaty. The new kings . . . well, there was really no way of knowing. So Ivinscont needed to be prepared, always prepared, in case those black horses rode from the east once more.

"Koravia?" James tugged at his chestnut curls, now gone entirely to frizz. "What, are we supposed to just go east? We're fugitives!"

"We're not going east."

"But—Vel, was it?—Vel. That's where Koravia is."

Brella sucked her teeth. "We'll explain on the way. We need to get into the forest before the sun rises and the King's Guard figures out you've gone."

"The *forest?*" James turned desperately to Scratch for support. "We'll die there. We have no weapons!"

"We have weapons," Vel volunteered.

James looked unconvinced. "Such as?"

"Bows."

"And Scratch? I can handle a bow—" a gross understatement "—but Scratch is for swords."

Vel tapped a thoughtful a finger against his jaw. "We have kitchen knives?"

"There isn't time for this," Brella snarled, a braid flopping over her shoulder. "If we don't get out of here soon, it's your heads."

"Can I borrow some pants?"

Everyone turned. Scratch stood, picking at her waistband, her skin aflame. She didn't know whether to cry or fight or vomit or lie down and let the exhaustion carry her away. In her chest, ribs squeezed around a ragged heart, too drained for fear, or perhaps beyond it. She was spent, her final stores empty. Anything she did from here on out would be drawing strength from muscle and bone, depleting her.

Everything had been taken from her. The least she could get in return were some comfortable pants.

"These, uh, won't suit," she continued. Brella's eyes were narrowed, her gaze a burning thing. "If we'll be riding."

Brella shook her head. "We're walking."

"Regardless. Do you . . ."

Vel made towards a chest in the corner. "I've got something that might fit. They're Leif's."

"Our brother," Iris called from the couch. "He's eleven."

"Here." Vel tossed her a wad of cotton. "You can change over there."

She shuffled toward the indicated partition, keeping her back to the wall, and struggled out of her pant-manacles. Sure enough, a neat rip gaped in the seat like a dark, mocking mouth.

You've had nothing before, she reminded herself, though her own voice was weak in her heavy head. *You can make it all up again.*

And there in her mind, as if summoned, was Frances. Her woods-wild eyes revealing truth after truth, melting off Scratch's armor, revealing skin that stung with newness. The princess, at least, deserved the rest of her life.

"I'm coming to get you," she whispered into the dying fire. "Whether you like it or not."

Chapter Four

From the second the small party slunk into the streets to the moment they crossed the forest's tree line, Scratch barely took a breath. She allowed herself to fill her lungs when the forest rose up around her, the heady scent of damp earth and piney wilderness sluicing the filth of the dungeons from her insides. The dawn crept pale blue on the trees, chill and gentle, staining the brown bark gray. She breathed and breathed.

She didn't miss the irony that the forest, dangerous, mysterious, and largely avoided, would be her refuge. It was unforgiving, a home earned by those who could survive it. There were the animals, of course—bear, coyote, wild dog—as well as the packs of bandits who staked their claim to swaths of land, camps with unmarked barriers so subtle an intruder wouldn't know they had trespassed until the blade of a bandit's knife kissed their throat.

But the threats of beasts and bandits were nothing compared to danger of the fair folk, the magical creatures who not only occupied these woods, but had, according to legend, drawn every tree from the earth. The clever Ivinscontian might call the fae a myth; the cleverest wouldn't say such a thing out loud, for fear the fae could hear. People disappeared in these woods, lured by ghostly light or the crying of a baby who didn't exist. Scratch's mother, being from the Lakes, was more concerned about sirens and kelp spirits, but even she knew to warn her daughter: stay out of the forest.

"Okay. We're safe." Brella dropped her pack and sat herself on a mossy, flattish rock. Here in the woods, she looked marginally less stern. "We should rest a bit."

"We've just arrived," James objected, though he sat anyway. He had stopped drooling, but rusty gunk caked his split lip and his black eye had gone purple. "Surely we ought to get some distance between us and the city."

"We have time." Vel picked a few leaves off of a nearby bush, crushed them in his palm, spat in them, and offered them to James. "Press this against your lip."

James blinked. "If that's what you enjoy, we can discuss it."

"It'll help." Vel seemed to try for firm, but a smile crept through. "Trust me."

"Only because you asked so nicely," James replied, unsuccessfully batting his fluid-caked eyelashes. He pressed the mess to his mouth. "Oh, that's lovely. You're a witch then? Convenient."

"Not a witch. Just a woodsman."

"A bit of both," James insisted.

"Not a witch." Vel grinned—a real one this time—and flopped down beside his sister.

Brella eyed him warily. "Enough of whatever this is. We have matters to discuss."

Scratch joined them on the forest floor, taking pains to be careful of the weapon hanging from her new trousers: a kitchen knife, sharp and sturdy, with a wooden handle. It wasn't much, but it would have to do. She had fashioned a hasty sheath for it from the formerly useless pocket of her too-tight pants. If she had been one for poetry, there might have been something there, but she wasn't, so: *ooh, shiny sheath*.

Brella smoothed her unnecessary apron over her thighs. "Where should we begin?"

"What's the plan?" Scratch asked. "Are you fighters?"

"We aren't fighters. I'm a brewer and Vel is a seamstress."

"Seamster," James interjected. "Surely."

Vel shrugged with one oversized shoulder. "I actually don't mind seamstress. Brella's a brewer, not a breweress, you know?"

"That's why we brought you," Brella continued with the air of one who had been through this breweress business before. "You're the muscle. As for why we're out here, Iris is—"

"The princess's lover," Scratch supplied.

Brella tensed. "How did you know that?"

"Intuition." Not entirely true, but it wasn't worth explaining that it was the only scenario that fit. How else would the palace maid have known about a secret passage out of the dungeons? Why else would she have had Frances's ear? "Why didn't she come with us?"

"She's in the palace. She can keep an eye on what's going on for us. Besides, if she left, it would send suspicion her way."

"Logical." Scratch shifted in her seat. "How do you know that Frances is in Koravia?"

"Frances has been catching whispers for months. She said to Iris that if she were taken, that's where she'd go." Brella reached down to retie a boot that looked awfully tight already. "But in the end, it doesn't really matter where she is. We'll get to her regardless."

"How—"

"Listen." She winced, her mouth twisting. It was, Scratch thought unhelpfully, a rather lovely mouth, with thick, dark lips that turned down at the edges. "What we're about to explain, it's . . . a little unbelievable. So just, please try not to judge anything out of hand."

"Me?" James raised his eyebrows. "Judge?"

Vel snorted into his fist.

"There's a place in these woods," Brella began, her voice taking on the timbre of a storyteller. She had a musical, deep sort of voice, more bassoon than flute, resonant through her broad shoulders. "A nexus kind of place called 'the Between.' It's fair folk territory. We cross a blood gate to enter, and once we're there the fae take us where we need to go. They're no threat to us while we're in the forest."

"Wait." James raised a finger. "Blood gate?"

"It's not as unpleasant as it sounds," Vel assured him. "It's a gift. Our family's blood allows us to pass through this forest unharmed and then enter the Between. We've been able to do it for generations."

"That's all well and good for you," Scratch objected. "But what about us? We're not related to you."

Brella paused before answering, and when she finally spoke, she didn't meet Scratch's eye.

"We'll form a blood bond. We'll slice our hands and hold them together. That should be enough to get you in and out."

Scratch nodded, choosing not to press. There certainly was more to this. Brella's determined foot-focused gaze gave that much away.

"And how long until we get to this 'Between?'"

"Ten days." Vel held up the appropriate amount of fingers. "Once we're in the Between, it's only a day. Then, we'll be in Koravia. Hopefully, we'll be wherever Frances is. And then," he gestured to the two bedraggled King's Guards, one of whom was equipped only with cutlery. "You do your thing."

Scratch narrowed her eyes. "Our thing?"

James cleared his throat. "Before we get ahead of ourselves, does this mean the fair folk will leave us alone?"

"Until we need them, yes," Vel confirmed. "We're safe."

"Jolly good. Hoorah. But what of the bandits?"

The seamstress, thankfully, had enough awareness to look a bit chagrinned. "That, uh, we figured would also fall under the heading of 'your thing.'"

Scratch sighed. "Of course." Gods, she was wrecked. She was running on two hours of sleep, and the adrenaline of her daring escape was beginning to seep away. Now that she no longer had to be actively afraid, her mind had room for other things: anger, mostly. Yesterday, she was ready to claim her deserved knight-hood. Now, she was rescuing the lost princess of a country that had used her for her skill and rejected her for everything else. A country that—oh yes—planned to execute her for a crime she didn't commit without even the dignity of a trial.

It was a good thing she had a knife. She was ready to stab something.

"Scratch?"

"Hmm?" She blinked out of her red haze. James was staring. "You all right?"

"Sure, Jamie. Peachy."

He crossed his arms, muttering something that sounded like "Well *I* haven't done anything."

Brella had her defensive face on, the one she had worn back in the city. The smooth planes were jagged, her freckles like chips of ice on a mountain face.

"If you're not happy out here," she drawled coolly, "feel free to go back to the dungeons."

Scratch could have fought. It was tempting, but she knew better. It wasn't her place to be angry here. Not her place to complain. If she were in charge, she could breathe; but Brella commanded here, so Scratch pressed her anger down—kindling to light a fire when she was safe.

"I'm fine." She squeezed her grimace back into her gums. "Really. Just adjusting."

"Please do. You need to be at your best out here."

"For the bandits?"

"Yes, and . . ." Brella's shoulders lifted, just a touch. "You might be tested."

Scratch's mind flashed to the day a war medic had smeared her blood across a piece of fabric to determine whether she had Campfire Flu.

"Tested?"

"The Between is a really, really special place. The fae are protective. Hopefully, if you stay near us, you won't have anything to worry about. But if you get too far . . ." Brella spread her hands. "They might give you a test."

"Ah." Scratch had a pretty good idea of what sort of test this might be. "And passing looks like surviving, right?"

"You got it." Brella wiped a hand across her forehead, depositing a little trail of dirt. Now that the sun had risen, Scratch could see the circles under Brella's golden eyes, little pouches of darkness dampening her dappled face. "Anything else we should cover before we keep moving?"

Of course there was.

There were still holes. How did these two merchants expect James and Scratch to rescue Frances on their own, with no backup? This was a lark at most, a hopeful little gambit that would, best case scenario, get them all killed quickly. Besides, if the king was plotting against his own daughter, where would Frances be returned to? Would Scratch save her princess's life, only to have Frances spend the rest of her years as a fugitive? And what of the rest of them? Would she, James, the princess, and the Shaes make a bandit camp in these woods, smoking pink flowers until the king keeled over?

When Scratch added the confusion over Frances's potential escape to this hellish tangle, she found herself clutching a string connected to the biggest snarl of her life.

The only certainty so far was that these Shaes, whoever they were, couldn't be trusted. At least, not entirely. Their explanations were too neat. Their plans were wildly inconsistent, too straightforward in some places, too loose in others—*our thing? Really?* Still, Scratch had seen enough liars to know that the business with the Between, implausible as it seemed, had the ring of truth. Liars? Certainly. Friends of the fair folk? That, too.

Which meant there was a real possibility that Scratch would end up with Frances, wherever she was. And maybe, by virtue of "her thing," Scratch could retrieve the princess unharmed. If the Shaes were telling the truth about the King's deception—*if*—then surely the public would be moved by the plight of their beloved princess. Could Frances take her father's throne? And if she did, could Scratch be beside her?

Sure, Scratch could do something different with her life, just as Frances had advised her. But what if she could do the same thing—the only thing she knew how to do, really—as the hero who had saved Princess Frances? Not even the God of Kings could keep her from her rightful knighthood after that.

It wouldn't be simple. The first few paces were clear enough, but anything after was clouded in the fog of confusion. She needed more information.

"I think Frances left," she said, watching Brella's face for a reaction. It was a risk showing her hand, but if Brella knew anything, she might be goaded into revealing it.

"What?" Brella had been halfway to standing. With a thump, she sat back down again. "What do you mean, left?"

"We had a conversation—"

"Wait. You know her?"

"Not really." Scratch watched Brella's nostrils flare, her mouth tighten into a puckered scowl. "We just talked last night."

She slowly, haltingly, told the Shaes about the princess, the pipe, the brief moments of scale-scraping honesty. She skirted around her humiliation, letting only the necessary droplets run through, keeping the rest close. Still, her face burned.

"Something else." Brella stared blankly. "She gave you advice. And you think, what—she left the palace?"

"I just think that—"

"Did you not hear the part," Brella ground out, color high in her cheeks, "where my sister is her lover?"

"I don't understand why you're getting so heated," Scratch retorted. She had been looking for a reaction, but she hadn't expected rage. Brella's eyes flashed with it, heated and over-bright. "I just thought, you know, in case."

"In case what?"

"In case you're wrong."

"I'm not wrong!"

They were both standing—*when had that happened?*—and panting—*and that, too?* Brella flushed dark, Scratch feeling the inevitable pinkness crawling from collar to forehead. Curse that Lakes complexion. It revealed everything.

"Scratch, don't do this." James hauled himself up and toward her, determinedly casual. "We don't know the whole story.

Besides, you obviously hit a nerve."

Brella scoffed. "There's no nerve."

"Oh, really?" James cocked his head to the side. "Do you always get so flushed and pant-y over silly little theories, hmm?"

"Whether the sergeant major is right or not is no real matter," Vel added. He, Scratch noticed, had barely reacted at all. "The Blood Gate will take us to wherever Frances is. Iris will either get her Frances back or she'll get answers."

"Or we'll all get killed," Scratch mumbled.

"And what a lovely bridge that will be to cross when we come to it, hmm, darling?" James's green eyes darkened with unspoken warning. "Now, I don't think we'll reach the princess—or, y'know, whatever—just standing here, will we? I say we get our trot on. What say you, women?"

Brella rolled her eyes and stomped away.

James strolled after her. "I'll take that as a yes," he called back to Scratch and Vel, sauntering between the trees like a wisp, humming a wartime jig.

Chapter Five

They trudged on. Vel and James took the front, chattering like maids at a sewing circle, curse them. Brella, who had lost her lead almost as soon as she claimed it, lagged silently a few feet behind. Scratch, short-legged and overtired, hung back. Her hand hovered over her sheathed knife, eyes on the trees. She told herself she was covering their rear. Really, she was too spent to keep up.

The farther behind Brella she fell, the less friendly the forest seemed. It was as though proximity to the Shaes formed a protective bubble around her. Without Brella nearby, the sounds of the forest grew louder and more ominous—chittering where there had been chirping, scraping in the place of scurrying. Shadows danced in the corners of her vision, twining between the trees. Something that could just as easily have been a rabbit's paw as the toe of a bandit's boot flashed by a nearby tree root, subtle as a floater in her eye.

Ah, yes. Tests.

From the moment she had arrived at the Academy, everything had been a test, and not just for her. If she won a fight, she proved a woman from the Tangled Lakes could win a fight. If she survived in battle, it was a Lakes woman surviving. The only upside to a fae challenge was that her background wouldn't factor into it. The thought of fighting without that weight was nearly appealing. Maybe she'd chase a shadow later on for a change of pace.

At least the weather was pleasant. The sun was fully risen now, its golden light giving a deceptive sense of warmth to the cool, hazy path. It was fresh summer, the early days of heat and sweat. Soon would be high summer, when the king's council did little but drink and bathe, and guards cooked in their armor like crabs in a stewpot. The heat wouldn't turn oppressive for a month yet, but hints of weather to come already showed in the heady perfume of summer flowers, the chirp of the bright birds who basked on upper branches, their iridescent feathers alight like gems.

Snippets of James and Vel's chatter floated back on the breeze.

"Well, I met him in the pub." James was laughing. "He told me he dealt in exotic snakes. How was I supposed to know what he meant?"

Loneliness cramped her stomach. Stupid, charming James. Stupid, dumb, rich, fancy, ridiculous—

"So . . ." Brella materialized beside her. "Nice sheath."

It was an attempt, and not a great one. "Don't strain yourself."

Brella scoffed. "Make this harder why don't you?"

Scratch studied the woman. Brella's shoulders were set, her arms straight with locked elbows. She radiated effort.

"We don't have to talk."

"Might make for a more pleasant trip," Brella said, unconvincingly.

You want to keep an eye on me, Scratch thought, her blood fizzing at the thought of working through this new puzzle. *Why?*

"Do you . . ." She searched for some tact. It was scant out here. "Do you generally not get along with people?"

Brella turned quickly, her braids whipping around after her. "I get along with people just fine."

"Not me, though."

"Forgive me," she said stiffly. "I don't know many people in the Kings Guard."

That was odd. According to most people, being in the King's Guard was the least objectionable thing about Scratch.

"We're regular people," she explained. "Just, with helmets."

"Sure."

"And swords." She fingered her knife. "Generally."

"Yes. I gather."

"So what's the problem?"

Brella smoothed her hair. It held the pattern of tight waves, even tied in two braids. Scratch's hair was thick and ropy, but when she brushed it back into its daily bun, it lay obediently flat. "There's no problem."

"Really? Because you look like you're about to pop a vein." She gave Brella a once-over. "Or crack a nut."

"Soldiers," she mumbled.

"What?"

"You certainly aren't poets."

She wasn't sure if that was an insult. Regardless, she didn't like it. "Would you have us be?"

"Poets have a great deal of empathy." Brella shrugged. "Makes the poems better."

Tension crept along her spine. "For?"

"Reading, I suppose."

"No, I mean, who am I supposed to have empathy—"

"I know what you meant." Brella shoved her hands into her pockets. "I heard about your octagon."

Scratch didn't know whether to be pleased or offended. Brella had said "octagon" like a curse.

"Yeah." She cast around for words. "It . . . worked."

"So it did."

They walked in stiff silence. The chatter from the lads up front fluttered back like mockingbirds caw-cawing in Scratch's temples. The borrowed pants were a touch snug around her thighs, but they fell at perfect length—a trifle humiliating, since their previous owner was an eleven-year-old boy. And, not that it

43

should matter, of course, but they were, well, ugly. Stripy brown and white linen with too-large pockets and a tie at the waist that flopped like old carrots. It was a testament to the circumstances that James hadn't mocked her for them yet.

Still, they were comfortable. And, crucially, in one piece.

"Thank you," Scratch choked out, "for the pants."

Brella hummed acknowledgment. "Not for rescuing you?"

"That too."

"I was sorry to see you demolish that other pair."

Scratch raised a shoulder with a nonchalance she didn't feel. "They were tight."

"They looked expensive."

Another weak shrug. "They had already been ruined." Even before they ripped. Her knees had spat blood onto the fabric when she was shoved to the hard stone of the dungeon, and who knows what filth had ground its way into the weave. She hadn't seen much in the dim light of the Shaes' living room, but she had caught the dark, wet stains that bloomed like bruises in the red fabric.

"So . . ." She tapped a nervous rhythm on the borrowed pants. "Do you come here often?"

"To the forest?" Brella raised an eyebrow. "Yes."

"And who guards you against bandits then?"

She shrugged. "I have more brothers. They're a little more, uh, weapon-proficient than Vel is. And I have . . ." She mulled over the word. "Friends."

Scratch chose the least thorny path. "How many more brothers?"

"Not including Vel? Six."

Scratch stumbled. "So, with Iris, there are . . . eight of you?"

Brella shook her head. "Seven boys, seven girls. Fourteen."

"That's a lot," Scratch commented, realizing only after the words spilled out how unnecessarily obvious they were.

Brella snorted. "I hadn't realized."

"Sorry," Scratch mumbled. "I was surprised." She leapt over a branch that Brella, with her long legs, had calmly stepped over.

"It was only me and my mother growing up."

Where was Purpose now? Probably tucked away in her nice little house with thick walls and windows that kept the draft out. It had been a gift of sorts, from daughter to mother, bought with saved-up soldier's wages. It hadn't been a peace offering as much as a cashing out of obligation. *Here, Purpose, take this house and leave me alone.* Now, Scratch didn't have to feel guilty when she thought of her mother servicing men well into her middle age. Scratch had, at least, spared her mother that effort. Normally, she didn't think about Purpose Keyes at all.

How long until Purpose heard that Scratch was a fugitive of the crown? Surely guards would show up at her door, demanding answers. Would they believe Purpose when she said she hadn't spoken to her daughter in two years? It was implausible, sure; they both lived in the Royal City and Scratch had plenty of time off to go visit. But it was the truth.

Scratch imagined her mother answering the door in her house dress, her uncut blond hair hanging limp and stringy around her small face. Were her cheeks still hollow, bugging out those blue eyes like twin siren's pools? Would she cry when the guards told her what her daughter had done? Would she smile?

"It's a big family," Brella conceded with a heavy sigh. "It's strange to be in the forest without them, though."

Scratch wanted to ask where all those siblings thought Brella and Vel were now, but, savoring this tenuous peace, she decided to save the harder questions for later.

"How often do you go to the Between?" she asked instead.

"A few times a season."

"Where does it take you?"

"Oh gods, where doesn't it?" A sunbeam shot across Brella's face, and she raised a hand to shield her eyes. Then, in an instant, she caught herself. "Lots of places."

"Like . . ." Scratch prompted.

Brella eyed her warily, her face carefully blank. Assessing. It was a look Scratch recognized from her own face: a cautious, deliberate shell that hid the skilled work of deciding whether to share something truly worth sharing. It was apparent that Brella, like Scratch herself, rarely doled out precious things, meaningful things, and only then to the people who deserved to hear them.

It hit her with the blinding brightness of a sun suddenly unimpeded by cloud cover: she wanted Brella to tell her about the Between. She wanted it desperately. Because Brella, for some reason, didn't like soldiers. Because Brella, for some reason, didn't like her.

Everyone thought they had the measure of Scratch, that they could see the parts of which she was composed and decide what sort of person those combined bits made up. Everyone had been wrong. And so the need built (and built and built) to show Brella that Scratch was worth the telling. That it would be a pleasure—no, an honor for Brella to lay her stories at Scratch's feet.

Brella, for whatever reason, thought she knew exactly who Scratch was. Scratch didn't know much about the other woman, but she knew at least that Brella was wrong.

"I'll listen," she tried. "I'm not just trying to make conversation. I'm curious."

Brella's eyes narrowed further, little lines appearing beside them. At last she sighed. "All right. Koravia, sure, but once my sister Maisie and I went to the Bargard Cliffs. We were so high up, I thought I could reach out with my tongue and taste a cloud." She paused. A dark flush spread across her cheeks and nose. "I couldn't."

Scratch's mouth went dry. "Where else?"

As she talked—and as Scratch listened—Brella's tension eased. She had seen the deep eastern caverns, glistening striations of ore spinning down into the darkness. She had seen the sulfurous pools of Kerir, steaming swaths of impossible green reflecting sunlight like stained glass. She had even smelled the flowers of Gundoor; those had made her pass out for a few hours.

"Worth it though," she said. "I still remember the smell. Nothing smells like that."

Scratch had never smelled exotic flowers or sat atop the edge of the world. She had spent her life in the Royal City. There had been a few expeditions—accompanying the King to the Hillen Lands or guarding a noble on a political expedition to Crather's Keep—but those had hardly been remarkable. She had taken the King's Road there and the King's Road back. Most of her experience had been stomping, her only view the inside of her helm.

She didn't even remember the Tangled Lakes. Her mother had taken her to the Royal City when Scratch was only a baby. She often thought about going back, dipping her toes in the lakes she knew only from her mother's stories. But within that twined a thorny vine of apprehension. She had been called a Lakes girl her whole life. What if she went there and found out she . . . wasn't? That being raised elsewhere made her something different, something even more singular?

And then there were the Western Wilds. Her mouth ran dry, remembering. "They live in trees," she had told the commanders. Homes up high with bridges between them, wooden grins with slats like teeth. Clotheslines and pulleys strung between branches. Children nestled in hammocks like pupating caterpillars. A whole world above the ground.

Octagon had been an oversimplification. The real term was octagonal prism. Soldiers pointed out, then up, then further up still to catch fighters as they fell. Lines that weren't lines, but angles, shapes. Soldiers in graduated groups, their bodies forming honeycombs, leaving room for the Westerners' spears to catch only air. Climbers with daggers in their teeth and boots, clad in leather armor for close treetop combat that the Western spear fighters would never expect.

"Scratch?" Brella was peering at her. The sunlight filtered through the trees and onto her freckles, two overlaid patterns of dappling. "Where'd you go?"

"Nowhere," she answered, and they walked on in silence.

Chapter Six

When evening fell, they stopped in a clearing conveniently located by a small trickling stream. Wildflowers burst in bunches all around, tiny clumps of pinks and yellows and purples smiling up from the roots of trees and the edge of the water. Scratch watched as a small brown rabbit hopped through the glen, briefly stopping its course to munch on a flower before darting away.

She scowled. "It's like a children's story, James."

"Be nice." He gifted her a light slap on the arm before joining Vel on his quest to find fallen twigs to serve as firewood.

Brella had gone off to forage for edible berries and roots, leaving Scratch alone at the campsite. For want of something better to do, she laid out everyone's bedroll. It took roughly thirty seconds. She then searched the stream's bank for the heaviest stones she could find and arranged them in a circle so that the fire might burn a bit longer. She knew it to be a wholly unnecessary move. The night was warm, and between the food the Shaes had packed and the foraged roots, it was unlikely that they'd be eating anything that required more cooking than a cursory grill. But her hands were restless, as was her mind. If she were to sit, she was sure she'd be set upon by visions of disaster and ruin, too-clear memories of her worst failures. Her brain was used to working at speed, and now, sidelined like a racehorse with no rider, her mind was frothing and stamping, a confined, muscled machine making itself sick with unspent energy.

"Nice stones."

Brella stood at the edge of the forest holding the hem of her apron. Roots and berries weighed down the cloth that now served as a makeshift basket, the red juices from burst fruit dappling the fabric.

"You're going to stain your apron."

Brella shrugged. "That's what aprons are for."

"But the embroidery!" It was fine work, the stitches tiny and immaculately placed, depicting strange plants Scratch didn't recognize.

"Vel can do more."

"Vel did that?"

"Did he not say he was a seamstress?"

Brella upturned her skirt, unceremoniously dumping the spoils of her foraging by Scratch's stones. She then took a small knife from her boot, plopped down awkwardly, and began peeling the vegetables.

Scratch scoffed. "You're making a mess of that you know."

Brella flicked a chunk of mangled root from her lap. "I expect that the maids at the castle have a somewhat lighter hand."

"A bear would have a lighter hand." She made a noise of impatience and held her palm out to Brella, who gamely plopped a fat root into her outstretched hand. She removed her kitchen knife from its fancy sheath and set to work, grinning to herself when she received Brella's anticipated low whistle of appreciation.

"You're good at that."

She shrugged. "Knife work is knife work."

"Ah. So you'd skin a man with the same sort of finesse."

"What? I'd never skin a man! I only mean—"

"I know, I know. You prefer women." Brella smirked, knowing eyes twinkling. "I know the type."

Prickling heat crawled up Scratch's face as she gaped, speechless. Luckily, James and Vel chose that moment to return, flushed and grinning, arms laden with twigs and branches. James looked a bit punch drunk, his eyes glazed and sparkling, his lips reddened.

"Shall we set this mess on fire then?" His eyes were on Vel as he cheerily tossed the twigs toward the circle of stones, managing to get only a few to their intended destination while the rest scattered like spillikins.

They dined on bread, cheese, and the roots, which turned out to be somewhat spongy and rather pleasant.

"I could set up some snares," Vel offered as he tore into a root. "Maybe we could have meat tomorrow."

James smirked. "Snares?"

"Uh, yes?"

James reached for his bow and nocked an arrow. Before anyone could ask what he was doing (or, in Scratch's case, roll her eyes), he loosed the arrow into the brush. When he retrieved it, a hare was in his hands.

"If anyone could skin this, I would be much obliged."

Brella, openmouthed, pointed at Scratch.

"Fine," Scratch said. "Gimme."

She skinned the poor beast in silence, the Shaes too stunned to speak.

"I'm an archer," James supplied, after a moment or two.

Vel nodded slowly. "I gather."

They didn't follow, so James led harder. "Sometimes I go by another name."

"Oh."

Scratch snorted into her elbow. James glared at her.

"It's a nickname. Have you heard of any . . . archery-related nicknames?"

The Shaes blinked blankly at him.

"Arrow?" Vel guessed.

Undeterred, James puffed out his chest. "Bowstring. Have you heard of a Bowstring in the King's Guard?"

"Uh." Vel spread his hands. "Now we have."

"Does everyone have a nickname in the King's Guard?"

51

Brella asked quickly, James reddening beside her. "Bowstring, Scratch. Is it about the scar on your face?"

"Brella!" Vel whacked her. "You can't just ask someone about the scar on their face."

"No, no. I'm fine about the scar," Scratch assured them. "That's a boring story. I got it fighting a girl who hadn't cut her nails in a while." She slipped off the rabbit's hide in one piece like a shirt and handed the meat to Vel to roast over the fire. "That's not how I got my name, though." She turned to James. He pouted down at his bloodied arrow. "You wanna tell it, Jam . . . uh, Bowstring?"

It had been their first day at the Academy, and Scratch had already become a target. Her sergeant, a stone-faced brick of a man, had called a group to the sparring ring and was setting up children to fight in pairs. "Separating the wheat from the chaff," he had called it, and although the ritual was informal, it was important all the same. The winners and losers were split into groups after their spars, and Scratch knew that if she lost, she would be forever hampered by the weight of her first failure. There was no option but to win.

Perhaps for his own amusement, the sergeant paired Scratch, the smallest of the bunch, with a dense, brutish boy at least twice her size. The boy, a well-dressed, proud son of an earl, immediately complained of the indignity that was fighting a Lakes-milky slum rat in dirty clothes. He pleaded with the sergeant for a more suitable opponent, perhaps his cousin, a reedy, green-eyed youth with a perpetually bored expression and overgrown eyebrows. The sergeant didn't budge, however; and after a few minutes of pointless wheedling, the son of an earl finally relented, stomping into the ring, grumbling all the while.

Ten-year-old Scratch sized up her opponent. In the mid-morning sun, his skin was as pink as a plucked chicken, and when he pouted, his stuck-out bottom lip was a ripe cherry. He was coated in a layer of baby fat that hid a robust well of strength, as she discovered when he threw his first punch, knocking her onto her ass in the dusty earth. Even now, she could feel the spreading ache in her seat of a bruise to come, the sting of humiliation prickling behind her eyes, and the terror of being dubbed worthless before she even had a chance to prove her mettle.

Then, someone shouted, "Get up and fight!" And she did as she was told.

She fought as only a girl who had tasted the first bitter hints of failure could. She spat the poison from her body by sinking fists into flesh. The terror and anger of teetering on that precipice fueled her, and she fought with terrible, unsteady desperation. She would not go home, could not, and the unfortunate boy before her was taught the cruel lesson of her determination. She landed punch after punch in his soft belly, and when he went down she boxed his ears and head, then his hands when he brought them up to protect his skull. Only after the sergeant had called "Enough, girl," did she finally relent, leaving her bested foe bloody-nosed and trembling in the dirt.

Pity for the boy rose like bile. He lay on his side, wiggling like a frantic maggot suddenly exposed to light. Her assault had left him leaking blood and mucus from his nose and mouth, bubbling frothy red with his ragged panting. Limpid threads hung at his shoulders and collar where his fine clothing had torn at the seams. He looked smaller somehow, deflated; and glassy-eyed like a gutted fish. He trembled.

Something inside of Scratch told her to turn from him, to avert her eyes from this boy at his weakest. She did him this mercy, looking instead to her classmates, all wearing similar expressions of shock and horror, commingled with freshly earned respect. The combination left her with a feeling both terrible and intoxicating. Searching for a friendly face, her gaze landed on the boy who had yelled earlier, who had told her to "get up and fight" when she feared there was no fight left in her. It had been the cousin of her opponent, the green-eyed boy. He was smiling.

"My name's James. Do you want to be my friend?"

And then there was madness, a cacophony of shouts and cheers, faces near her and hands slapping her back. The defeated boy was all but forgotten in the fray as low and highborn spectators alike introduced themselves. Some came to offer congratulations, but more hid thinly veiled threats beneath supposed praise. They had seen what this nobody girl could do to one of their own and wanted to tell her that they would not be next.

She had let these new faces melt into one exhilarated blur and, trembling, had fallen into the blissful relief of her survival.

". . . and someone shouted 'She doesn't have a scratch on her!'" James told the rapt Shaes. "And it stuck."

Scratch generally didn't mind the story. Sure, there was a tint of guilt over the pride, but it didn't bother her when she didn't think too hard about the boy she had beaten. But today . . .

It had been her moment of renaming, when she went from Nobody to Soldier. She had planned to be a soldier forever.

Her hands were still red from rabbit's blood. She wiped them on the grass.

"And Brella?" she asked, too quickly. "Where does that come from?"

"It's actually short for Umbrella."

James was in no mood. "Don't tease us."

"Not teasing. Vel can verify."

"Not teasing," Vel verified.

"Why Umbrella?" Scratch asked, receiving a roast quarter of rabbit from Vel.

Brella lifted a shoulder. "It's a long story."

"We have time."

Brella paused for a moment, caught in knit-brow consideration over whether Scratch and James were worth her story. "I was born during a rainstorm," she began, apparently finding her audience satisfactory. "My parents wanted to name me Rainbow. Vel was sick when my mother was pregnant, and my parents hoped that when I was born, Vel would get better. The rain would stop and everything would be okay." She squinted up at the sky as a bat swooped above their heads, squeaking in the moonlight. "But it wasn't. He stayed sick for months, and that rainy season was the heaviest in a generation. Still, I was a happy baby, and I was Vel's favorite thing. My parents said that

I wasn't able to clear the rain, but I made it easier to bear. Like an umbrella."

"I'm better now," Vel offered.

"Yes." James arched an eyebrow. "We can see that."

Scratch was stuck inside her own head. There was no Brella without Vel; she was his Umbrella. What was it like, she wondered, to be so connected to someone else? It sounded warm. Safe.

When she had beaten the boy at the Academy, she had beaten him alone.

"We should sleep," she announced, skin prickling. She had barely touched her portion of rabbit. "I can take first watch."

No one objected. While James and the Shaes slipped inside their bedrolls (which Scratch had so expertly laid out), she found a good, mossy spot under a thick maple and settled herself. Through the leafy branches she could just make out the stars. They looked strange out here, as if they had scrambled just to unmoor her. Where was the God of Dirt, with his giant feet of mulch twinkling overhead? Where had the God of Stillness run off to? And, horrors upon horrors, where in the infinite hells was the Cheesemonger?

Deep breathing speckled with snores drifted up from the bedrolls. Now she was truly alone.

Her name was Scratch, and she had earned it. She had every reason to be proud of escaping that first fight and every subsequent challenge with her dignity intact. But there was a reason the story made her skin itch tonight, a snag in the fabric of it. Alone, under the stars the gods had abandoned, she opened herself to the why of it: the boy. Pathetic. Ruined. Stripped of his dignity so that she could take her first hard-won step toward a life of her own. To best him had been the only way forward. Now, sitting alone and lost in an unfamiliar wood, with no title to her name and no home to speak of, it felt like a terrible waste. He was destroyed so that she might thrive, and to look directly at the memory of him meant the weight of her victory nearly choked her.

She had learned afterward that his name was Heiryn. He'd left the next day, sent home in shame. Soon, the only mention of his name was in the story of how Scratch had earned hers.

Chapter Seven

Scratch woke at dawn. The fresh blue light of early sunrise tinted the campsite, washing it in dew-damp refreshment. She greedily sucked in the morning air like cool, cleansing water.

Brella slept beside her, her brown skin glowing faintly in the morning light. She looked younger while she slept, her face smoothed of the little tics and tensions that shaped it into something sharper. Her freckles stood out like bits of spice on a pound cake. There were so many, some crossing the friendly border between skin and the darker, softer expanse of lip. Scratch couldn't help but think of stubborn shoots that sprouted between cobblestones, nature so wild it burst even in the inhospitable landscape of the Royal City.

Umbrella Shae wasn't a fighter. She was a brewer, and she was sleeping on the forest floor on day two of the rescue mission for a kidnapped princess. A dangerous mission, one touched by conspiracy and unknown threat. Still, if Brella was to be believed, she was determined to bring Frances back, and to do it herself.

Why? Yes, Brella's sister was the princess's lover, but there had to be more to it. Brella was strong-jawed and fierce. Charitably, Scratch could conclude that Brella was doing the work because no one else would. Still, even if Scratch had been prone to such generous conclusions, it was a stretch. There had to be a simpler answer. Unfortunately—and infuriatingly—it seemed to be just out of reach, a butterfly mockingly darting inches beyond her grip.

The bright crack of a twig splitting by the tree line cut through her butterfly-crushing thoughts. She scrambled to her feet, then crashed to the ground with an unceremonious thud and a very undignified shriek. She was still in her bedroll.

"I feel so much better knowing I'm traveling with a real-life King's Guard solider." James grinned at her from his seat between the exposed roots of a thick, old oak. "You're a true inspiration."

"Shut it." She rubbed her bonked rear as she made her way over. "Are you reading?"

"Yup." He closed the book he had been paging through and laid it in his lap. "Don't be cross. No one is coming for us in this glen. I half expect a kindly bird to fly down with a little cake for me."

"What is it?"

He shamelessly handed over the clothbound, pale blue book.

"Really, James? *The Centaur and His Boy* again? You know, the same thing happens every time you read it."

"Yes, well, I like what happens. And maybe something different will happen this time around." There was a wink to his voice. "There are fae about."

"Don't remind me."

He leaned against the tree, closing his eyes and breathing deep. "Someone woke up on the wrong side of the blade of grass."

"Forgive me if I'm not jolly enough for your liking."

He smirked. "I shan't."

"They're lying, James." She rested her head on his shoulder. It was, as usual, far too bumpy. She often requested he eat more so that he could better reach his highest calling, becoming her pillow. "I don't think they're lying about the blood gate and all that, but there are missing pieces."

"Oh, Scratch." His chuckle sounded irritatingly put-upon. "I expected this, you know."

"What?" She lifted her head to glare at him. He stared off, green eyes soft in the shade. "You think I'm wrong?"

"Of course you're not wrong." He lifted a shoulder. "I just don't see why it matters."

"James. If we don't prepare—"

"Then it'll be our fault when we lose. I know, I know." A big yawn cracked his jaw, and he stretched up against the tree bark. "But we've already lost. We aren't King's Guard anymore. Inevitably, there is a price on our heads. I don't see a way of preparing for anything because there's no way of knowing what's ahead."

A jolt of annoyance stiffened her shoulders. "James. It isn't over. We could bring Frances back and bring her story to the people and—"

"And what? Depose the king?" He shook his head, smiling softly. She wanted to hit him. "Aren't you tired?"

She bit back the reflexive *no*. "Of?"

"Of fighting, Scratch. It's all we've ever done. Don't you want, I don't know, something else?"

Tension bloomed across her brow. "Not you, too."

"Look around." He swept an arm out. The forest glowed, blankets of moss crawling up trees and over stumps, green and vivid and inviting. Birds chittered on branches, tweeting their morning missives, visiting and departing. The air smelled of split-apple freshness, wet and sharp and brand new.

"The way I see it," James murmured like a visitor in a quiet temple, "there are no paths for which we can prepare. That doesn't mean there's nowhere to go from here, darling. It means there are so many possibilities, we can't possibly plan for all of them. Like it or not, we'll be surprised."

Her heart felt heavy, low slung and drooping behind her ribs. "I'm very angry at you."

"You need a distraction." He arched an eyebrow. "Brella would suit."

"If I had a pillow, you'd be fighting your way out from underneath it right now."

"She's lovely." He tipped his head in acknowledgment. "Yes,

a bit prickly, and doesn't seem too fond of soldiers, but it looks like she's grown to tolerate you."

"Oh, yes. All girls dream of tolerance."

"Naturally." He elbowed her lightly. "It could be fun."

"I don't date."

"Wrong. You haven't dated. And I'm not talking about dating."

"You're talking about getting inconvenient splinters." She fixed her gaze, trying hard not to look at the woman sleeping at the other edge of the glen. "It's not something I do, Jamie. Even if I wanted to, it's too much of a—"

"Distraction, I know." He slung an arm around her shoulders. "I swallowed that excuse for years, Scratch." He pitched his voice higher. "I can't step out with a woman because I can't be distracted, darling. I'll find someone to kiss after I get my knighthood."

"I don't sound like that."

"You do rather." He squeezed her. She took it, unsmiling and squished. "But there's nothing to get distracted from anymore. And besides, you're a romantic, at heart."

"You're a puddle, at brain."

"Well, if I can't convince you to make a move on Brella, could you do a bit of something else?" He tapped the book. She had forgotten she was holding it. The cloth cover was stiff and jarring between her fingers.

"No, James."

"If you—"

"No, James."

"But you could—"

"No, James."

"Fine." He snatched the book from her, dropping it in his lap and folding his arms across his chest. He pouted.

She waited a moment before admitting defeat.

"What part are you up to?"

He grinned, handing her back the book and opening it to a page about a quarter of the way through.

"The man just escaped the ogres." He eagerly tapped a section of black print. "Start there." He cuddled into her side, tipping his head up to give her a meaningful look. "Go on then." She sighed and did as she was told.

The centaur studied the traveler who had entered his magical glen. He was frail, probably having run for days from whatever creature, man or magical beast, had been in pursuit of him. His clothes were torn. Through the large rip on the front of his shirt, the centaur saw a set of well-formed abdominal muscles, dusted with a light smattering of fair hair.

"What ho, human," he called. "Why do you traipse through my magical lands? No human is given welcome here!"

"I have nowhere to turn." The human was on his knees, hands clasped in a sign of prayer. "Please allow me safe rest and I will be forever indebted to you."

The centaur scratched his chin and ran his fingers through his short magical beard. On his knees, the traveler was at his mercy. He could bring the man back to the Council of Centaurs, which was magic, and receive a magical reward. And yet, something about the man drew him in. Perhaps it was the openness of his wet mouth, or the flush of his pale cheek. Or maybe, and most likely, it was the erection tenting the front of his tattered trousers.

"I have never seen a centaur before," said the man, bringing the heel of his hand to his member and pressing down. "You are unlike any other creature I have laid my eyes upon. Is it . . ." the man bit his lip, "true what they say about centaurs?"

"That we have the girth of the horse? That our manhood is solid like a rod of brass? That we can give a man pleasure so great it will ruin him for human men? Ha! All true. Also, we are magic."

The man was panting now, wantonly rubbing

his hand along his turgid length. "And that you have a
stamina so great you can spend hours, even days, making
love?"

"Why don't you come here and find out, weary trav-
eler?" purred the centaur, beckoning the man like a fish
to a magic lure.

She reseated herself and winced.

"What's wrong?"

"Fell. In my bedroll. Perhaps you remember. It was your fault."

"Was it?" He smirked. "Because I broke the twig?"

She snapped the book shut. "You did that on purpose."

He tilted his head with a completely unconvincing *moue* of innocence. "I could see you were awake. I wanted to get your attention."

"Yes, well. My ass thanks you."

She glared at him. He smiled back serenely.

"Shall I tend to it for you, darling?"

"I think Vel would take objection. Speaking of, what's going on between you two?"

James blushed, turning to hide his face. "*Nothing* is going on."

"Nothing? You always tell me about this sort of thing. Are you sick? You look flushed." She pressed the back of her hand to his forehead.

He swatted her away. "No. I'm just choosing to exercise a little restraint. Haven't you told me to keep things to myself from time to time?"

"Yeah, but that was when you were telling me about that time you went home with the vegetable seller and he took out that big carrot and—hey!"

In one practiced move, he had her pinned, his weight pressed against her forearms. She struggled against him, her back rubbing uncomfortably against the roots of the tree.

"Get off me, you ass."

"Make me, speck."

And they were off, twisting and turning, pressing and rolling, wrestling like they hadn't done since their teens. They were punching and kicking and pushing and then, all of a sudden, laughing, breathy and gulping, run through with giddy freedom and exertion. Their moves grew increasingly ridiculous, and as they scrapped Scratch felt warm, liquid calm seal a few of her tension cracks. So she went harder. She threw a handful of leaves into his face. He sat on her head. She got a finger up his nose. He threw her into the woods.

"Ouch!"

"Oh, sorry. Did you fall on a rock?" he panted, wiping sweat from his eyebrows, which now resembled snarled skeins of wool. He was certainly missing the bespoke golden eyebrow comb she had bought for him. She treasured the memory of the jeweler laughing aloud when she explained what sort of comb she had wanted made, and what its absurd purpose would be.

"No," she told him. "Just fell on my ass. The same spot from earlier."

"Earlier? Oh, you mean when you fell in your bedroll like a complete fool?"

She led with her shoulder as she ran, colliding into his midsection and lifting him up so that he was slung over her back, head and feet dangling on either side of her body. She rocked back and forth so he swung like a gangly human pendulum, the tips of his fingers grazing the earth on each pass.

"Put me down! Put me—oh."

He was staring through her legs, so she had to turn to see what had caught his attention. Both Shaes were awake. They sat up, mouths open, staring.

Without thinking she dropped her burden. He tumbled into the grass in a bundle of limbs and fabric with a muffled *oof.*

"Well." Brella yawned deliberately, exposing a pink tongue and white molars. "When Vel suggested we bring you along, I wasn't convinced. But seeing the fighting prowess of two of our nation's best up close, well . . ." She smirked. "I've never felt safer."

Chapter Eight

The canopy was denser today, filtering dappled sunshine that illuminated the party like scattered gold flake. James and Vel gravitated toward the front while Scratch and Brella lagged behind. James looked entirely at ease, which was hardly fair. He barely seemed bothered by Scratch's fully formed, totally unassailable assertions of treachery. It was as though he didn't care, which was patently absurd. He *had* to care. He must have been just as tangled as Scratch was over it all.

"It's the tragedy of the centaur, you see," he explained to Vel, waving around that damned book. "Even though he has an irrepressible sexual appetite, he can't touch himself because his hands are all the way up front."

"Halt!" shrieked a little voice.

At the command, all four travelers stopped in the middle of the road to watch a small figure drop from a tree directly ahead. They wore a wide smile on their youth-pudgy, dirt-smeared face. Bits of tree bark clung to their hodgepodge clothes, the thin fabric littered with mismatched patches. Their mouth was stained pink, likely from stuffing their face with wild berries.

Wow. Were all bandits this adorable?

"I'm terribly sorry, my friends," the sweet confection of a woods rogue apologized in a chirrupy voice, "but I will be requirin' your purses. Quick as you like now."

Scratch opened her mouth to talk—well, to laugh and then talk—but Brella got there first.

"Lollie, is this one of yours?" She craned her head around, squinting up into the nearby branches. "She's cute, I'll give you that."

"Shit." Another bandit, this one larger than the first, fell from above, landing deftly on the forest floor. "Call it off, gang. These folks don't have two coppers to rub together."

"Lovely to see you too, Lollessandra," Brella said in dry greeting.

The cute bandit let out a sharp, bright pulse of laughter. "Is your name really Lollessandra?"

"Shove off," mumbled the larger one. "This one's called Umbrella."

"Naw, really, Lollie? That ain't a name. That's a household item."

"Excuse me." James raised a hand. "Can someone please clue me in on what's causing this little diversion?"

The larger bandit—Lollie, the little one had called her—strolled around, planting herself in front of James. She was tall and slender, fair skinned with dark hair cropped to her chin and a small, peaked hat perched jauntily on her head. Someone had patched the elbows of her hide jacket with a green checked fabric that matched the pale hue of her canny eyes. Scratch felt those eyes take her in, sly and assessing, as the woman ran her tongue over her teeth and hooked her thumbs into the waistband of her trousers.

"This your new one, Brella?"

Brella scowled. "None of your business, Lollie."

Lollie opened her eyes wide and took a step back. "I know who she is. There's a bounty on her head."

Scratch's stomach sank. She knew that there would be some commotion back in the Royal City over her and James's disappearance. She had hoped—foolish, foolish—that it might not find her out here.

Her hand hovered over her knife. She could take Lollie easily (she didn't even want to think about fighting the adorable baby bandit), but there had to be more adversaries around. She could sense eyes on her, burning hot on the top of her pale head. What if they were kids, too? Yes, soldiers weren't poets, but they weren't child killers, either.

Brella's gaze flicked between Scratch and Lollie, then up into the surrounding trees.

"She's with us, Lollie," she said eventually, voice tight. "They both are. Go against them and you go against us."

Scratch didn't have time to think about what Brella's steadfast allegiance meant. She was too busy glaring at the bandit, waiting for an attack. It could have been her imagination, but for a moment it seemed that genuine pain flickered over Lollie's slight features. In an instant, the pain was gone, replaced by narrowed eyes and a sly little grin. It all happened so quickly, she could almost believe she hadn't seen anything at all.

"If she's with you, Brella, she's safe with us." Lollie bowed her head. "And, of course, it would be rude to ask why you and Vel—"

Vel waved. "Hello."

"—would be escorting two fugitives of the crown, would it not?"

"Yes." Brella's gaze was unswerving. "It would."

"So we should accept, without explanation, why a seamster—"

"Seamstress," James coughed. Vel beamed at him.

"—and brewer are traveling with two people who are worth a thousand crowns each—"

James choked. "How much?"

"—without even so much as an excuse. Even a transparently fake one, for my benefit."

"Indeed." Brella smiled. Scratch couldn't understand how Lollie didn't shiver under the malice of it. "We'd also like a meal if you would be so kind."

For her part, Lollie didn't hesitate. "Anything for an old

friend. You don't mind saying hello to the family, do you? Come out, everyone!"

Brella groaned. "No, don't call everyone—"

But it was too late. Figures, a dozen or so at first glance, melted out of the landscape, emerging from behind boulders and the trunks of trees. A few, one of whom carried an unsettlingly large, loaded crossbow, jumped down from high branches. Most were young. Scratch placed the oldest—Lollie—at around her own twenty-five years, while the youngest hovered near eight or nine. Many wore green handkerchiefs tied around their throats, the two tails popping merrily from open collars.

As the Shaes greeted the throng, it immediately became clear that Brella's impatience had just been for show. She smiled as she opened her arms to the merry band of child criminals, smoothing down cowlicks and stroking cheeks, receiving what was no less than adoration from the raggedy crew.

Feeling a bit disregarded, Scratch sought out James, who stood beside Vel under the shade of a large maple tree. A rangy long-haired teenager chatted with them, wiggling with excitement.

James leaned toward the girl. "You're good at making what, my dear?"

"Pokies!" She pulled a long brown object out of her satchel and handed it to James. "Well that's what we call 'em at least. They're just thick branches I whittle into a point. The trick is, don't make 'em too smooth. You wanna leave some splinters in there. Three coppers a pop, and I'll throw in a fresh chipmunk hide."

"Lovely, but I'm all set on weapons and dead animals. Scratch, darling?" James held out a hand. Scratch eyed it until he dropped it back to his side. "This is Ylla. One of the Tree Grabbers."

"Tree Snatchers." Ylla rolled her eyes. "Boy, for a rich man you sure aren't that quick."

"That's enough, Ylla." Lollie appeared, laying a slender arm over the teen's shoulders. "Be nice to our guests."

Scratch compressed her jaw. "We don't plan to stay. We're on a bit of a timeline."

"Don't be silly." Lollie smiled widely, but her icy eyes brooked no argument. "You'll spend the night with us. We've got a camp nearby. Don't we, Brella?"

"Huh?" Brella wandered over, a young girl clinging to her waist. "Yeah, it's not bad."

Something about this situation rankled, and it wasn't just that Brella hadn't prepared her for a harmless band of armed infants.

"We don't want to inconvenience you."

"Scratch—"

Lollie smirked. "Your name is Scratch?"

Annoyance bloomed red behind her eyes. "Yes." Not that anyone named Lollesandra had room to judge.

"Fine name," Lollie replied without a hint of irony. "It's not every day our Brella brings a Passenger. She is your Passenger, is she not?"

"Yes, she is. And more to the point, Lolls, I wasn't aware I was anyone's Brella."

Scratch had barely enough time to wonder what in the infinite hells a Passenger was, and whether Lollie had been referring to her before the bandit volleyed back a tart reply.

"Of course, my mistake. Ah, I do miss our banter. Follow me, all."

Lollie led their party deeper into the woods, making sharp turns and quick jumps over split logs and mossy boulders. Scratch kept dogged pursuit, short legs be damned, until the trees parted and she found herself in a wide, sun-drenched clearing. Ten squat canvas tents sat around an extinguished fire pit, over which a char-marked spit squeaked as it shifted in the afternoon breeze. Laundry hung on lines stretched between trees, small hats drying beside mended britches and the occasional tunic. Someone had created a makeshift altar out of smooth river rocks, but it was entirely unclear which god was meant to be honored by the little display, which included featureless cloth dolls and a bulky whittled statue of what might have been a bear.

Lollie swept out an arm. "Home sweet home."

"Looks a little permanent for a bandit's den." Scratch crossed her arms over her chest to muffle the sudden mysterious pang therein. "Aren't you concerned about getting arrested?"

"As if King's Guard would ever come out here, present company excepted. Besides, the forest takes care of us." Lollie stood close—too close—and lowered her voice. "The trick is, when you ask the forest for something, you really have to feel it. Gotta put everything you have into it. Hasn't Brella told you? She understands this place better than anyone."

Scratch bristled. "She's mentioned a few things."

"She used to love it out here you know." Lollie took a hunk of wood out of her pocket, followed by a small knife. She began to whittle, dragging the knife across the wood in slow, rhythmic strokes.

Scratch didn't know how Lollie had managed to get her alone but somehow it had happened. Chalk it up to being out of her element, or maybe the wily magic of the woods. Brella was nowhere to be seen.

"It's nice that she's back here." Lollie's dark voice spread slowly over her like spilt ink. Her knife moved against the wood, loosing ribbon after ribbon. *Thwack, scrape. Thwack, scrape. Thwack, scrape.* "She didn't tell you about us, did she?"

"Funny enough, you hadn't come up."

"Funny. Indeed." She didn't laugh. "I do wonder what other things haven't come up. Brella has such stories to tell."

And with that, the queen of the bandits strolled away, melting into the chaos of her domain.

Chapter Nine

Lollie was, without a doubt, a threat of incalculable danger. That said, the woman was a rather good host.

On her orders, two strong boys presented a goat, skinned and stuffed with herbs and vegetables from the bandits' surprisingly well-stocked garden. The band must have robbed a spice merchant at some point, because they managed to liberally season the beast on the instruction of a discerning adolescent, who appeared to be in charge of the culinary proceedings. Scratch, James, and the Shaes were plied with mugs of ale while the Tree Snatchers, Lollie included, took turns turning the spit. Scratch offered to help; her palms itched for something to do—but was shouted down by little voices, proclaiming her a "guest" who therefore "shan't lift a finger." She did as she was bid, planting herself on a split log and setting to the task of convincing herself that she enjoyed being served by feral children.

Brella was breezy here, guard down and smile wide. Her cheeks were lightly flushed from the ale, and she had at least three children clinging to her person at all times. To see Brella like this gave Scratch an inexplicable warm feeling, somewhere down in the parts of her she generally chose to ignore. A favorite poet of James's had written of "dark cellars of the soul, covered in cobwebs," or some such rot. Flowery nonsense, but Scratch couldn't help but relate in this particular moment. She felt as though she were unraveling spider's silk in corners of her being that had long gone to seed, ignored in favor of "Being A Good Soldier."

Scratch didn't date. Not because she didn't want to, but because she couldn't. One slip up, one deviation from the path she had been on since her first day at the Academy, and all was lost. Now, at twenty-five years of age and without a future to fret over, there was no excuse not to pursue Brella, were either party interested. Well, no excuse other than the fact that the brewer was more than probably a liar. Really, James had been reading too many silly love stories. Not everyone was looking for a centaur to get their hands around.

Brella laughed in her periphery, snorting ale over the rim of her mug. She glanced at Scratch as she wiped her nose and leaking eyes. She grinned. Scratch briefly forgot what to do with her arms.

Dinner was served after nightfall when the untouched darkness of the forest welcomed a thick, twinkling canopy of starlight. Scratch stared up, unable to name a single constellation. Unlike last night, she knew to expect a sky full of strangers. Still, her internal compass spun.

"Stargazing?"

Brella sat down beside her and held out a plate of meat and veg. Scratch stared down at it and up again.

"For me?"

"No, for the God of the Heavenly Fast. Yes, for you, you tit."

Scratch waited to tuck in until Brella returned with her own plate, piled high with steaming slabs of meat.

"Hungry?"

Brella grinned sheepishly. "They like to feed me. For some reason, the Snatchers think I need tending."

"You?"

She shrugged. "Lollie always worried about me. I really think it was more about her needing to feel like she took care of someone than me needing the caring."

"Seems like she's got enough people to care for already." Scratch indicated a pair of boys wrestling a few yards away. One kicked the other in the stomach, sending him directly into the side of a tent. It went down hard, tentpoles skittering away into the night.

"Quite." Brella sipped her ale. "It's her calling. All of these children grew up poor. Bad families or dead families. It was this or fend for themselves."

Or the Academy, Scratch thought, but it wasn't worth saying, especially now in this tenuous peace.

"She doesn't take advantage of them," Brella continued, biting into a steaming turnip. She held the hot morsel between her teeth for a few moments, then remorselessly spat it back onto the plate. "The robbery is mostly to cover the operating costs. That, and something to do. A common goal binds a group together."

She thought of the octagon. Soldiers pointed out, then up, then farther up still.

"True enough."

They ate in silence, surrounded by the songs of awakening nightbirds and chattering bandits. Someone brought out a mandolin and began to play, strumming wordless melodies into the warm night. She could hear James's laughter drifting up from the other side of the fire, sweet and familiar, as he and Vel entertained a group of beaming youths with what sounded like a rather bawdy tale. She thought about scolding him but, well, these weren't her kids. If Lollie had a problem with it, she could get up from the log she shared with one of the older Snatchers, the two of them murmuring together and shooting quick, unsubtle looks Scratch's way.

Her skin prickled. "Hey Brella, what's the story with you and—"

"Do you stargaze?" Brella stared heavenward, eyes far away. Her finger twitched, subtly pointing at one of Lollie's older bandits. Scratch raised her eyes and the girl turned quickly away, making an unconvincing attempt to appear interested in the untouched plate on her lap.

"Um, yes," Scratch murmured. "But these stars are . . . different."

"Different stars, different gods." Brella reached a hand upward, then dropped it to her side. "Do you see that cluster with the three stars? The one with the red star to the left?"

She did. The God of Storms should have occupied that spot. "Yes."

"That's the God of Bladder Stones."

"There's no God of Bladder Stones."

"Oh yeah? Then who do you pray to when you have bladder stones?"

"Uh, the God of Healing?"

Brella waved her away. "He's too busy with consumptive children to concern himself with bladder stones. And there, the green star with two below?"

"Uh huh."

"The God of Falling Asleep Whilst Reading."

Scratch laughed. She couldn't help it. And then, "I think I've spotted another."

Brella arched an eyebrow. "Have you?"

"Look there." She pointed up, and Brella drew close to follow her finger. Brella was warm against her side, solid and real. She swallowed. "There." Her voice was barely a whisper in the inky night. "The God of Sneezing with Your Mouth Open."

Brella cackled, pushing her away, and Scratch bounced back as if drawn. They went on like that for a while, invoking the God of Three-Legged Dogs with Sad Eyes and the God of Spilling Beer on a Rude Man at a Pub and the God of Posh Eastern Accents, the last of which caused James to poke up his head and demand an explanation for why they were laughing at him, and could they kindly stop. Of course, they only laughed harder.

While Brella pointed—"Up over there, the God of Un-pickable Wedgies"—Scratch allowed herself an indulgent look. She watched Brella's full mouth as she spoke, gazed at the bronze locks that fell down her back. This was what Brella really looked like, without fear, without anger. Even in the deep blue shade of night, she radiated the warmth of sunrise, her hair as brown and warm as a loaf of fresh bread. The woman was all break-fast—bright, welcome breakfast, like the yolk of an egg or the underside of a griddled cake. She was an apparition of morning time, and Scratch had always liked morning best.

Oh, yuck. James had been right: Scratch really *was* a romantic.

Still, that hardly mattered when the truth was that Brella, without doubt, was a treacherous liar. It rankled not knowing what the woman could be hiding. Maybe the attraction was that Brella was a mystery, a puzzle like a battle plan. Upon further examination, the theory made perfect sense. Scratch didn't want Brella; she wanted to understand her. Brella filled the hole the absence of strategy sessions left behind. There was nothing more than that. Relief melted through her muscles, calming the tension she'd been holding all day. Brella was nothing more than a riddle, and all riddles had solutions.

Before she could refocus her eyes on the night sky, a little poke came at her shoulder. She turned to find a girl, younger than the rest, perhaps five or six. She had long white-blond hair, unkempt in a way that made Scratch's fingers itch to pull it into some sort of manageable coif. Her skin was blue-vein fair, her eyes portholes open to the stormy sea.

"I welcome my cousin to my home in the spirit of gratitude," the girl squeaked.

Scratch bowed, her head reverberating with memory like a sudden gong strike. "I enter my cousin's home in the spirit of peace."

The little girl squealed and threw herself into Scratch's arms. It was only by the grace of her fighter's reflexes that she managed to catch the child without toppling over.

"I'm Temperance." The girl's sticky nose bobbed in the air an inch from Scratch's face. "What's your name?"

"Scratch."

Temperance gave her a curious pout. "That's not a Tangled Lakes name."

"I don't like my Tangled Lakes name."

"Boy, me neither." Temperance plopped onto Scratch's lap, which she had apparently decided was now her seat. "When did you come here? Do you miss the Lakes? Do your mama and papa live in the Lakes? I don't really remember the Lakes that much, but my mama used to tell me stories. She said it was wet and salty. Do you have a grandma and grandpa? Have you been on a boat? I wish there were lakes here. If there were, I'm sure I would be the best sailor. Do you fish? What's the biggest fish you ever caught?"

"Temperance." Brella laid a steadying hand on the girl's arm. "Why don't you give a moment for Scratch to answer before you ask another question, hmm?"

"Sorry." Temperance waited patiently for just under three seconds before she launched off again. "Do you know how to make a lobster trap? My papa was a lobster trapper. Can you read? Do you read books? Do you have Lakefolk friends? Do you know anyone who's little, like me? Why is your hair tied so tight? Where do you keep . . ."

Scratch answered as much as she could. No, she didn't miss the Lakes. How could she, when she had come to the Royal City as a baby? No, her mama didn't live in the Lakes. She lived in a house in a nice part of town with thick windows and a big lock on the door. No, she didn't have a grandma and grandpa. Or, if she did, her mother never told her about them. Purpose hadn't told her daughter about any of their family.

"Really?" Temperance stuck her thumb into her mouth. Brella gently pulled it out. Temperance didn't seem to notice. "Not even about your papa?"

"No."

"Oh." Temperance considered this. "I had a mama and a papa, but they both died. You seem sad. Lollie says it's okay to be sad. I'm sad sometimes, too." She patted Scratch's face, a gesture meant to be comforting but was undeniably a series of tiny, painful slaps. Her thumb was still wet from when it had been in her mouth, and it left damp smudges on Scratch's cheek.

Brella wasn't looking at either of them.

"Do you want to sing a song?" Temperance cocked her head. "Mama used to sing songs while she brushed my hair."

"Mine too," Scratch rasped. Tangled Lakes hair was thick and scraggly, prone to knots. Her mother said it was because the hair wanted to be rope for ships. Scratch had always complained while her mother brushed her hair. "Let it be rope!" she would cry. "I don't care!"

Temperance jammed a finger into a nostril. "Could you brush my hair?"

"Sure."

A few minutes later, Temperance sat between her legs, humming absently while Scratch combed through the tangles and snarls. Brella had drifted away. She sat with Lollie, having quiet conversation by the dying fire. Scratch turned from them, settling her mind on the meditation of drawing thick, yellow locks through Temperance's gap-toothed comb, leaving them smooth and glossy.

"Brackish, brackish, brackish," Temperance sang, "are the waves awaiting me."

And there it was, stored in another one of those dark cellars of the soul, coated in cobwebs. It crested before she could stop it, as much instinct as catching Temperance had been when she had leapt into Scratch's arms.

"Brackish, brackish, brackish," she sang, before she recognized that she was singing, "are the waves awaiting me."

Temperance whipped around. She stared for a moment, then smiled.

"From the beginning," she instructed, and Scratch could do nothing but nod helplessly and sing:

Brackish, brackish, brackish
Are the waters of the sea
Born was I in brackish swell
And so my grave shall be
Spill the lager, spoil the milk, and scald the bitter tea

Brackish, brackish, brackish
Are the waves awaiting me

I sail amongst my fellows
For my cousins all they be
No better men to take
When you are facing down the sea
Hoist the sail, men, hoist it high, and onward hard alee
Brackish, brackish, brackish
Will our journey surely be

But, oh! The water's churning
Men, watch out, for do you see?
The hungry waves are reaching out
And they are calling me
Remember me, don't weep for me, I was but one of ye
Brackish, brackish, brackish, boys
My grave is now to be

But on the shore a woman waits
She holds a child of three
Inside of her, in brackish swell
There rests a babe to be
She waits, while in her heart she knows her love she'll never see
Brackish, brackish, brackish
Are my lover's tears for me
Brackish, brackish, brackish
Are my lover's tears for me.

There was noise in the camp when she finished, the same murmurs, the strum of strings, the clank and clang of tin plates and earthenware mugs. She must have imagined, then, the quiet that came over her while she sang. Imagined the low swell of waves, or perhaps her mother shushing her, *shush, shush,* then an ebbing, silent like sleep. Imagined—invented—the tenderness of hands on her skin, smoothing down her hair and kissing her eyelids. That couldn't be real. Her mother would never treat, had never treated, her so sweetly, with such care. But why then did she see in her mind's eye the flickering of a low tallow candle, the wooden walls of her childhood home? Why did she hear her mother singing? Or—oh, gods, had she confused her own voice for her mother's? If she hadn't felt sick already, that certainly did the trick.

"Temperance, I'm going to take a quick trip to the woods. I'll be right back."

Temperance nodded sagely. "Remember, 'Leaves of two, you'll scream when you poo.'"

"Thanks, I'll keep that in mind."

She walked toward the tree line, not looking around, just putting one foot in front of the other. She was dizzy and unnerved, like she had just been transported somewhere else. The return trip had felt like falling off a speeding horse. She was fine, she was fine; she just needed a moment to breathe. A moment away from frizzy-haired Lakes girls and Brella's false gods and Lollie's cold, inscrutable eyes. A moment to collect her wits.

She found a leaf-free tree on which to rest her head. The damp, earthen smell of the forest filled her nose and throat, raw and fecund. She missed her world with walls, where she woke early and gave orders and served a king she could trust. The forest was too old to respect order. It was not built for her, nor she for it. She was built for lakes apparently, their songs imbedded in her bones.

But, she reminded herself, she had been built twice. Once, when her mother birthed her, and a second time when she spilt blood at the Academy and took her new name. She had adapted before, hadn't she? Fine, she'd adapt to this. This strange life she found herself inhabiting. How hard could it be to become someone new again? Someone who could understand this place. What was wild earth anyway but potential? She could—

A thud sounded behind her, two feet hitting the earth from a height, and then there was a knife to her throat.

"Hello, Keyes," Lollie purred. "You and I have much to discuss."

Chapter Ten

"Lollie." She dared not breathe. Lollie held the knife mercilessly close, an inhalation's breadth from Scratch's skin. "If you wanted to have a conversation with me, you should have just asked."

"Shut up, you royal lapdog. I need to know what you're doing with Brella."

Looking at her too long. Trying to solve an impossible puzzle. "Nothing."

Lollie brought the knife closer. Scratch could feel the metal kiss her skin. "Is she your prisoner?"

"No."

"Have you threatened her?"

"No."

Lollie's breathing was harsh and high. "You didn't kidnap the princess like they're saying, did you? You're going after her. You and the Shaes and that decorative item you call a friend."

It shouldn't matter if Lollie knew the truth. Still, it rankled. That information wasn't hers to know. Couldn't Scratch have something to her damn self anymore?

"I don't see how that's any of your business."

"Brella's worth more than that, you know." There came the sound of crackling as Lollie ran her tongue over dry, chapped lips. "I told her to be quiet about the gate. That the King's Guard would eventually use her to get to it."

"You know Brella. If she's anywhere, it's because she wants to be."

"Oh, don't act like you know Brella," Lollie spat, venomous. "I know you're not really her Passenger. Not like that. And you don't care, do you? You don't care that you're stripping her of that?"

There was that Passenger again. Brella owed her an explanation. Until then, she'd have to pretend. "I think you're jealous."

Lollie growled as the knife made contact with Scratch's skin. She felt the warmth of a few beads of blood trickling down her throat and onto her shirt.

"You should be scared of me." Lollie's whisper sliced the air. "I could kill you out here."

"Is that what you teach those children? To kill their guests?"

Lollie's breath stuttered. She shifted her grip on the knife and exhaled, the cool air ghosting over Scratch's nape. "Probably no worse than what you learned at the Academy. What do they teach you?"

What had she learned at the Academy? To wake early. To train every day. To hold a sword. To stand by a brother or sister on the battlefield and stanch their bleeding wounds, to get them to a healer before they expired. To stare down an enemy and not cower. To become someone.

"Honor." The word was sour with longing.

Lollie choked out a raspy chuckle. "You don't know anything about honor."

"More than you."

"You don't seem scared." Lollie angled the blade upward, like a barber shaving close. "Why is that?"

"Because I could kill you twice out here and no one would know." A bluff, of course. She couldn't reach her knife. She was only buying time. What would happen if she screamed? Could James get there faster than Lollie could slit her throat?

The answer was probably no. Thankfully, she didn't have to try.

"Drop the knife, Lollie," Brella said.

All she needed was a second's hesitation. She felt the knife drop away, just for a breath, and—there. She edged into the silent moment, like a key into a lock, her hands fitting perfectly around Lollie's fingers as she pulled the knife from the slack grip and flung it far into the undergrowth. Her fingers pressed tight to Lollie's flesh, her back taut, muscles working as she gripped the bandit and bent forward, taking her up and over and slamming her into the earth. And then, a few practiced moves—an arm here, a leg there—to get the woman facedown, Scratch's knee pressed into her lower back.

"*Ow*," Lollie grumbled.

"Damn right, *ow*." Brella retrieved the knife from the bush where it landed, examining the blade. "I didn't think you were stupid enough to hold a soldier at knifepoint."

"And yet I did." Lollie wriggled like a trapped lizard, legs kicked out behind her, knees bent at a right angle.

"And yet you did." Brella squatted down next to the captive bandit's head. "Did it even occur to you that you could really mess things up for me—for all of us—by hurting her? That I might be keeping things from you to protect you?"

"Fine excuse. Well, you never told me a damn thing when we were together. Why should now be any different?" Lollie's muscles worked against Scratch's grip. "I thought—I don't know what I thought."

"I have an idea." Brella seated herself, cross-legged. "You did what you always do and assumed I needed rescuing."

"Can you blame me? You never told me anything. Anything about your life, anything about what trouble you were getting yourself into. All I could ever do was guess. Guess and worry."

Brella stiffened. "I didn't ask you to worry."

"Well, too bad." Lollie dropped her cheek to the earth, sighing. "It's my nature. I look after children."

"I'm not a child."

"I didn't say you were."

"I don't need looking aft—"

83

"It's what people do for each other!" Lollie flailed, but she was no match for Scratch's knee pressing firmly into her spine.

"I didn't need you to—"

"It isn't about what you needed, Brella. It's about what you wanted." She gave up the fight, going limp in the dirt. Her hat was missing and her short, sleek hair was dusty and mussed. "No one does anything alone. And I know you have Vel, but you're so close to each other you never let anyone else in."

Scratch cleared her throat. "I could go."

"No, Scratch." Brella held up a hand. "Stay."

"Yes, Scratch," Lollie added. "Stay. Bear witness to my total humiliation."

"I'm not trying to humiliate you, Lollie." Brella looked away, drawing little patterns in the dirt with the blade of Lollie's knife. "I came to tell you to let her go. Whatever trouble I'm in is trouble of my own choosing."

"Fine."

Silence rang out in the dark wood. Scratch wanted to run. This felt like reading someone's diary: an intimate trespass, devoid of any clarifying context. She had both the most power and the least out here with these women, and the tension tugged at her spine.

Lollie wriggled. "I'm losing feeling in my arm."

"Oh, sorry."

"Don't apologize to her, Scratch."

"I really could go. You two seem to—"

"Scratch, stay."

Lollie tensed. "Don't tell me there's really something between you."

"I don't see what business it is of yours." Brella rose stiffly, wiping dust off of her trousers. "This is a warning, Lollie. Don't get in the way of things you don't understand."

Lollie glared up at Brella from where she lay in the dirt. "It kills me that you don't get it."

For one moment, Brella's composure cracked, that full mouth falling open, those hot-coal eyes going round. Then she swallowed, setting her jaw. "Get what?"

"That I'm not your enemy. That it's not weakness to ask someone to help you. That whatever you're doing, you can't do it alone."

"I'm clearly not alone." Brella waved a vague hand in Scratch's direction.

Lollie chuckled darkly. "Of course not. Sergeant Major, if I promise not to knife you in your sleep, will you let me go?"

"Oh, yes. Pardon me." Scratch scrambled off and Lollie rose, wincing as she shook out her arms and rolled her wrists.

The bandit scrubbed her face with dirty hands, depositing smudges on her cheeks and forehead. "Well, I'm off. Who knows what chaos your brother's new beau has incited in the camp." She made to walk off, but stopped. "I just . . ." She breathed, and Scratch imagined she could see the words crumple on Lollie's tongue. The bandit shook her head and disappeared into the trees.

Brella dropped her head into her hands and groaned. "Oh, God of Chaos. I'm sorry you had to see that, Scratch."

"What's a Passenger?"

Brella went wide-eyed, caught like a doe. "I wasn't sure you had heard that."

Anger sparked in her chest. "What are you hiding from me, Brella?"

"Nothing! Well, nothing important."

A lie, of course. She had been prepared for this, for knowing that Brella lied remorselessly, boldly. It shouldn't have stung. "So, what? Lollie just keeps bringing it up for fun?"

"Lollie is just . . . Lollie." Brella spoke the name with irritated familiarity, and it struck Scratch how little she really knew about this woman. She knew Brella was defensive. That she had a whole slew of brothers and sisters who were . . . somewhere. She was a brewer, supposedly. And despite the clenched-jaw care with which she approached the world, she was either the sort of person who careened headlong into an impossible quest, or a skilled and practiced liar. Disappointment dripped through Scratch's body, slowing her blood and weighing her down.

"Tell me what a Passenger is," she demanded, but there was nothing behind it but resignation.

"A blood bond," Brella began, after a careful pause. "It doesn't just get you through to the Between. It connects us."

"Connects us how?"

She lifted a shoulder. "I don't really know. I've never done it before. Supposedly it's intense. Fae magic," she added. "It'll make us close. Apparently, we'll be able to sense each other's emotions while we're Between."

"Why did Lollie get so bothered about it? Is it . . ." She struggled for the word. "Special?"

"I guess. My mom always told me . . ." She broke off, staring at nothing. "She said it was something to do with someone I cared about. I was waiting. I never brought Lollie. It didn't seem right."

"And you're bringing me."

Brella's eyes hardened. "I don't have a choice, do I?"

Anger warred with guilt. "You chose to take me with you."

"I had to. There was no other way. And I don't see you complaining. Would you rather still be in the dungeon? Or perhaps hanging from that slender little neck, hmm?"

Her stomach churned. "Brella . . ."

Brella covered her face. Scratch thought for one horrified moment that Brella might be crying. Should she . . . go to her? Touch her? Every option looked like it might end with a broken finger, so she stood and watched while Brella breathed behind her closed hands.

"Look, Scratch." Brella ran a hand over one of her long brown braids. Someone—a child, probably—had poked flowers in between the strands, little blue buds that looked like they belonged in the loamy earth of Brella's hair. "We barely have a plan. We love our sister, so we're doing whatever we can to get her princess back. And because . . ." She breathed for a moment, eyes closed. "Because it's the right thing to do. You might not understand—"

"I understand."

Brella winced. "He's not a great king, Scratch."

Had it been only two days ago that she was passed over for commander? It felt like an eternity. "He has his faults."

"A great deal more than faults."

"Well, if what you say about a conspiracy is true . . ."

"Scratch. Do you really not—" She tugged at a braid. A flower popped out and landed on the ground, disappearing into the brush. "Of course you don't."

Scratch bristled. "Of course I don't what?"

Brella's nostrils flared. "I keep forgetting you're a soldier."

"If you could refrain from making these cryptic little comments about how you disapprove of me being a soldier, never mind that the cornerstone of this excellent plan you have is for me and James to do 'our thing,'" she curled her fingers in quotations, "and 'our thing,'" more quotations, "is what we do as soldiers. We fight. You got us so that we could fight. I don't see what the problem is."

Brella stared at her for a moment. Then she exhaled, all the fight floating off her body like dew.

"You wouldn't," Brella mumbled as she turned away, walking off toward the chatter and firelight of the bandit's camp.

Chapter Eleven

If Scratch had lived through a more awkward morning, she couldn't remember it.

On one side of camp, Brella hunched over a plate of eggs, spooning them into her mouth while Vel looked her over with concern. Across the fire, Lollie silently waved off a band of older Snatchers, several of whom were making a valiant attempt to keep the littlest of the bunch away from their leader. Tension hung over the camp like wet canvas, the atmosphere close and uncomfortable.

Scratch didn't quite know what to do with herself. Luckily, Temperance spared her the choice, nuzzling into her shirt and making low, mournful noises.

"I don't want you to go."

"I know." Scratch petted the girl's head and made what, to her best recollection, were sounds of comfort. "I will miss you," she said, finding as she said it that it was true. It was odd. She had spent years fighting alongside the same soldiers, yet had grown attached to only one: James, who was presently handing over a few shiny coins to a delighted teenager. No one besides James had managed the feat of getting her to care. But something must have sloughed off her when she left the castle, a layer of dead skin turned armor by the force of routine or order or some calculable rubric of where she belonged in the world. Now, she was like a freshly molted snake, her scales too soft and too bright, her eyes stinging from reflected newness.

Actually, that might be due to the tears.

She discreetly wiped her eyes with the back of her hand and held on to Temperance like an anchor.

"Got you a present." James bounced over, both hands held behind his back. "Pick."

She indicated his right arm. He brought it forward, and—

"James, what am I going to do with this?"

"Poke someone," he drawled, as if it were the simplest thing in the world. "They're called Pokies, Scratch. Shouldn't be too hard for you to puzzle out."

"I have a knife."

"And now you have a Pokie as well. Keep up."

"What was in your other hand?"

He showed her his left—another Pokie.

"I'm wanting for variety out here," he muttered. "Forgive me for presenting you with the illusion of choice. Gods, Scratch, you are no fun at all this morning."

"Scratch, if I could have a moment." Lollie stuffed her hands into her pockets as she approached. "I, uh, a moment."

Scratch gently extricated herself from Temperance with a soft word and followed Lollie to the edge of the woods.

"I'm not sorry," Lollie declared. To her credit, she didn't look away, her cold, pale green gaze unyielding. "I did what I thought was necessary."

"I understand," Scratch said, because she did, for the most part. She might have done more than hold someone at knifepoint for answers.

"I expect you do." Lollie scratched the back of her neck. "I have a favor to ask. About Brella. She can be careless. She is a thoughtful person, but when she gets angry . . ." She trailed off, shrugging. "Just make sure she doesn't end up launching herself into danger. That's all."

"What do you think I'm going to do?" Scratch replied tartly.

"Throw her to the wolves?"

"She's charming," Lollie said in a matter-of-fact sort of way. "She acts like she doesn't need someone watching her back. She does."

"Everyone does."

Lollie threw up her hands. "Fine. I can see this was a hugely worthwhile conversation. Thank you so much, Scratch. Go on your merry way and do whatever-the-fuck it is you and the Shaes are doing. Never mind that I've known Brella for three years—"

"Three years?"

"And she never told me a thimble's worth of information about her life. And you two saunter in here like the God of the Sun and the God of the Moon, with all of your little secrets, and I can't learn shit about what either of you are up to."

"You ambushed me," Scratch hissed, eyes flicking to the curious Snatchers spying them from yards away. "What, are we supposed to be friends now? You decide that I need advice, and that I'm going to take it from you? I'm a Sergeant Major in the King's Guard."

"And she's not a soldier." Lollie dropped her voice to a hot, frantic whisper. "I don't know what you're doing or what you want, but if you put Brella into harm's way, I will kill you. That may strike you as sentimental, Scratch, but I look after children all day. I'm not as calculating as you. I'm not smart enough to hide what matters to me. I know that means I've made myself vulnerable to you." She glanced off into the trees. "Brella makes me stupid."

The back of Scratch's neck itched. "Oh."

"Yeah."

"She'll be fine with me," Scratch said, and it was an easier promise than it should have been—almost as though she cared about Brella's well-being.

"Thanks." Lollie looked a touch surprised, as if she'd expected an argument. "I feel like I should give you something in return. Oh, we robbed a wine merchant the other day. You want a cask?"

Yes, desperately. "Uh, no thanks."

"Your loss." Lollie shaded her eyes from the rising sun. "I already hate today," she declared by way of farewell. "You'd do well to keep your word, Sergeant Major. I have a very long memory."

"Great," Scratch mumbled once Lollie was too far away to hear. She tamped down a spike of fellow feeling for the cranky bandit. "Lovely."

Chapter Twelve

Children followed the traveling party as they left camp, strolling along like they were there to join the rescue mission. Brella smiled and waved while the pack was in view, but she visibly drooped as soon as the band disappeared behind the trees.

Vel floated up beside her. "Brella—"

"Shush, Vel," she muttered. Her posture drooped and there were bags beneath her eyes. "I've had enough talking. Can we just be quiet today? All of us?"

James pouted, but Vel nodded. "Fair enough."

They walked on through the morning, the Shaes leading the soldiers along the same inexplicable route. It had been easier when the prospect of bandits, beasts, and fair folk was only theoretical. After Lollie, it was easier to picture enemies in the trees, darting behind rocks, hiding their footprints in the shallow streams that wended their way through the uneven landscape.

Discounting the anxiety, the forest today was much the same, with no discernible path, nor any clear markers that even hinted at where they might be headed. Were they getting closer to the princess? Closer to the Between? Lollie had made it seem like Brella's ability to pop from one country to the next was not some sort of elaborate hoax. That was as reassuring as it was discomfiting. If Brella was telling the truth, that meant that

Scratch would really pursue the princess. And if she could get Frances back, she would really claim her rightful spot as Lady Commander. She allowed the thought to warm her, just for a moment. Not hope, but motivation. Incentive.

She set her mind to poke at the mysterious snarl of Frances's disappearance. If King Ingomar had really planned to stage his own daughter's abduction, the girl probably wasn't in Koravia. The whispered word that Frances and Iris had picked up—*Koravia, Koravia*—was the planted seed, not the culprit. If—a big if—the Shaes were telling the truth, then King Ingomar's plan was to start a war with Koravia by accusing their king of kidnapping Princess Frances.

Strength against Koravia was one of many reasons King Ingomar had led all of his mighty conquests, his "west, west, west to the ocean" pursuit. What if he wasn't satisfied with a strong defense? What if he had decided the safer path would be to take the offensive and attack Koravia before they got a chance to do the same? All he needed was a good enough reason to make the first move.

Scratch was so wrapped up in her thoughts she barely heard the crinkle of dead leaves. "Stop," she whispered, but by the time the word slipped through her lips, it was already too late. A rustle in the trees ahead, one beside, and one in a bush—they were surrounded. She dropped her hand to her knife.

"Do what I say when I say it," she breathed. Brella met her eyes, nodding mutely. Something lashed around Scratch's insides at the sight of her, squeezing tight. She blinked it away, finding James. His brows were drawn, his tongue darting across his nearly healed lip. He reached for his bow, nocked an arrow, and—

"I wouldn't, if I were you." A man stepped out from behind the trees ahead, tall and broad and instantly familiar.

"Branch," Scratch breathed.

The last time she had seen him, he was tossing her into a dungeon. The intervening days hadn't been kind to the man. His clothes were torn, his face and hands grayed with dirt. He had a wild look in his eyes that she hadn't seen before, hungry and narrow. Normally, he was hulking. Now his bulk tipped into a forward lean, low like a wolf. He was armed, but Scratch was more worried about what he'd try with his bare hands.

He grinned, his teeth stained berry purple. "Found you, Keyes. And Bowstring? I'd lower that if I were you. Hester's right behind you."

James slowly lowered his shot, peering over his shoulder as Hester edged out of the brush, his sword drawn. Opposite James, Gultin strolled out from his hiding place, hands in his pockets. He leered.

"We're traveling with two civilians," Scratch said, fingers floating by the hilt of her kitchen knife. "Let them go. Your quarrel is with us."

"Actually, Trout, it's with all of you."

It had been so long since someone had used a Lakefolk insult against her that she was more surprised than offended. "How's that?" she asked, stalling. "The Lord High Commander must have sent you out after me and James. Nobody else needs to be involved."

The minute she said it she knew she was wrong. No one had sent these soldiers out to get her. They weren't equipped for travel, their packs thin and clothes tattered.

"You were fired," she murmured, recognition dawning. "Banished." Branch said nothing, but the hot flare of red over his face revealed the truth. "You were banished because of us. Because we got out. I'm sorry."

"You're sorry?" His laugh was reedy and wet. "Sorry won't help you now. Lucky it's us that found you. We'll be good enough to take you in alive."

James inhaled sharply. "Is the whole city after us then?"

Branch gave him a pitying look. "With that price? Not only the city, ponce. Nowhere's safe for you. Besides, everyone thinks you killed her. Who wouldn't want to be the one who brought you to justice?"

"We didn't!" James reached for something in his pocket, but

Hester was faster, lunging forward to poke the tip of his blade into James's shirt. James stilled. Scratch's heart leapt into her throat.

"James." They locked gazes. She breathed deeply, dropped her shoulders, and let the air out through her mouth. Then she turned to Brella and Vel. There was fear in Brella's eyes, tightness around the long lashes and a bright wetness in the warm brown of her irises. Scratch's heart stuttered sluggishly.

"Run," she hissed. She felt the hilt of her knife between her fingers for a moment, then flung it. The weapon sprouted from Branch's chest, blood spurting under the blade. He looked down, dumbstruck, then up: and he fell to the ground with a limp crunch. She reached down, found nothing, and swore; the knife was her only weapon. She darted over and yanked it from the dying man's chest, blood gushing from the dark red wound. A sound made her pivot. Gultin approached, huge and hulking, his sword drawn. He had the reach, but Scratch had her own advantages. She darted under his thrust, slashing at the tendons behind his ankles. He shouted as he fell, hobbled in the dirt. His sword slipped from his fingers.

"Thanks for this," she garbled through a mouth numbed by adrenaline, "been meaning to pick up one of—"

"Ahh-hells!"

She had felt fear before. There was the dull, final fear of waiting to be executed in the dungeons. There was the thrill-tinged anxiety as she watched her octagon bloom on the battlefield. But there was no fear that compared to the ragged terror that tore her chest at the sound of James's broken, horrified scream.

He was on the ground, his leg splayed out at a nauseating angle. Blood soaked the side of his pant leg, and his face had gone ashen white.

Her mouth hung open. She closed it with a click. "James . . ."

"Hello, Sergeant Major."

She had been so focused on James that she hadn't realized Hester was still fighting. He lunged at her, short sword out and glistening with blood. *James's blood*, she thought, swallowing the fear, sour in her tight throat. There wasn't time for fear. Instead, she forced herself beyond the fear into the anger. It came to an instant boil, every moment that had scalded her since her last meal in the castle rising up, shrieking. Frances's truths. King Ingomar's dismissal. Her last hours in the dungeons. Vel's and James's laughter. Brella's fiery eyes and vague insults and stiff jaw and evasiveness and the cold knowledge that everything Scratch had worked for was now meaningless. It was all meaningless.

She screamed and slashed with the borrowed sword, but it had been Gultin's and he was a big man. She misjudged the balance, spinning out with the momentum, and Hester seized his opportunity. She blinked, and she was disarmed, the sword slamming against the earth, just out of reach. She bore down instead, fists up, looking for an opening, not letting herself believe this was the end. It couldn't be. Not after she had come so far. It didn't make sense that she would die here in the forest at the hands of a mediocre sergeant because she had had to leave her own sword behind.

She chanced a look at James. He was alone, which chilled and warmed her in equal measure, because it meant that the Shaes had escaped at least. They would be protected by their magical forest. Would they go on, or would they go back to the Royal City to regroup, maybe recruit more fighters? Mercenaries this time, fighters that Brella respected more than soldiers. They would go on, and she and James would die and there would be no one left alive to grieve her.

She squared her shoulders, and—

There came a loud squelch and a wet, choking noise as something red erupted from Hester's throat. He glanced down, hands gripping haplessly at nothing, blood dripping from his open mouth. Then he fell, a heap of blood and limbs and nothing, on the forest floor. His arms twitched once, twice, and he lay still.

Brella stood in the clearing. Her eyes were wide and bloodshot, and her warm brown skin had taken on an unpleasantly sallow shade of yellowy gray. When she met Scratch's eyes, she sank to her knees.

"I killed him."

Scratch moved without thinking, rushing to Brella's side and scooping the larger woman into her arms. Brella fell into her, pressing her face into the shoulder of Scratch's shirt. Hot tears worked their way into the weave, dampening her skin. Brella grasped wildly at her, and questing fingers demanded more, closer, tighter. Her hands roved like spiders as she squeezed at Scratch, her tears turning to sobs, her sobs to wails.

"I killed a man. I killed a man with a fucking Pokie."

Chapter Thirteen

Relief hit Scratch in a rush, momentarily freeing, then suddenly exhausting. Her hands shook.

"It's all right, Brella," she mumbled. Her tongue felt thick and heavy. "It's okay."

"It's not all right." Brella shivered. Her trembling lips had gone pale. "He was going to kill you. So I killed him. I killed him. Oh gods, I killed him."

She wasn't the only one wailing. A few feet away, Vel huddled over James's wounded leg. Every time he touched the bloody mess, James shouted, his scream piercing the air like the call of a dying prey animal.

Scratch desperately met Vel's eyes. *What do we do?*

He wiped away a tear. "Brella, we have to."

"No!" she shrieked. "We can't. There isn't time."

"His leg is b-broken." He was shaking, his fingers coated in blood. "He'll die without m-medical care. And then there's . . ." He indicated Gultin, breathing shallowly on his stomach. He bled freely from the back of his legs, not even attempting to get up. "We need to figure out what to do about him."

"Don't kill him," Brella cried, high-pitched and warbling.

Scratch tightened her hold, pressing Brella close to her chest. "We won't kill him," she said gently, "but we need to do

99

something. If we just leave him, he'll die."

Brella gripped Scratch's arms with bruising force. "Scratch. You need to know. The fair follk. They don't give anything out for free. She'll take something; she always does." She made a sound somewhere between gulping and choking. "Usually, it's time."

"Time?"

"She'll help. But please, please, if she offers you anything, if she takes you aside and says she has something special for you, don't take it." Tears clung to her long eyelashes. Her hair was slipping from its moorings, little bits of bronze forming a frizzy halo around her head. "Tell me you won't."

"I won't." She felt dizzy. Nauseated. "Who is—"

"Nana!" Vel shouted into the trees. "Nana, we need you!"

Nothing happened for a few moments. With numb hands, Scratch stroked Brella's hair. Over the top of Brella's head, she watched Vel whisper gentle words of comfort to James, who panted and sweated on the ground before going limp. Vel gasped.

"James? James!"

"It's good, Vel," she told him, though her throat twisted and tears stung her eyes. "It's good. He passed out. He's not feeling the pain that way."

He looked distraught, but he nodded, and it hit her afresh that the Shaes weren't soldiers. They hadn't seen violence like this before. Brella had never killed. Of course she was wrecked. After Scratch's first kill, she had vomited against a tree.

The Shaes were liars, yes, but not about needing Scratch and James to fight for them. That had turned out to be horribly, sickeningly true.

"Oh, thank the gods." Vel pointed into the woods. In the distance, a cottage came into view. As Scratch watched, it got both clearer and closer. The house didn't move, but every time she blinked it was somehow nearer. It was a squat, sky-blue little thing, coated like confectionary in pale trim. A low white fence bordered flowerbeds teeming with bright, healthy, entirely unrecognizable blooms. A few stones formed a makeshift walkway up to the gleaming yellow door, on which a brass knocker bearing the face of a goat grinned at them.

"Well," bleated the knocker, "this is rather unexpected."

The door burst open and a woman bustled out. She was clearly old, though she moved quickly. Her crinkling, worn cheeks had all the rosy plumpness and warmth of a full teapot. Long white lashes framed sparkling eyes, with irises a blue so pale it verged on white, and dark, rectangular pupils that stretched nearly the entire length of her eye. Her hair was a fluffy cloud, brushed back and away from the large, thick-glassed spectacles that sat atop a genial little nose, as smooth and as well-formed as an acorn. She wore a pale yellow blouse topped with a dusty rose pinafore, the lace-trimmed skirt skimming the tops of her—

Those weren't knees.

"Oh dear, oh dear." She scurried up to James with remarkable speed, tutting over his prone body. "Oh dear. Gogo, fetch me the blanket."

"Yes, Nana," the door knocker replied. How he was meant to fetch anything Scratch had no idea, but in a moment a roll of fabric zoomed out of the door and unfurled next to James.

"There, there," the woman cooed as the blanket gently edged its way under James. "Good job. Almost got him now. Drop him in the rose room and then come back for the other. He'll go in the daisy."

The blanket rose and carried James into the cottage. It returned in a moment, a touch blood-stained, and repeated the process with the sputtering Gultin.

"What's going on?" he slurred, floating through the cottage door. "What is this? What's going on?"

The woman turned, giving Scratch a clear view of her full form. Two reddish-brown furred appendages jutted from the bottom of her skirt, knees bent backward. At the ends, where there should have been feet, the woman had hooves.

"Now," the goat-woman declared, a serene smile beaming from her wizened face. "Why don't you children come in for some tea? We have much to discuss."

101

Chapter Fourteen

Scratch entered the cottage in a daze. She had never been in the home of a fae before. Was there some sort of etiquette she had to follow? Did she need to bring a gift? All she had on her were weapons: Gultin's sword, her kitchen knife, and a Pokie. Perhaps Nana would enjoy a slightly used, bespoke silk knife sheath. Unless—did the fair folk even have knives?

She could have slapped herself. Of course they had knives. They certainly had cottages, and fairly regular-looking cottages at that. The room she entered was wood-paneled, with a pair of well-worn couches occupying most of the space. Before them squatted a low table laid with a small dining set: one plate, one spoon, and one cup, all done in mismatched, colorful ceramic work. Low beams latticed the ceiling like the top of a pie, bundles of dried herbs hanging at all four corners. At the center of the ceiling an upside-down dangling bouquet of flowers emitted a soft, yellow light, like an unblinking flame.

Scratch reached up to touch the glowing flowers. Brella slapped her hand.

"Don't."

"I wasn't going to."

"Yes you were." Brella frowned. The moment Nana had directed the brewer to enter the cottage, she had stopped crying, sniffling so hard Scratch could almost believe Brella was sucking all her tears back into her face. She was stiff, crinkles of tension blooming beside her bloodshot eyes. Scratch wanted to touch her again, but her hand was still stinging from that slap. She couldn't risk another.

"Sit, sit." Nana indicated the couches. "There's plenty for everyone."

Scratch blinked. The table, which had before held an empty plate, now groaned under a platter laden with freshly baked scones, steam curling off them in the form of what Scratch could have sworn was a beckoning finger.

She looked to Brella for approval. *Can I?* Brella ignored her, flopping onto a couch and grabbing a scone for herself.

"Thanks, Nana," she mumbled through the crumbs. "We were in a pretty tight spot."

"I gathered. Sit, my new guest. And you too, Vel."

Vel trembled, his eyes darting toward the two closed doors Scratch only now noticed sat on either side of the room. "Our friend." He gulped. "Is he . . ."

"He's fine, Vel," Nana tutted. "Now, come sit. I made your favorite: gurgleberry."

Scratch followed Vel to the unoccupied couch and reached for a scone. Fruit dotted the surface like garnet in ore. She bit. Sweetness zinged across her tongue, a mixture of cherries, chocolate, and the memory of one sunny day she and James had spent laughing over dirty books by the Academy pond.

"This is," she whispered reverently through her mouthful, "the best thing I have ever eaten."

Nana beamed. "Thank you, child. You're just like my Umbrella. A healthy appetite." She pursed her lips. "You could use some fattening up, though. If you stay for a while, my dear, I'd be happy to—"

"We're only here for a little while, Nana." Brella wiped her mouth on the back of her hand. "Just until James heals."

"James." His name sat in the fae's mouth for a moment, a little ball of sunshine. Then, as Scratch watched in dumbstruck fascination, she swallowed it. "And the other?"

"Uh, Gultin?" Scratch supplied. There was a danger, she suspected, in this fae knowing names. Not just knowing—keeping. But Nana already had Brella's, Vel's, and James's names, so it couldn't be that bad. Besides, Gultin had just tried to kill her, so her empathy was somewhat limited where he was concerned.

"Gultin." She ate his name, too, the little ball of light traveling down her throat. "And you?"

Brella flinched. "Nana—"

"She ate of my table, Umbrella."

"Yes, but she doesn't need you like—"

"She does." Nana's nostrils flared. "You all do. Or would you prefer to be discovered by one of the dozens of parties pursuing her?"

Vel looked up from the untouched scone in his hand. "Dozens?"

"Yes, child. I may not know who she is, but I can certainly feel the eyes on her. The hands reaching for her, too. And the steel." She licked her lips. "I can taste it."

Scratch's stomach clenched. "Swords."

"There's wealth around her." Nana held out her hands, palms forward, grabbing at nothing. "A bounty. The people are desperate for her."

Brella made a sound that might have been a growl. "They can't have her."

Well, that was surprising. A jolt zinged across Scratch's stomach, followed by a fizzing warmth. But, no—it probably wasn't personal. Brella needed her to fight off more pursuers, or to factor in whatever mysterious end, whatever secret, the woman still held close. Despite herself, Scratch felt her ribs tighten.

"Of course, they can't, Umbrella. I can smell how important she is." The fae's tulip nose twitched. "In ways you haven't begun to understand."

Scratch raised a hand, confused and tired and a little warm with anger. "How am I important?" There was enough she didn't know, enough knots to unpick. She couldn't stomach another.

"It's not for me to tell, child," Nana replied, infuriatingly calm. "Things will be revealed as you're meant to know them. Now." The fae's focus was palpable, a poke rather than a caress. "Your name."

"Patience," she croaked, stiff and uncomfortable. "Patience Keyes."

Nana opened her mouth. It was dark inside.

"Not that name, child," she hissed, displeasure curling her lips.

"That is my name." Though it lifted the hairs on the back of her neck. She still heard it in her mother's sharp voice, raised in anger. *Patience. Patience!*

"No." Nana's voice took on a strange timbre, an added chorus of voices underneath hers, pulled from somewhere deep. "I need the name you are called. The name you are known by. That is the name with power. Far more power than the name you were given at birth."

"I—" Her words died in her throat. She felt ten years old again, rising from her first fight with scraped knees and dust in her eyes. "Really?"

Nana's fire dimmed. "Really, child."

"Scratch." As she said it, something like the reverse of a shadow, a little negative space of light, traveled from her mouth to Nana's. The goat woman opened for it, held it on her pink tongue, then swallowed. As she did, the room came into sharp focus. The wooden walls weren't simple at all. Symbols and words etched in an inscrutable language ran the length of the beams, glowing with faint light. The gurgleberries glistened in the scones, lightning bolts of yellow energy running beneath each rosy membrane. The glowing flowers dangling from the ceiling opened their mouths, revealing rows of tiny, needle-sharp teeth.

"Oh," Scratch said.

Nana rose, holding knitting in her gnarled hand. A long scarf with shifting patterns trailed from two golden needles to the wooden floor. In the yarn Scratch could make out the images of four people, three tall, one short, traipsing through a tree-thick wood.

"Now that we've all eaten," Nana declared with a satisfied grin, "I should go take care of your friends. It seems as though I have a great deal of mending to do."

Chapter Fifteen

"He'll be okay, right?" Scratch asked, watching Nana disappear behind a closed door. "James. She's not going to hurt him?"

"No." Vel fell back against the couch and closed his swollen eyes. "She'll help him. For now."

"For now?"

"She has his name." Brella took another scone—it must have been her third—and chomped into it. She wasn't looking at Scratch. "She knows him. And now he owes her."

"Owes her what?"

Vel shrugged. "It varies. After she rescued me from a pack of bandits, I had to give her a phial of my blood."

Scratch recoiled. "For what?"

He shrugged again, absently fingering the tan skin of his elbow pit. "Not sure. Time works differently with her. Maybe she'll use it after I'm dead."

"How old is she?"

"Time. It's . . . weird." He fluttered his hands around as demonstration. "I don't think even she knows."

Scratch ran out of questions after that, so she let her mouth fall shut, her eyes closed. She was wrecked, battle-fatigued and mentally sluggish. She wanted to sleep, but feared missing any information, any bit of truth that could get her back to her feet.

Brella cleared her throat. "Scratch, can I talk to you?"

She opened her eyes. Brella was staring at her warily, with defensiveness writ across her set jaw. "Uh, sure."

"Alone?"

Vel scowled. "I'm comfortable. And I'm sad. You can go elsewhere."

"Fine. We'll go to the lavender room."

"Where is—oh." As Scratch spoke, a new door appeared in the far wall. Or maybe it had been there all along and she hadn't noticed it before. Actually, come to think of it, she had seen it before. In fact, it was the first thing she had noticed about the room: a wooden door decorated with a painted sprig of lavender. And, gods, it was beautiful.

"Oh," she cried. "Of course. The lavender room."

Brella's melancholy cracked, letting a smile shine through. "You'll get used to that. You can only find things in here you know about. But once you know, it feels like—"

"A treat."

"Yes, Scratch. A treat." Her smile broadened, then fell. "Come on."

Scratch practically skipped toward the door, flinging it open and tumbling into a much larger room than should exist in a cottage. The air inside had a sleepy, perfumy smell. Four windows opened to lavender fields, stretching off in lilac waves toward the horizon. A massive bed with purple dressing took up the majority of the space, with two towering side tables against the head and a trunk big enough for Scratch to lie in at the foot.

"I forgot there weren't chairs in here." Brella glared at the bed like it had wronged her. "Scratch, do you need a leg up?"

As it turned out, she didn't need a leg up, but her ascent wasn't exactly graceful, and she face-planted into a mound of lavender pillows.

"Why is it so big in here?"

Brella lifted a shoulder. She had managed to hoist herself up cleanly and was now lying against a neat stack of cushions. She was roughly twice Scratch's size, but even Brella looked like a doll in this bed. She stared at her feet.

"Not all of the fair folk are the same scale."

"So are you saying . . ." Scratch peered over the side. "Giants?"

"Try not to look so delighted."

"Why not?" She fell back against the pillows, sinking into the soft plushness. "It's delightful."

"Of course it is. It's meant to be." Brella pursed her lips. "You saw what she did with your name. She's kind, as kind as she can be for what she is, but she needs to eat. She would love to keep you here forever."

Scratch sat bolt upright. "She'd eat me?"

To her horror, Brella didn't respond with an immediate *No*. "Not exactly," she said instead, after a pause that went on far too long. "Not your body, anyway. More like your spirit. The rest of your life. Your potential." She smoothed her apron. "You see why we can't stay here long."

Scratch stifled the urge to fling herself out the window. "Just until James is healed."

"Yes. Nana's told us she'll have a way to avoid people coming after you. I have an idea but . . ." She gazed out at the swaying lavender. "She'll know best."

"Sure."

They sat in silence, two tiny figures on a giant's bed, under the nowhere-ish eyes of hundreds of lavender stalks.

"I should . . ." Brella tugged at a braid. "I should apologize to you."

Scratch stilled, the tantalizing prospect of answers dancing before her. "For what?"

"For coming apart like that. It wasn't fair for you to have to, um," she winced, "care for me."

Heat licked at Scratch's cheeks. "It was fine."

"It wasn't. I'm supposed to be guiding you. I know the woods better. I shouldn't have left you alone like that."

"You didn't leave me alone."

"Of course I did." She pulled a frayed thread at the corner of her apron. "I know I was unreachable. When I was . . . crying, I mean. If you needed me for anything."

"But I didn't." Scratch reached out, laying a hand on Brella's. She took it as a victory that Brella didn't flinch away. "You saved us. You and Vel, calling Nana. And if you hadn't gotten Hester—"

"Hester." She licked her teeth. "That was his name? The man I killed?"

"Yes." It wasn't worth telling Brella how mediocre Hester had been, how mean and petty, even as early as the Academy. He was still a person. That was the rub of it. No matter who you killed, no matter how antithetical to your needs their living was, they were always people. "Hester. And, Brella, of course you felt ... bad." Brella was right: soldiers really weren't poets. "This was your first kill."

Brella snatched her hand back, face paling. "My first?"

"Maybe your only one. I just, I mean that we're on a rescue mission to get Frances. We don't know what we'll run into. You might have to—but hopefully not." The last bit of color drained from Brella's face. "This could be it. One and done."

A line of tension appeared by the corner of her mouth. "One and done?"

"I don't mean—" She cursed herself. "I just mean that everyone's first kill is difficult. When I had my first—"

"How many people have you killed, Scratch?"

The question hit with the abruptness of a blast of sunlight. Her eyes stung, angry tears gathering that she dared not spill.

"I ... I don't know."

"You don't—"

"A lot, okay? I've been in the King's Guard for years. I've killed people."

Brella's nostrils flared. "You don't know how many?"

"Fine," she said, her own voice muted in her ears, like she was speaking from the fuzzy, algae-coated floor of a lagoon. "You want to know how many? I'll tell you. From the most recent one, today. Before, at least four in the Western Wilds. One because she struck at James and was winding up for a second attack. She had a flail. Weapons like that cause so much chaos on a battlefield. It's possible—likely, even—she killed some of her own. One came at me with a spear. I took him under the ribs. It was a clean kill. Another I knocked off her horse and I'm certain she was trampled. And I say at least four because I wounded three more. One was close to fatal, but the other two didn't fare particularly well, either. I don't know what became of them, but it's highly unlikely that all three survived. Before the Wilds, I killed an assassin that sneaked into the King's quarters. He had been hired by a mad earl. I stuck him in the back as he lifted his dagger to the King's throat. Then, in Kyria, I was fighting with a battalion in our second wave. I was at the battle of Killjean, when—"

"Enough," Brella rasped. "Enough."

"I didn't enjoy it, if that's what you think." *Believe me, please believe me.* "Being a soldier is not just killing people."

"Then what is it?"

"It's . . ." What was it? An organizational purpose for a child born in chaos? A prism for the unfocused light of a mind that burned and burned?

"It's figuring out how to leave a battle with the fewest losses possible." That was true. That was *true*. "It's strategizing so that we do only the necessary violence to achieve our goals. It's teaching a group of individuals to fight as one. It's—" She choked as a lump rose in her throat. "It's mattering. It's doing something that matters."

Scratch knew that unless she performed a miracle, she would never get back to the Guard. But here, in this absurdly large bed, she understood what never going back meant. That her mind, so quick and deliberate, so specialized to her work, would go unused. That, most likely, whatever she did next would be something new, and that she probably wouldn't be particularly good at it.

"You've killed a lot of people." Brella's voice was dull.

"I . . ." She took a deep breath, then let it out. "Yes. I don't like to. And the first one was—"

113

"I don't need to hear about it."

Brella finally looked at her. There was something in her eyes, something off. With a sickening lurch, Scratch knew, with uncomplicated certainty, that what she saw threaded through that amber gaze was disappointment.

"You asked," she said, more pain than logic.

"We're so different." Brella's words were barely a whisper. "I shouldn't have thought . . ."

"Thought what?"

"Nothing."

It was just a moment. Only seconds squished together, a blip in time that could have so easily been arbitrary, except that Brella had molded those seconds like liquid steel into a piercing blade. The disappointment in her eyes. The dismissal as she turned away. It was a moment that scraped and scarred.

Perhaps the moment was the blade that finally pried off the last of her armor. Perhaps, under her armor there was nothing.

"Brella, I—"

"I should go see what Vel's up to. You can get off this bed yourself, right?"

"Brella—"

"Scratch." She held up a hand. "Give me a moment, all right? Just . . . a little time."

She left Scratch alone in the bed, her parting gift something sad and small in the shape of a smile.

Chapter Sixteen

Nana grinned across the dining table, which had either recently materialized in the middle of the living room or had been there the entire time. It was laden with dozens of small bowls, each housing some sort of aromatic, vibrantly colored dish. A basket of freshly baked flat bread released curling steam up toward the low buttressed ceiling. At the center of the table, garlanded in greens like a woodland noblewoman, lay a whole grilled fish.

"I've figured it out," the goat woman announced. "How to keep yourselves safe out there, I mean."

Vel paused, a bite of food halfway towards his open mouth. "Are we meant to guess?"

"Blood bonds." Nana grinned. Her plate was entirely empty. "You're doing them tonight."

Brella pushed a piece of fish around her plate. "That's what I thought."

"Why do you look so morose, Umbrella? A blood bond is a joyous occasion."

"I am joyous," she drawled. "You're just not familiar enough with human emotion."

"Oh." Nana furrowed her brow. "Of course. My mistake."

"And James?" A bit of something bright green clung to Vel's upper lip. "Will he be up for it?"

"Of course! He's been awake for hours. The other one's up, too, but he's rather sulky."

Scratch perked up. "He is? Can I go see him?"

"The sulky one? I can't imagine why. Oh, you mean James. Not yet, Scratch child. We are not through with dinner." Nana pushed a bowl of something red and chunky in Scratch's direction. "Do you not appreciate the Tangled Lakes food I made for you?"

"I, uh . . . Tangled Lakes?"

"Of course, child. I smelled the water on you the moment you crossed my threshold. Now eat up, there's a dear."

Scratch sheepishly surveyed the food. She didn't recognize a single dish.

"Oh, goodness." Nana wrung her hands. "You don't know any of these, do you?"

"Well, no." She felt Brella and Vel looking at her. She cast her eyes down at her lap. "I was raised in the Royal City."

"Yes, child, I do know that. But didn't Purpose make you food like this?"

She laughed, rough and mirthless. "No, she didn't." A thought occurred to her, bright and bloody. "How do you know my mother's name?"

Nana ran her tongue over her teeth. "Ah, now. Yes, by the way you greeted me I could tell she hadn't told you."

"Told me what?" She could feel her heart pounding in her ears. The few bites of food already in her stomach danced along her ribs. "How do you know her? Was she here?"

"She's been here, yes." Nana gestured to the door, the walls, the threadbare rug twined with glowing threads. "But the rest is not for me to tell."

Acid burned Scratch's throat. Purpose had never told her daughter about the life she had led before the Royal City. She had said nothing about the Tangled Lakes or why she had left. Nothing about the journey. Nothing about Scratch's father. Nothing about who she had been back then. Scratch was used to being left in the dark, but this, that her mother had stepped across this magical threshold and decided to withhold the wonder, stung like fresh betrayal.

"Of course." She ran her hands over her hair, her scalp buzzing. "Of course she's been here."

There was a hand on her arm. "Scratch?"

She blinked. Brella stared at her, the gold tint in her eyes bright against the warm brown.

A spike of anger slammed through her temples. "Did you know about this?"

Brella recoiled. "Of course not. Why would I know?"

"I . . . you . . ." The anger seeped away, just as quickly as it came. Maybe if she had learned to expect more from Purpose, she'd have huffed off. Cried into a pillow. But she had learned to hope for nothing. She couldn't even be surprised. "You wouldn't. Of course."

Brella's cheeks darkened. "Right."

"Oh, I do love human dramatics!" Nana clapped her hands. "Now, should we go discuss our plans with your lovely little archer friend?"

Scratch followed morosely, her mind gluey and elsewhere. Purpose had been here with Nana. How? Why? The Shaes had some sort of magical woodland inheritance, but her mother? She was nothing but a Lakes fugitive, a nowhere person with no one to share her days. A harsh sentiment, but from Purpose's own mouth: *"Patience, girl. Do you know what I did for you? Do you know what I gave up to get us somewhere safe? Do you understand that I mean nothing? I have nobody?"* Scratch had no idea what great, dangerous bogeyman they had run from, nor could she vouch for the relative safety of her own childhood. Her own bogeyman was her emaciated, wild-eyed mother.

Swallow it down, she told herself, compressing acid over rings of muscle, through a tight throat, a burning chest, a churning stomach. Maybe bile would dissolve the feeling. Hopefully there wasn't a wound. No rough edges, nothing to fester.

She had James to think about. He was sitting up in bed, very at home in a white-and-gold embarrassment of pillows and throws.

"Hello!" he cried, cheeks pink with health. "I hear you all wept over me. How fun!"

Vel trembled from his very large feet to his high-up head. "Can I touch you?"

"I'd be offended if you didn't."

Scratch dutifully stood back as Vel launched himself into the bed, devolving immediately into quiet, shaking sobs. She dug her heels into the wooden floor. Loneliness spread before her, a crevasse.

There were two fingers on her elbow, warm, a centimeter deep in an arm she hadn't realized was shaking. Brella looked down at her with unblinking amber eyes. Scratch turned away.

"You almost had us, idiot," Scratch croaked, because the air was stifling and if she didn't use her voice, she couldn't be sure she still had one. "If it weren't for—" she gestured around the room "—you'd be dead."

James held out the arm not teeming with Vel. "Come here, fool."

She hesitated. He rolled his eyes.

"Come on."

So she did, settling in to his other side. The bed was wide enough, and though her skin prickled at being so close to the large and weepy man who had claimed her best friend, she didn't bolt.

Brella flopped down in a round, sculpted chair beside the bed, the seat so low her legs popped off the ground, crablike.

"What's the prognosis, Nana?"

"He requires rest," Nana said meaningfully. James blushed, wriggling into the sea of down. "But the bond will hopefully accelerate the recovery."

James let loose a carefree smile that Scratch could only envy. "The blood bond? We're doing that now?"

Nana nodded. "It's the only way to keep you safe. Vel and

Umbrella have certain protections in these woods. You do not. There's only so much that being beside them can do without the bond in place."

"Ooh, is there a ritual?" James's eyebrows danced like a pair of voles engaged in a mating dance. "Robes? Candles? Sacred symbols drawn on the floor?"

"Ah, humans!" Nana clapped her hands, her bosom bouncing jovially. "You always have such funny ideas. No, all you need for this is a knife, a good friend, and a few sacred words."

Nana pulled two scraps of parchment from her apron, handing one each to Scratch and James.

"Now, the Shaes know the words. They've been taught to speak them all their lives. But you two are new to them." Nana's smile was wide and crinkly, and Scratch noticed for the first time that the old woman's canine teeth were sharp and pointed. "Read them, but don't say them out loud yet. Get to know them for a moment. If you just recite the words, the bond may not take."

Scratch glanced down at the paper. The ink was a black so dark it looked like holes, deep portals through paper to flesh and beyond. She ran her finger over the print. It seemed like it should have been wet, but it stayed put, firm and glossy. She read:

I enter a room through a borrow-bought
pass twixt where swiftly-sweet grasses a
dew'd

With her blood in my blood tilly-tumping
through vein we emerge rolly-polling
renew'd

I escape my mean flesh through between-
gate refresh'd and touch world through
the room to explore

'Tis a gift I receive, so I promise to leave
of myself when I pass through the door

119

"Leave of myself?" Scratch swallowed thickly. The words rattled around in her mind, pieces meant to fit but slipping away, skittering under the folds of her brain like cockroaches exposed to light. "What does that mean?"

Nana smirked, her lips newly plump and youthful. Or perhaps they had always been that way. "Come, now. Nothing is for free."

"She always takes something," Brella murmured. "So does the Between."

"But it's not always bad." Nana planted herself on the bed. The mattress barely shifted underneath her. "You could be holding onto something. Tension. A difficult memory. Perhaps the Between could free you of a curse like that."

She already knew the answer, but she had to ask. "And do I get to choose?"

Nana's eyes twinkled. "Everyone loves a surprise."

She could turn back now. She could run, scoop up James and go. But where? Back to the Royal City, where she would be hanged or beheaded as a killer? To build a new home in a forest riddled with bounty hunters? To her mother's house, to suss out the woman's newly discovered untruths? The only way forward was the wet and thorny path, where unknowns hunkered in inky darkness.

She chanced a glance at Brella and immediately regretted it. The woman, usually so golden and tall, was slumped and gray, her ember eyes cooled and miserably cast down. She fiddled morosely with her apron. She frowned.

Scratch was sick of the lies and sick of the loss, but Brella had lost something, too. She had killed someone today, and Scratch knew from personal experience how that changed a person. Brella would have to be made of stone not to ache. And the woman wasn't done losing. In forming a blood bond with Scratch, a Passenger she hadn't chosen, Brella would lose the promised, special thing her parents had told her to wait for. Scratch had told Lollie that Brella would be fine. Brella wasn't fine. Only Vel and James, gazing at each other like a pair of loons, seemed to be on the good side of all right.

"Well." James looked up from his parchment, green eyes gleaming. "Shall we get bloody?"

Chapter Seventeen

Brella and Scratch were dispatched to the lavender room by a giddy Nana, who insisted the pair perform the ritual on their own. Brella trudged silently to the giant's guest room, Scratch following nervously behind. When they got inside, Brella stood in the middle of the room, her shoulders hunched. She stared out a window, watching lavender set ablaze by the orange light of the setting sun.

"Brella," Scratch tentatively ventured, "are you sure you want to do this?"

"It's not about what I want." She didn't turn around. "We're doing this. We have to."

"You seem . . . Do you want to . . ." She searched for the word, which, all things considered, wasn't a particularly good sign. "Talk?"

"You want to talk."

It didn't have the inflection of a question, but Scratch answered anyway. "Uh, yes?"

"About . . ."

"I get that this is a big deal for you." Scratch jammed her hands into the shallow pockets of her borrowed pants. "You know those magic words by heart. Your parents did this together. They told you it was—" She swallowed. "Special. If you don't

123

want to do this with me, I get it. We can find another way."

Brella turned to face her, expressionless. "Another way?"

"Look, I get it." She cursed the lack of easily accessible chairs. This conversation was knocking at the back of her knees. "I've run out of options. I had this whole life planned." Her voice broke. She swallowed shamefully, hoping the lack of direct sunlight hid the redness around her eyes. "I had a whole plan, you know? I thought I would be a commander. And then the king I spent my whole life either serving or training to serve declared me his enemy without even affording me the dignity of an interrogation. So I get it. I've lost . . ." The list was too long. "I've lost everything that matters to me, aside from James. I don't have a lot of choices left. I can either come with you to rescue the princess or die in the forest, I guess." She managed a weak laugh. It hung sticky in her hot throat. "But you . . ."

She forced herself to look up at Brella, blinking away the sting. Brella was staring back, open-mouthed. She was flushed, her freckles dimmed by the dark honey warmth over her cheeks. "This was supposed to be special for you. And I'm taking that away."

"You aren't." Brella's voice was nearly free of inflection. "It's not your fault."

"Maybe not entirely, but I can't . . ." She choked. "I can't do to you what's been done to me."

The silence was thick. Through the enchanted windows, the lavender swayed in an impossible breeze. It was nighttime out there, but Scratch couldn't vouch for the truth of that. It could be any time, really. The two of them could be anywhere, or nowhere. The realest thing in the room was Brella's gaze on her, those eyes like wet, fresh earth, her skin like rain-dappled road.

Brella opened her mouth. Closed it. Opened it again. "Why are you like this, Scratch?"

"What?"

"Like—" Brella tugged on her braids so hard Scratch's eyes watered. "I mean, you're a person." Her topaz eyes were open, her voice heavy with meaning. "A whole person."

Scratch shifted on the balls of her feet. "Yes? I am."

"You know what I mean."

"I don't. I could . . ." She swallowed, feeling unsteady ground beneath her feet. "Try?"

"The octagon." Brella's breath was high, her chest rising and falling. She began to pace the room, window to window, looking so small in the shadow of the oversized furniture. "Ivinscont wasn't supposed to come back with victory in a day. Victory after one battle, Scratch. Do you realize how unlikely that was? And the things I thought when I heard that the person who had made that call, who had devised that plan was—was just a nobody from the Tangled Lakes."

Her lungs clenched around something hot and hard. "A nobody."

"Like me. A nobody like all of us. I just . . ." She groaned. "I needed to know who you were." She looked down, then back up again. Her eyes were so huge. Criminally huge. Who gave them the right? "So I asked around. I know you were the best in your class at the Academy."

Her shoulders tensed. "Okay."

"And that you bought your mother a house in a nice part of town. And that you don't visit."

Scratch's nails cut into her palm. "That's none of your business."

"Who are you, Scratch? And why did you work so hard for a country that doesn't give a shit about you?"

"Because I didn't know." Her mind was a morass, wet and foggy. Her skin stung from sharp-edged questions. "I thought if I worked hard . . . The Academy saved me, okay? They saved me. Without them, I would have been nothing."

"I doubt you would—"

"I didn't have another choice, Brella. I had to get out of that house."

Brella stopped pacing. "What house?"

"My mother's house." Scratch gave up, flopping onto the floor, crossing her legs. Brella reluctantly joined her, slowly lowering herself onto the oversized wooden planks. "It wasn't great."

Brella raised her eyebrows in dawning awareness. "Oh."

"Yeah. I bought her a new house so she'd stop harping on about everything I needed to be grateful for. The things she supposedly did for me." Scratch sucked in some air. It shuddered through her. "I send her money so she doesn't have to . . ." She absently scratched a line across her thigh. "Work."

"What sort of work?"

"Trade." She shrugged. "When she worked in brothels, it was okay. But when she had men in the house, I didn't really have anywhere to go. I liked the brothels, though. We always had food."

"You were hungry."

Scratch nodded. "The Academy recruiter saw me nicking apples. Thought I looked trainable."

"You looked hungry."

She turned her face to Brella's. There was something new there, strange and soft. "What is that supposed to mean?"

"Nothing. I—Scratch." Brella furrowed her brow, considering. Then she reached out. "Can I?" Scratch held her hands open, and Brella clasped them loosely, so gently. Brella's hands were warm and rough, bigger than her own, with very square, very clean nails. "I want to do this with you. The blood bond. It's my choice. I'm making it."

Shock struck her, cold and then warm, seeping into her shoulders and down to her ribs. "But you hate soldiers."

"You're not a soldier anymore."

Scratch tried to pull her hands back, but Brella gripped, firmly, keeping them in place. "You're not, Scratch. Not anymore."

"I could be again," she insisted, and tugged.

"Do you want that?" Brella asked. Her fingers were strong on Scratch's palms, digging down into the flesh. "Really. Think about it. For that king? The king who denied you the promotion you deserved."

126

"Not for him. For her!"

Brella let go so abruptly that Scratch nearly tipped over backward.

"For her?" Brella asked, stunned.

"Frances." Heat rushed to her face. She cast her eyes down, feeling stupid and juvenile. "I know it sounds . . . wishful. I just thought that if we brought her back and the people knew, or we told people . . . I don't know, that their king was corrupt? They like Frances, I know they do. We could keep her safe. And she could . . ." She winced. "Take the throne?" she squeaked.

Brella didn't move for so long that Scratch was sure the magic of the room had frozen her in place. Then, her lips curled into a small smile, then bigger, showing her teeth, and she was laughing, gulping in air as she whooped and giggled.

Scratch pouted. "It's not that funny." She hunched into herself, crossing her arms over her chest.

"No, Scratch." Brella wiped her eyes and reached forward to cup Scratch's elbows. "It's great. It's so great. I want that, too."

"You . . ." She looked up. Brella wasn't laughing anymore. "You want that?"

"The king. He's terrible in ways you can't imagine." Brella bit her lip. "I think Frances would be better."

Scratch had never really considered the merits of King Ingomar. It didn't matter what sort of king he was in the end. He was the king, so Scratch served him. Whether or not he was good for the people hadn't been a pressing factor while Scratch busied herself rising through the King's Guard. Ingomar would be king until he died and then Frances would be queen and on and on it went, and Scratch had nothing to do with any of it. Why should it matter to her? She cared that she and James lived comfortably. That she could be proud of herself. That she saw in herself something greater than the world saw in her. That she could make the world see in her the things they refused to.

King Ingomar had seen, and still he'd disregarded her. Then he'd thrown her in a dungeon.

"You have a plan," Scratch said, savoring the feeling of knots coming untied. "A plan you kept from me."

"Not so much a plan." Brella pulled her knees up to her chest defensively. "An idea. A hope. Did you think I was risking my life just so my sister could get her lover back?"

Of course not. "I wasn't sure what to think."

"If I tell you about the king," Brella asked carefully, quietly, "will you listen?"

Scratch didn't hesitate. "Of course."

"Okay then." Brella smiled, and she was breakfast, warm and sweet. "I'll tell you everything."

Chapter Eighteen

The rest of the night was a swirl of loose memory and magic. Brella promised to explain King Ingomar's faults after she and Scratch formed the blood bond, but she didn't get the chance. The last thing Scratch remembered from the night was slicing her palm with the kitchen knife. A moment later, she was blinking herself awake on the floor of the lavender room, comfortably swaddled in a sea of monstrous pillows and blankets.

A few feet away, a mound of quilts rose and fell, a sort of plush tortoise shell, out of which a sleeping, bronze-tufted head emerged. The cool, purple-tinged light from the lavender windows illuminated Brella's sleeping face, her lashes forming a perfect line of wheat stalks resting on the warm, brown sunrise of her cheek. Scratch nearly raised her hand to touch that cheek. Would it feel smooth? Warm, like the heat from a hard-boiled egg still in its shell? Soft, like a glistening, yellow-dough morning loaf? Did freckles feel different on skin? Scratch didn't have any, nor did James, so she had no frame of reference. Were they just bits of color, or did they feel like the seeds of a strawberry—little divots of tucked-in pebbles, sleeping on top of skin stretched taut over juice?

She supposed she was rather hungry, on top of everything else. She cleared her throat.

Brella slept.

She poked a leg out from under the blankets and stamped her heel against the floor.

Brella slept.

She yawned loudly, stretching her arms over her head until her back and shoulders clicked.

Brella mumbled a bit, nestling deeper into the quilt. She snored.

Well, there was nothing for it. Scratch raised a cautious finger and poked what, in her best estimation, was Brella's shoulder.

"Mrgh," said the quilted thing.

"Brella. It's morning."

"Na."

"Yeah. I was thinking we should eat a bit of breakfast."

As though "breakfast" were her name, the sleeping thing raised her head. The quilt fell back and Scratch was treated to the full, undiluted Brella of morning. What ochre hair had not formed a startlingly vertical nest atop Brella's head was plastered to her face with nighttime spittle. Her cheek bore the imprints of the pillow, a written history of a night spent in rock-solid sleep. Her eyes, usually so alert, were dazed and soft, dying firelight instead of sparks.

And, gods help her, Scratch felt her mouth go dry.

Brella was a mess. She slept like a hibernating bear, and she did it remarkably. Resplendently. As far as Scratch was concerned, Brella was the best ever at sleeping. How many people knew that this sleepy softness lurked underneath that hot, hard glare?

Scratch pressed her small skinny hand against a chest that suddenly burned.

"I'm going to go," she whispered hoarsely. "You'll wake up?"

Brella nodded, or perhaps just shifted in sleep. Scratch raised herself from the sheets and left, closing the door behind her. Her hands were in fists. Slowly she opened them and breathed.

Vel and James sat in the living room, having a leisurely breakfast of scones swirled with mysterious fruit alongside eggs with yolks so bright they could not possibly have come from a chicken.

"You seem livelier," Scratch told James, pushing down the discomfort that she had meant to leave behind in the lavender room. "More upright at least."

"Kind of you to notice." James kicked a chair away from the table for her. "Join us, why don't you?"

The lads, as it turned out, also had no memory of forming the blood bond. They had woken up dizzy and tangled before stumbling into the living room to discover Nana, who helpfully assured them that this sort of memory lapse was to be expected.

"Nothing to worry about," James trilled. "Just your average, run-of-the-mill fair folk stealing memories, blood magic ritual, our minds are too mortal to understand, blah blah blah sort of thing." He winced. "She's in there with Gultin now. Apparently, he's not doing as well as I am."

"How can that be?" Scratch accepted Vel's proffered mug of something steamy and coffee-like but somehow . . . sparklier? "You got hit much harder."

He shrugged. "Apparently his struggle is not of the physical sort. Nana said we could talk to him when you woke up. I figured we ought to do it together."

"How about we don't and say we did?" she muttered, but she was already standing, reluctantly leaving the beckoning baked goods behind. She followed James to a door with a cheerful white daisy painted on its face. He opened it, releasing a cloud of warm air scented with rot.

"Oh, gods." James covered his mouth. "It smells like the field hospital in Kyria."

"Come in," Nana called from the dank darkness. "He's awake."

With a shared wince, they entered the dim room. Curtains were drawn over every window, letting in only slivers of orangey light. Nana sat in a rocking chair beside a low, small bed. The covers were crisp and white, like a healer's robes.

Gultin lay propped on stiff pillows. He had always been big, even as a kid at the Academy. Scratch remembered the first time she had seen him, this galumphing thing with too-large ears and a nose that had already been broken so many times it had morphed into a multi-planed prism of flesh. He rarely smiled, only grimaced, pacing the grounds with the sure-footed stomp of a man who looked for fights and won.

He smiled now.

"Hello, Keyes. Bowstring." There was a blankness about his face, his open eyes and docile, pleasant mouth. He looked both younger and older, less hardened of expression, but wizened beyond his years.

"Gultin." A small bench appeared—or had always been—beside the bed, and Scratch took a tentative seat. James remained standing, hovering near the door.

"Gultin," he squeaked. "You look well."

"You always look well," Gultin replied, regarding James with lightless eyes. "I rather fancied you at the Academy. I thought of asking you to walk with me, but Father would have disapproved, so I beat you instead. Do you remember?"

"You beating me?" James swallowed. "I remember."

"Sorry about that." He turned to Scratch. "Did you take the princess?"

"No."

"Kill her?"

"No."

"Ah, well." He smoothed the blanket down over his legs. They looked impossibly small under the tight bedding. "You still escaped the dungeon. That's a bit illegal."

"We shouldn't have been there in the first place."

"True enough." He turned his eyes toward the door. "Hello, Bowstring. Did you know, I rather fancied you at the Academy."

James was shivering. "Did you?"

"Your eyes are so green. Did you know?"

"Yes, Gultin. I know."

"All right." Gultin blinked slowly, like a cow. He yawned. "Well, I ought to get back to sleep soon."

"Gultin," Scratch said, unease creeping along her spine. "Are you getting any better?"

"Better?" He cocked his head to the side. "Why would I get better?"

"So you can leave." She pressed her hands against her thighs to keep them from shaking. "Don't you want to get back to your life?"

"What life?" he asked. There was no bitterness in it. No anger. It seemed to be a real question.

"Your family?"

"Oh, they don't like me." He waved the thought away like a gnat. "That's why I went to the Academy. I had Branch and Hester, but you killed them."

He said it so simply. Not an accusation—a fact. A dull knife, slicing her from belly to throat. "I'm sorry, Gultin."

"Don't be." That wave again. "I know why you did it."

"You could come with us," she offered, trying not to think of what a terrible idea that was. Something in Gultin's nothing face was making her desperate. "We're rescuing Frances."

His smile didn't shift. "No, thank you. I'm perfectly content where I am."

James made a strangled noise. "*You.*" He rounded on Nana. "You did this."

She eyed him narrowly. "I did nothing different than what I did with you. This one decided not to fight."

"There's still time." Scratch grabbed Gultin by the shoulder. His bones, under papery skin, pressed against her fingers. "Gultin, come on. You have to move. You can get better."

"What for?" His eyes were splotched green and brown like algae over a murky pond. Scratch had never noticed the color before. There had never been reason. "I can't be in the Guard anymore."

"We can't either," she protested.

He blinked. "It's nice to talk to you, Keyes. I forgot to say, I liked your octagon."

She fell back onto the bench, dizzy. Nana rose with a sigh.

"Say your good-byes, you two. You're leaving after this." She patted Gultin's covered foot. "The good news for you is, since he's staying, I'll only take something minor from you lot as payment. This one's feeding me up well, isn't he?"

Gultin smiled dopily at her. "Yes, Nana."

Scratch watched Gultin breathe. His chest rose slowly, and there was a whistle to it, like consumption. She had the uncomfortable urge to swaddle him up and rock him.

"I have your sword, Gultin," she said, realizing too late that it came out as a motherly coo. "It's in the other room. I'm sure Nana will give it to you if you ask."

"That's sweet." He blinked once, twice, and then turned toward the ceiling.

A powerful urge to leave struck her, and she grabbed on to James's hand on the way to the door. He didn't move.

"Gultin." James sniffled. "You know I fancied you at the Academy."

Gultin's face went still, his eyes wide with wonder. He sat forward slowly, dreamlike. "You did?"

"I wanted t-to—"James's breath hitched. "To take you walking. But I didn't."

"I fancied you too. Your eyes are very green."

"Will you come with us? Please?"

Gultin leaned back against the pillow and closed his eyes.

"I won't, James. But you've given me a very nice dream."

Chapter Nineteen

It was morning, which meant Mama was about to send Patience out for the day. She hated mornings, always shutting her eyes against the sun and wriggling down under the thin blanket, bits of hay from her under-stuffed mattress poking through the old, threadbare sheet to scrape at her skin. If only she could wait a few moments, stay in the relative warmth of their little house. This season, mornings were cool and drizzly more often than they weren't. Evenings were worse, the sky heavy with the sort of soft, cold dampness that could barely call itself snow. She wasn't ready to leave. Besides, her left shoe had a big hole and she hadn't had socks in months.

"I'm having men over, Patience. For work." Mama tied herself into a new frock, miraculously intact and free of patches. "Make yourself busy. Come back an hour after the sun has set."

Patience flopped out of bed and tugged at her hair, an unruly, tangled mess of mats and knots. She pouted. "What work do you do for them, Mama? Why can't I be home? I'll be quiet."

"No," Mama snapped. "It is not for little girls. Now go."

"But the other kids. They don't like me, Mama." Patience scrubbed at her snotty nose. From Hunter's season through the dawn of Rider's, it never stopped running. "They hit me."

Mama closed her eyes and pinched the bridge of her nose.

"What have I said about that, Patience?"

"Hit them back or run. But—"

"No buts. Go." And with that, Mama slammed the door, leaving Patience no choice but to occupy herself until dark.

As luck would have it, that day turned out to be rather pleasant, despite the damp and the cold. Patience managed to evade the other children, finding solace with the butcher at his stall at the covered market. On slow days he allowed her to help him with his meats.

"You're good with a knife," he told her. "And you've got quick hands. Cut along this tendon here and you might earn a few coins for your trouble. Wash your hands under the pump first. And for the gods' sake, don't touch your nose!"

She sliced and sorted while the butcher sold his cuts. He chatted affably with the men and women of the neighborhood, all the while pointing out his little helper for the day. She smiled and preened and cut, and before she knew it, the sun was low in the pinking sky.

The butcher grinned as he packed up his knives.

"Here." He tossed her a few coppers. Her eyes grew wide at the sight of them, so shiny in her blood-caked palm. "And you can have this as well." He handed her a package wrapped in waxed cloth. She squeezed it, feeling bone and meat.

"Really?" She could hardly believe it. All of this, just for her and Mama?

"You earned it. You did a hard day's work, Patience. Hard work is the most important thing." He patted her on the head, then added in a conspiratorial whisper, "Don't let the other kids nick that off of you. It's good meat!"

She sped home, little legs beating the ground hard, kicking up clouds of dust behind her. Sure, Mama had said not to come back until an hour after sunset, but she couldn't wait to display her prize. Besides, the longer she stayed out in the streets, the higher the risk of the other children stripping her of her coin and her dinner.

Mama will be so proud, she thought as she ran. *Mama did*

hard work and so did I. And tonight we'll have a feast.

She skidded to a stop outside the little shack. Through the cracked window, she could see the flickering of a candle—the good, wax one that Mama never let her light. Moans and cries floated from inside the house, setting Patience's little heart to racing. Was that Mama? Was she in trouble? Was somebody hurting her?

The door was locked, but the wood was soft enough. With the mighty force of her tiny leg, Patience kicked the door open and bounded inside, dropping the package of meat at her feet to free her hands, which had already curled into fists.

"Mama! Are you all right? Is someone hurting you?"

The look on her mother's face was nothing short of murderous.

"What did I tell you?" Mama hissed, reaching for her robe. She was naked. Why was she naked? "Get out of here! Now!"

There was a man on Mama's shabby hay-stuffed mattress. His face was purple with rage, and he grabbed out for clothes far finer than anything Patience or her mother had ever worn.

"I hope you know you won't be getting paid." He had an accent Patience couldn't place. Long *o*'s and rolled *r*'s. She would learn, in later years, that the man had been an aristocrat. But she didn't know, when she was seven or eight, why the man had talked so oddly, or why he was so angry, or why Mama was begging him to stay, promising him that next time there would be no interruption, next time she would be entirely his, she promised, please, don't go, please, please . . .

When he left, attempting to slam the door behind him though it hung off of its hinges, Mama crumpled to the floor. Patience ran over to her.

"Mama, don't cry. I got us dinner. A lot of meat and a bone, too. And a few coppers. Look!" She dug the coins out of her pocket, holding her palm open. "We'll be okay. You don't need that man."

Mama slowly lifted her face from between her folded arms. "Did you steal this?"

137

"No, Mama. I worked. Do you know the butcher at the covered market with the blue handkerchief around his head? He—"

"What did you do for him?" Her words pierced Patience's skin like butcher's knives. Beside her, Scratch noticed with horror, was Mama's new dress, a gaping tear in it like an open mouth. "Why did he give you this money?"

"I cut meat." What else would she have done for him? "I cut it and wrapped it up for people who were buying it."

"Oh yes?" Mama snarled. "Do you know why grown men are nice to little girls like you?"

"He said I have small hands, and that I'm good with a knife."

Mama's coarse laugh scraped her skin. "Don't go back to him. Men like that are never nice."

She remembered the butcher's smile, his insistence that Patience deserved payment for a job well done. She wanted to defend him, to tell Mama that there were good men, good people, in the world. That not everyone would hurt a poor Lakes girl with no friends.

"Okay, Mama," she said instead.

"Okay, Mama?" Mama's nostrils flared, eyes blazing. "Is that all you have to say?"

"Um, yes, Mama?"

And Patience folded into herself as Mama's fists began to fly.

Chapter Twenty

Scratch jolted awake with no idea where she was or how she got there. Dawn was creeping overhead, cool blue and fresh. She spread her fingers, feeling blades of grass. A breeze zinged across her skin, slightly dew-damp and chilly, no blanket covering her. How had she fallen asleep like this?

"Scratch?"

Brella stared at her. She also lay in the grass, her bronze hair dimmed by moisture and plastered to the side of her head.

"Where are we?" Scratch asked hoarsely. "How did we . . ."

Then it came to her, the splash of a memory. Nana had handed the Shaes their packs and pushed them toward the door.

"I'm separating you," she had said, tongue darting out to lick her plump lips. "Are you afraid?"

"Separating?" Vel shrieked. "You can't do that. They'll die!"

"By pair, Vel." She had rolled her eyes, her squared pupils tumbling like dice. "You'll be with James, Umbrella with Scratch. I'll take your fear. Your confusion. And if anything blooms, I'll take that, too."

"Blooms?" Scratch asked. "What do you mean, blooms?"

Nana grinned, wide and inscrutable. "You're both two days from the gate. You're welcome for that. You'll meet each other there."

Scratch, realizing quickly that there was no negotiation, no time to think, reached for James's hand. "You good?"

"I suppose I have to be. But I'll—"

And then there was darkness.

"Is your pack here?" Scratch felt around and sighed in relief when her hand hit familiar cloth. "Are you all right?"

"I saw your dream," Brella murmured, a bit green.

Scratch's stomach liquefied into icy slush. "You did?"

Brella took in a ragged breath as she sat, brushing leaves from her face. "I guess it's the blood bond. I didn't mean to. I tried to wake up when I realized what I was seeing."

"It's all right. Not your fault." The memory was sharp-edged, razors of shame and anger poking through the threads of it. She had been weak then, at the mercy of a miserable woman. Had Brella seen the contempt in Purpose's eyes when she glared at her daughter? Did Brella know how unlovable Scratch had been before she reworked herself into something worthwhile? Scratch had the urge to scream. *That isn't me anymore! I don't even have the same name.*

Brella swallowed, a loud gulp in the quiet forest. "If I'd have known . . ."

"It's fine." It was like a poking. Phantom fingertips on her most soft, secret places. She didn't want to see Brella's face, afraid of what she would find there. Pity, she imagined. Pity for her weakness, and maybe delicate words after. Coddling, horrific tenderness. And she'd take it, because, even though she hated the thought, she wanted it. A desperate, scraping bit of her needed it, and the needing was shameful. She'd betray herself, and her weakness would be discovered.

Please, don't pity me. Please, please.

There was no pity on Brella's face. It was flushed dark, her freckles disappearing into the rising color. Her eyes shone bright. Her mouth was a small, fierce knot, mirroring the tangle between her drawn eyebrows. She breathed shallowly and loud.

"You're angry," Scratch mumbled, swallowing the mad urge to laugh.

"Mm," Brella grunted. "Mm."

"You're angry at . . . my mother?"

"Mm." Her nostrils flared. Her jaw worked.

"It was a long time ago, Brella."

"Still." Her upper lip curled. "You bought her a house?"

"Yeah."

"Mm."

"To get her off my back mostly. Obligation fulfilled."

"What obligation?" Brella spat. "She didn't seem particularly obliged to care for you, Scratch."

"Oh, didn't she? I hardly noticed." She raised a hand to stroke Brella's stiff arm. The muscles jumped. "She isn't worth this. But, uh, I do appreciate it."

"Mm. I'd like to—" Brella clamped her lips together, startling a laugh out of Scratch.

"What? Storm her house? Brella, she's been through hells, too.'"

"I know lots of people who have dealt with the worst sort of shit, and they don't go around treating their kids like . . . like . . ."

Scratch shook her head. "You can't go back in time and teach her how to be a mother. Or, I don't know, maybe you can. Maybe the Between will drop you off outside her old shack and you can bust through the door and shout the house down."

"Mm. I don't want to teach her, Scratch."

"What?"

"I don't want to teach her how to be a good mother. I want to throw her through a window."

Scratch's laugh erupted so suddenly it nearly frightened her. It was loud enough to bounce off the trees. "Charming. I appreciate it." And she did. It was odd perhaps, that she might take Brella's threat of doing bodily harm to Purpose Keyes as a kindness. And yet . . .

Brella stared at her for a moment, eyes glowing bright. "Do you want to braid my hair?"

The whiplash made her brain rattle. She giggled, laughter spilling out of her. "Braid your hair?"

141

Brella nodded, pulling a few strips of leather from her apron. "I can do it myself, of course, but it's better when Vel does it. I saw you doing Tempest's hair, so I thought . . ."

"Sure."

Brella's hair was soft in her hands, and not as thick as she had imagined. The curls and waves had the illusion of density, but when Scratch squeezed, the hair gave way, thin and easy to separate into halves. Brella handed her a comb, and she drew a straight line in Brella's scalp with it. Scratch had known a menial task would calm her. As she drew the strands through her fingers, she felt her shoulders loosen, and the nervous laughter subsided. The act seemed to have the same effect on Brella. Her stiff rage abated, her breathing growing deep.

Purpose had done something like this with Scratch every so often, brushing the ropes out of her hair. Being touched by Purpose was a dangerous thing, and there was shame in the wanting of it. Most of her touches were slaps, but they came with a certain satisfaction. When Purpose raged, Scratch was the center of her mother's world, if only for that brief moment.

When Purpose combed Scratch's hair, Scratch always complained. She was afraid that Purpose would stop if she knew how much her daughter liked it.

Brackish, brackish, brackish, her mind sang like a taunt, *are my lover's tears for me.*

"I've always had a difficult relationship with my parents," Brella murmured.

Scratch froze halfway down the first braid. "You don't have to tell me this. Just because you saw—"

"I want to. You didn't choose to show me that, so I . . ." She breathed, her shoulders rising and falling. "Do you not want me to? I can stop."

"No." Scratch swallowed thickly. "It's fine."

"I'm the oldest girl of fourteen. They expected that I would do a lot of parenting for them. I'm not very good at that."

"Did you ever talk to them about it?" Scratch asked, though she wasn't sure if that was the right question. Discussing families was like speaking a different language.

"Eventually, yeah. It helped that Vel and Iris were better with kids."

"Do your parents know you're out here?"

Brella was quiet so long Scratch wasn't sure whether she had heard the question. When she spoke, her voice was so low as to almost be a whisper.

"My parents disappeared a year ago."

Scratch's fingers felt numb as she tied off the last braid. "What happened?"

"They went to the Between and they never came back."

Scratch cautiously lowered her hands onto Brella's shoulders. Brella shivered.

"Can we sit here for a bit?" Brella asked. Her voice was low and smooth as a river rock. "Just a few moments."

Scratch nodded, though Brella couldn't see. It felt like enough.

The forest smelled rich around them, warming in the waxing morning light like baking bread, rising gold.

"Two days." Brella peered into the light. "Nana said we were two days away from the gate, but we're four at least. Unless— oh." She slapped a hand to her head. "Of course she did this."

"What?"

"We have to take Hatter's Pass if we want to meet the lads in time."

"And Hatter's Pass is . . ." Scratch prompted, though she already suspected the answer.

Brella turned, grimacing apologetically. "More fair folk."

Something fluttered in Scratch's stomach, a lightning bug composed of fear, irritation, and curiosity in equal measure.

"Anyone dangerous?"

Brella shook her head. "Just irritating. He doles out favors and then expects something big in return. It's easy enough to say no."

Scratch somewhat doubted that she and Brella shared the same definition of "easy" but she decided not to make a fuss.

James had been right. There were so many possibilities ahead, Scratch couldn't possibly plan for all of them. Like it or not, she'd be surprised.

The thought wasn't as unnerving as it should have been, which, in itself, was unsettling. She ached for a steaming mug of coffee and the largest, cleanest parchment she could get her hands on.

Chapter Twenty-One

Brella led Scratch out of the clearing, passing through trees coated in thick, damp moss. It was darker here, shaded and cool. The landscape had a sort of wild quality, like no one had left footprints in this mulchy earth in generations. The trees twisted, as horizontal as they were vertical, with trunks wrapped like adders around rocks, and bark knotted from root to branch.

Brella ambled across the rough landscape at an alarming pace. She moved like an animal, seemingly without thought, swinging around tree branches and hopping between exposed roots. When Scratch had envisioned the fair folk before, she hadn't pictured a jumbled grandmother of human-and-animal parts living in a cottage outside of time. She had pictured a creature like Brella, so at home in the wilderness, a gust of wind darting through the leaves. She was mesmerizing to watch, all confidence, not even pausing to make sure she was on the right track, not planning any step before she took it.

Was it really possible that Brella's only ulterior motive was installing Frances on the throne? Could every story of hers actually be true? That she impulsively agreed to follow an abducted princess, accompanied only by two confused guards and one of her many brothers? She had known, previous to their meeting, who Scratch was. She'd said as much back at Nana's cottage. Did that necessarily mean she'd had a hand in Scratch's imprisonment, or the princesses's disappearance . . .

Hope. It was hope, bright and eye-watering. Her stomach sank when she remembered where hope had led her before.

She had nearly forgotten to expect a fae interruption when an oily voice slunk out from the treetops.

"I told you not to come back," the voice purred.

Scratch shivered, reaching out to grab Brella's arm on instinct. Brella carefully clasped her hand.

"You did nothing of the sort, Hatter," Brella replied tartly, squeezing Scratch's fingers.

"Not you, Parasol. Her."

A man appeared in front of them, very tall and rather skinny, but of entirely human proportions. His sandy blond hair flopped over dark, canny eyes, light curls skimming a dark blue tailcoat entirely free of forest debris. He had dressed his slender legs in white stockings with bows, his feet in buckled leather. With every immaculate stitch, every too-bright hue, Hatter looked like a poor man's idea of a noble.

"Me?" Scratch pointed at herself with her free hand. "I've never seen you before in my life."

"Oh, very droll, Purpose," the fae trilled, his accent crisp and proper. "I told you in fairly certain terms that if you darkened my pass ever again, I would come to collect. Now then." He held out a manicured palm. "My price."

She wasn't sure whether she ought to feel relieved or frustrated. "I'm not Purpose."

"Oh, I'd recognize that dishwater hair anywhere, you old shipbuilder." He curled his fingers meaningfully. "Give it here or pay."

"This isn't Purpose, Hatter," Brella told him, angling her body protectively between Scratch and the fae. It was sweet—too sweet—but laughably unnecessary. The fae was a twig: infinitely snappable. As he leered, Scratch considered what a pleasure that might be. "This is her daughter."

Hatter's eyes widened. "Well, well. The fetus has emerged.

146

How long did you gestate? A year? Two?"

"Wait." Scratch shook her head, thoughts snapping together with the jarring force of her comprehension. "Do you mean to tell me that my mother was pregnant when she came to see you?"

"Well, that's what she said." Hatter shrugged, finally dropping his outstretched arm. "I assumed she had a rather large, fairly demanding parasite. Though I do suppose there was some truth to that."

Scratch pinched the bridge of her nose, stemming the first few shoots of a massive headache. "So not only did my mother never tell me about her many adventures in the forest, but she also failed to mention that I had been with her at the time?"

"Well." Hatter drummed his fingers together. "It depends on your definition of 'with.' And 'her.' And 'time.'" He leaned against a tree, crossing his arms. His body was too stiff, and Scratch noticed that he wasn't quite making contact with the bark, instead hovering a few centimeters away. "Doesn't change the terms, though. If she won't come, you'll do just fine."

Brella scoffed, but didn't retreat. "Oh, leave off, Hatter. Shaking down a child for a parent's debts? That's a little too human for you, don't you think?"

He raised an eyebrow. "As much as I detest your primitive race, Brella, they get it right every once in a while."

"What exactly is it that my mother owes you?" Because if she was going to argue with this irritating creature, it might as well be over something worthwhile.

Hatter smiled, revealing a mouth with far too many teeth. The more Scratch looked at him, the more she could recognize his inhuman qualities. The way he moved his eyes was animal, darting and quick like a shrew. His body was more reptilian, sinuous and snakelike. And his neck articulation? That was all chicken.

"Didn't I say?" he pecked. "Purpose owes me . . ." A long, dramatic pause. "Her hair."

Scratch nodded, letting go of Brella's hand so she could pull her hair from the leather strap she used to secure it. "How much of it? Is a few inches okay or do you want all of it? I don't have a razor."

Brella muffled a snort behind her hand.

"But." Hatter knotted his brows, his confident smile fading. "Purpose was so reluctant."

"I told you I wasn't my mother." She reached for the warm, wooden hilt of her trusty kitchen knife. She'd grown fond of the thing. "You're not going to do anything with it that'll, I don't know, curse me later, right?"

"I-I was going to make rope."

"Fantastic." She tugged her hair taut and held the knife at the nape of her neck. Her locks were tangled and matted from a few days without combing, but if Hatter wanted to make rope, there was no better condition for it. "Is this good enough?"

Brella let loose a stream of giggles. "Let me do it for you, Scratch. It would be my honor to help repay your mother's debt."

"Well." Hatter smoothed down his jacket. "This is perfect. Ideal even." He eked out a dimmed smile. "All settled."

Of course it was hair. Purpose had loved her hair, lank and thin though it was. And she had brushed Scratch's—*brackish, brackish, brackish . . .*

No. Scratch squeezed her eyes shut, listening to the swish and scrape of Brella sawing through her locks. It sounded oddly like an untuned fiddle. Dissonant, scratchy, and rhythmic— calming, in its way. "And now that we've done business . . ." She cursed the rasp in her voice. "You wouldn't be able to tell me what my mother owed you for, would you?"

Hatter's grin spread. "If you want the information, I could make you a deal."

"No thanks." With satisfaction, she watched his face fall. "I'm fine not knowing."

"O-of course."

"Here we are." Brella held up a hank of Scratch's hair, pale yellow and thick. "Is this what you were after?"

Hatter hugged himself, shrugging petulantly. "I suppose."

Scratch shook her head around experimentally. "What do

you think, Brella?" There was no response. "Brella?"

Scratch turned to face her and—*oh*. Brella stared. Eyes bright but unfocused, mouth slack, dazed. She looked with hungry abandon. Scratch burned under it. Her heart raced, leaping near painfully, as she watched Brella draw her pink tongue over those large, barely-dappled lips. Scratch felt hot, so hot, and still shivery, her body alive and lightning-struck.

"You look well," Brella murmured. She reached out a hand to tousle the soft ends, a touch that burned from scalp to toes. "We'll clean this up a bit tonight, hm?"

"Yes," Scratch breathed. Her knees unlocked, and she clenched her thighs to keep herself from swaying.

Hatter cleared his throat. Scratch jumped at the sound.

"Are we through?" he demanded.

Scratch blinked at him, slowly rejoining the world she had just transcended. "Uh . . ."

"We are, Hatter. Come along, Scratch." Brella clasped her hand once more, large and warm and sure, and pulled her down the wending path. Scratch could not see a foot ahead, but she didn't feel fear. *Hope is foolish*, she reminded herself, and like a fool she followed.

Chapter Twenty-Two

Brella sat at the base of a large oak.

"I want to show you something," she said.

Scratch shuffled over, past the dying embers from the fire they had used to roast the roots and leftover bread they had eaten for dinner. The glen Brella had selected for the night was small and tree-lined, with just enough space for two bedrolls and a tiny fire. They had huddled around the flames, close and giggling, while the sun set around them in pink and orange streaks, and the moon rose, fat and white and eager.

"What is it?"

Brella pulled something small and square out of her apron pocket. "A book."

"Why is it," Scratch asked, getting comfortable against the tree, so aware of her body pressed against Brella's side, "that everyone brought a book but me?"

"It's not my fault you didn't plan to be arrested and then broken out of the dungeons and then dragged along on a rescue mission." Brella sniffed. "Your lack of forethought is appalling."

"Myriad apologies."

"Anyway, it's not just a book." Brella tapped the cover. "It's a collection of every decree that's come out of the castle since the beginning of King Ingomar's reign." She indicated the last few pages of the book, which were in noticeably better shape than their brethren. "I add on new ones when I get them."

"How do you get them?" Scratch carefully took the book from Brella's hands, holding it in her palms like an unhatched egg. "Decrees are usually read aloud in the city square."

"I pay someone in the castle." There was a cocky sparkle in Brella's voice. When Scratch looked up in openmouthed surprise, she spotted a matching, wicked glint in Brella's eyes.

"You do?"

Brella nodded. "I have for years."

"Years?"

"And a very discreet printer." She snatched back the book, leaving Scratch stunned and empty-handed. "If I had my way, everyone would have one of these."

"Why? I imagine it's terribly boring."

Brella laughed in a soft, smooth sort of way that made Scratch's stomach clench.

"Shall I read some to you?"

Scratch's mouth went dry. "There isn't any light."

"I have remarkable vision." Brella opened to a page near the end and cleared her throat. "*This paragraph pertains to the citizens of the newly annexed lands, known forthwith as Kyria and the Western Wilds. The parties above indicated shall share in the triumphs of our land as well as our many offerings and spoils. The parties shall therefore be liable for yearly taxation, without exception. For the children, their national status flows from the maternal side, so as for a mixed marriage, the mother of the child provides official blood. In a second generation . . .*" She dropped the book. "Scratch, are you listening?"

"Of course." She stifled a yawn. "Thrilling stuff. Great read."

"I know it's boring." She closed the book, setting it on her outstretched legs. "That's sort of the point."

"Why would that be the point?"

"Because if it's boring," Brella explained, "people won't pay attention to it."

Scratch ran her hand over the nape of her neck, feeling the

newly shorn strands. When they had reached the clearing, Brella had tidied up Scratch's new haircut. There were no mirrors, nor a reflective pool in which she could admire herself, but, by Brella's satisfied glances, Scratch suspected she looked a bit of all right.

"Why wouldn't the king want people to pay attention to his decrees? I've met him. The man loves the sound of his own voice."

Brella paused for a long moment. "Do you know how nationality works in Ivinscont?"

"Um, if you're born in Ivinscont, you're a national of Ivinscont?"

"For most, yes. Not for all. Not for Kyrians or Westerners."

Scratch sat up at that. "Now, I know that's not true."

"Do you?"

"Yes. Once those states became part of our land, their people came under our flag. A strong and watched o'er people—"

"Under our banner high. I know, Scratch." Brella sighed and closed the book, laying it on her outstretched legs. "But."

"But?"

"But." She tapped the cover with a long finger. "Decree Seventy-Six: though they be lawful Ivinscontians, the people of Kyria will for life maintain their national status as Kyrians, as will the generations that they beget. Decree Ninety-Four added Westerners to that, too."

"You have it memorized?"

She waved her hand noncommittally. "Most of it. Anyway, Seventy-Six means they're Ivinscontians, but they're also not Ivinscontians."

Scratch scrunched her forehead. "But that's good, right? If they want to maintain any, you know, feeling for where they're from, what their region was like before it was Ivinscont, they get to keep that."

Brella tipped her head in acknowledgment. "Sure. But."

"More but."

She huffed out a laugh. "With me, Scratch, you'll always get more 'but.'"

How Brella managed to ignore the heat rising to Scratch's face, she didn't know. It felt like an inferno.

"But," Brella continued heavily, "that also means they're a different class of person. Kyrians and Westerners can't join guilds."

"They can't?"

"No."

"Oh." She thought for a moment. "They can join the Academy."

"Yes."

"I doubt they would have the coin to join guilds anyway," Scratch reasoned. "I certainly couldn't have. I didn't have a copper."

"Nor did I, not so long ago."

"So what's the trouble, really? The Academy is the only way for someone with no coin to end up with any coin."

Brella took a deep breath. "The Academy is another issue entirely."

"Oh gods, Brella. Not another 'but.'"

"I didn't say 'but'!"

"It was implied."

"I'll be more careful next time." Even in the dark, the fires in her warm brown skin were lit and shining. "So, the King says keeping Kyrians and Westerners from joining guilds is to encourage them to stay in their original regions. To keep the population strong and dispersed, and to curb crowding in the royal city."

"Well that sounds reasonable. I'm sure if—oh, hells, Brella. I can already hear the 'but' coming. You might as well get on with it and tell me why I'm wrong."

Brella laughed, gleaming gold like a temple idol.

"All right, Sergeant Major. I shall." Her lips quirked up at the corners. "Why does Ivinscont go west?"

"I thought you were answering a question, not asking one."

"Humor me."

Scratch's sigh was mostly for show. "Fine. Because a larger

country is a stronger country. Because having the ocean at our west would be a huge strategic advantage. Because the lands we're taking are primitive and could benefit from our resources. And because those lands have natural resources that we could use to strengthen our reserves and to boost manufacturing in the new mills."

Brella nodded. "And if, say, all the Kyrians come to the Royal City to join guilds, then who will work in their mines?"

"Ah."

"Yes. Ah."

"Well, that's not so bad." Scratch unfolded her hands. Gesturing always helped her think, and she was certainly thinking now. "If they're staying in their mines, they're basically doing what they've always been doing, aren't they?"

"Sure. Except instead of the ore going to sustain their own economy, it's going to the Ivinscontian economy."

"Yes, yes, but they get the benefits of being Ivinscontians, too." She didn't know when it happened, but Scratch was suddenly bright with excitement. For days, she had scratched the surface of all these new mysteries, never breaking through. It was a welcome relief to finally understand something, to hold the complexity in her hands like a gem, turning it carefully so light caught every facet.

"Such as?" Brella must have felt something too, because there was a familiar breathy thrill in her voice. The thrill, Scratch knew, of closing in on an answer—or, perhaps, of finding a new one?

"Such as mining technology," Scratch answered.

"That . . . that's actually a fair point. I hadn't considered that."

She felt unduly pleased. A hot flush crawled up her cheeks. "Well, there you are."

"Okay." Brella leaned forward, jumping from that point to the next. Scratch leaned in to match her, only slightly disappointed they couldn't stick around in her victory. "So we make mining easier. Say, a Kyrian mine owner becomes extremely rich. He takes a wife, fathers a few sons, watches them grow, and then one says 'Papa, I'd like to be a glazier.' So what does the Kyrian papa do?"

"Bribe someone? That is, apparently, your method." Scratch tapped the closed book on Brella's lap as evidence. And then, because she was feeling brave, elbowed her gently in the side.

Brella erupted into fresh giggles, bubbly like froth on cream. "Fine, he probably would. But that's not a system to build a new nation on, is it?"

"New? Ivinscont has been around for generations."

"West, west, west to the ocean. That's certainly new. Besides, most people aren't going to be mine owners. They'll be miners. Miners who will need to do a great deal more mining, because now the ore is needed by the crown."

"But the machines—"

"Don't require pay. Fewer jobs."

Scratch considered that. "So what do the miners do?"

Brella yawned behind the back of her hand. The sun had set hours ago, and the fire was down to coals. "Some of them come to the Royal City. Of course, there's no point in them taking up apprenticeships, since they can't join guilds. So they end up working jobs that pay less. Many become servants. They take the jobs they can get, and, because they have no room to grow or money to save, their families stay poor for generations."

"Or they join the Academy." Scratch's lips felt numb.

"Or they join the Academy." She didn't need to add *to fight for a land where they aren't full citizens*. The unspoken truth hung in the air like rotted fruit on a branch.

"How do you know all of this?"

Brella lifted the book. "Reading. Meeting the Kyrians and Westerners that come to the City. I'm a brewer. People like to talk over ale, so I make sure everyone who visits understands their rights." She smoothed her hair self-consciously, an odd gesture for someone so confident. Seeing it felt like a secret, or a private touch on the arm. "I'm not trying to, you know, save them or anything. I just . . ." She gestured vaguely, then sighed. "I just think they should know the whole of the situation. And that someone is paying attention."

"I'm glad." Scratch's voice was hoarse, so she cleared her throat. "I'm glad you're paying attention."

Brella leaned toward her. The place where their shoulders touched felt like a bright spark. "You are too, now. I find that this information isn't so easily forgotten."

She nodded, even as a sickly wave of guilt crested in her gut. "They were living in poverty before we came in. In Kyria, I mean."

Brella nodded. "They were."

"No sewers. Throwing waste from windows. The streets were filthy. Many of them welcomed us."

"That's true."

"And in the Wilds—"

In the Western Wilds, the people lived in trees. They rested on branches and built their homes among the leaves. She had seen slat bridges stretched between trees like toothy grins, connecting house to house, window to window. And on those bridges she had seen archers, lying flat on their bellies, waiting for the Ivinscontians to tear them down to earth. Spear fighters shocked by daggers, dropping one after the next. They hadn't come quietly, but they came.

She suddenly found it difficult to breathe.

"Scratch?"

"Hmm?"

"Are you all right?"

"Yes." She swallowed thickly. Her throat felt tight. "I'm getting tired."

"We should sleep." Brella stood, taking her little book with her. "Shall I take first watch?"

"No, I'll do it." She managed a weak smile. "I have a lot to think about."

Brella hesitated. She looked like she was about to reach out, her eyes darting between Scratch's hand and her own. Instead, she walked to her bedroll and slipped inside.

"Goodnight, Scratch," she murmured, her eyes already closed.

Scratch settled herself against the tree. She tried to think about what Brella had said, those unjust laws and closed guilds, but her mind had other plans. Each time she blinked, she was back at the Academy, staring down a pudgy, pink boy. And then she hit him. And she hit him and hit him and hit him until he was down and shrieking. And then someone said "She doesn't have a scratch on her!" and it stuck.

She had thought she knew what that name meant. Now, she was certain she had no idea.

Chapter Twenty-Three

Scratch was in a warm, shabby room. It was late. Darkness awaited outside the drawn curtains, but a fire flared on the hearth, bathing the room in yellow-orange light. A group of people sat in mismatched chairs around the fire, some sipping ale, others chatting in low tones. A tang of apprehension curdled the atmosphere, and every so often eyes darted toward the door, though it remained closed.

"How long should we wait for her?" asked a voice Scratch knew, a voice that meant comfort, even before she could assign it a name.

"Relax, Brella." She knew that one, too: Vel. "The head maid probably asked her to do some last-minute thing."

"Doesn't respect her time," offered a third person: an old, stout woman who perched on a stool, her body as round and smooth as a puffball mushroom. Her hand shook as she brought a long-stemmed pipe to her mouth and sucked. "Always keeping her after her shift's over. Never paying her her due."

"Mrs. Callin, I do hate to rush you," interjected a young man. He wore spools of thread on each finger like a handful of rings. "But if we wait too long, I think Vel's gonna wrap me up and eat me like a spider."

The old woman—Mrs. Callin—clicked her tongue at the

159

man. "Hush, Dale."

"Vel," the man whined. He was tall and thin, with dark freckly skin and bronze-brown hair. "Can't you get Hill to do this? You know I can't sit still."

Vel grinned, his eyebrows dancing. He held a needle and fabric in his hands and his fingers flew. "You said you wanted to flip a coin. You flipped a coin. Besides, this builds character."

A man sitting at Vel's side snorted. He was identical to the gangly Dale, down to the last freckle. "Yes, Dale. Do grab some character for the road."

An imposing man with a thick dark beard harrumphed from his too-small stool beside the fire. "I still don't like it."

"Agreed, Judah." Dale held his fingers out. "Would you care to take my place?"

"Not that, idiot boy." Judah pointed a meaty finger at Brella. "I still don't like that Brella's leading transport."

"I still don't care." She faced him, eyes narrowed in silent challenge. "We made a plan. You know the rules, Judah. Majority decision."

Judah crossed his arms over his sizable chest, hunkering low in his chair. It creaked. "Doesn't mean I have to act pleased about it."

"Aw." Brella's smile was cold and mocking. "I've displeased you. I'm so very torn up about it."

"Umbrella, stop." Dale's twin was stiffer than his brother, hands folded in his lap and feet planted firmly on the gnarled wood floor. "I voted in your favor because you said you could keep your temper in check."

Brella glared. "I can, Hill."

"And I'll be there as well." Vel held up a handkerchief half covered in colorful embroidery. Scratch couldn't see much in the limited light, but there seemed to be a bird among the stitching. "I'll keep her calm."

"I don't need anyone to keep me calm, thanks."

"All right," said Vel evenly. "Then I'll keep you company."

A man Scratch hadn't yet noticed rose from his chair and

came to sit by Brella. He was small and slender, with cunning green eyes and hair like a red fox's.

"Are you all right?" He placed a comforting hand on Brella's leg. "You don't have to say yes."

"Generous of you, Leverett. Then, no." She grinned at him weakly. "I'm not looking forward to the next few weeks if I'm honest."

"If we're lucky, it won't be that long." He squeezed her thigh. "You'll be good there."

"It's not me I'm worried about."

The door flew open with a bang. Nearly everyone started, including Dale, who, in his flinching, unspooled a rainbow of thread.

Brella frowned. "Of course you wouldn't settle for a reasonable entrance."

The woman in the doorway smiled, casually pushing a lock of shoulder-length wavy hair behind her ear. Her skin had a healthy golden glow, and freckles dusted her face and arms like spice on toast.

"Miss me?" the newcomer asked Brella with a smirk.

"I saw you two days ago."

The woman batted her eyes coquettishly, taking a seat next to Leverett. "If I had my druthers, I would see you every day."

Brella rewarded the woman with a two-fingered gesture, for which Leverett smacked her on the shoulder. Dale laughed. Vel whacked him on the back of the head.

"All right." Mrs. Callin's voice cut through the noise like scalding water in snow. "Everyone, shut it. Maisie is here. We have important business."

"Hear, hear," Dale cheered, while Hill gently rewound the thread around the spools on his fingers.

"Sorry I'm late." Maisie lifted a scarf from around her neck and draped it on the back of her chair. "I was with Frances."

Mrs. Callin raised an eyebrow. "Were you?"

Brella shifted on her seat. "Is she ready? Because if she—"

"Relax, Umbrella." Maisie had a rakish, confident smile, the

161

kind a dazzling swindler might take years to perfect. "She's the most eager of all of us."

"And she knows what's ahead, right?" Vel's mouth was tight with worry, "She knows how difficult it might be?"

Maisie sobered. "She's known hardships, Vel. She'll be fine."

"Good." Leverett clapped his hands together. "Everyone know their jobs?"

"Frances and I will leave in roughly—" Maisie glanced at the beat-up grandfather clock in the corner. "—twenty-six hours. After the feast."

"The fate ball is spooled," Leverett added. He snapped his fingers, and a discarded spool floated up from the floor to land delicately atop Dale's last unoccupied finger. "Our contact says the king is entirely convinced not to knight Keyes. During the feast, the ball will pull her away."

"And the other?" Hill asked.

"He'll follow," Vel assured him. "He always follows."

Mrs. Callin nodded. "When they're in the dungeon, Iris will take the path Frances laid out and retrieve the pair."

"Where's Iris?" Leverett whispered to Brella.

"Castle," she murmured back. "Working."

"Then Iris will lead Keyes and the other here, where Umbrella and Vel will be waiting to take them through. Any questions?"

Brella shrugged. "None from me."

Leverett raised a finger. "If you run into Lollie?"

Brella waved a dismissing hand. "I doubt I will. I could barely find her when we were together. But if I do, I'll cook up a cover with Keyes. Probably that she's my lover and my Passenger."

Maisie winced. "Ouch."

Brella sucked her teeth. "What 'ouch?'"

"You stop seeing Lollie six months ago, after years of telling her you're not ready to show her the Between, and suddenly you have someone you're willing to take through?" She shrugged. "Cold."

"You don't know anything about it."

"You're an absolute barnyard creature, Umbrella." Maisie

crossed her arms over her chest. "And I think I have a fairly good idea of how it would feel to have the woman I'm seeing—"

"Maisie, you're nineteen."

"Yeah, and my girlfriend is seventeen and the rightful leader of a nation—"

"Oh, and that makes you the expert on post-relationship etiquette, you jumped-up cowpat? Thank the God of Justice for you, Maisie."

Maisie snarled like a stepped-on cat. "Oh, shut your self-righteous hole, you absurd—"

"Who are you calling—"

Dale clapped his hands over his head, spools unspooling while Vel fruitlessly tried to keep his brother steady. "This!" *Clap.* "Is!" *Clap.* "So!" *Clap.* "Stupid!" *Clap.*

"I'm so tired." Hill dropped his head into his lap. "So tired."

"Girls!" At the sound of Mrs. Callin's voice, both women's mouths snapped shut. "You are revolutionaries, not feral cats. Might I remind you that this is a matter of national importance? If you can't put your differences aside, our entire plan will go right to the infinite hells, and the two of you along with it. I'll see to that myself."

Maisie and Brella lowered their heads like scolded children.

"I'm sorry, Mrs. Callin," Brella mumbled.

"Yeah." Maisie sniffed. "Sorry."

Dale elbowed a scowling Vel. "Callin's better than Mum, eh? Quicker too. And nobody lost any hair this time."

"I have a concern." Hill raised a tentative hand. "What if she doesn't want to go with you, Brella?"

Brella raised her eyes to him, cautious but no less murderous. "We've been through this, Hillary. She doesn't have a choice."

"I know she doesn't, but she's smart. She could easily figure out something's going on. I just want to know what kind of plan you have in place to convince her not to ask too many questions."

"Convince her?" Brella folded her arms over her chest. "All I have to do is keep the plan a secret, which I am perfectly capable of doing. Her only way of getting to Koravia is through me. I

163

don't need to convince that ridiculous, bloodthirsty imp of anything."

"You have a point, Brella," Leverett offered, forthcoming caveat written all over his shrewd face. "But consider, she has no way of knowing whether you're lying about the Between and Koravia. If she thinks you're a traitor—which, darling, you absolutely are—she'll have no reason to go on with you. And besides, once you get into the Between with her, it will be a great deal harder to hide what's under the surface."

She pointed a deadly finger at Leverett. "I am *not* a traitor."

Maisie groaned. "We know, Brella. You don't have to do the whole . . . ," she waved her hands around, "thing."

Brella ignored her, jaw set. "I am not a traitor. I love my country and its people. That's why I'm doing any of this: to make a small difference in the fight to save this country from that idiot on the throne, his heinous Hand, and that tiny, little—"

"Murderous raisin?" Maisie supplied.

"Stabbing squirrel?" Dale offered.

"Woman who very badly needs a haircut?" Vel piped up.

"Sergeant Major," Brella grumbled through gritted teeth.

Leverett nodded hesitant assent. "Sure. All right. You're not a traitor. But that doesn't mean our Sergeant Major Keyes won't disagree." He steepled his fingers, then brought his mouth down to meet them. "I have a proposal."

Mrs. Callin acknowledged him with a wave of her hand. "Speak, Lev."

"Seduce her?"

There was a second of silence. Then, the room exploded into laughter, claiming everyone but the stoic Mrs. Callin, the sour-faced Judah, and a stunned, openmouthed Brella.

"No," Judah growled.

"Judah, I can speak for myself." Brella stiffened her shoulders. "No."

"It's not a bad idea." Dale stroked his chin with the remaining spools. "She's gotta have a little incentive, and I know she drinks from the same pot as you do."

Maisie shuddered. "Yuck."

He shrugged. "All the same."

"I'm sorry, is this some kind of joke?" Brella's voice was dangerously high. "Do you think I want anything to do with that runt?" She cast a desperate glance around the circle. "Anyone want to chime in here, please?"

"It's actually not the worst idea."

Her shoulders drooped. She looked, if only for a moment, betrayed. "I expected better from you, Hill."

"I just—Velly, yes, I can see the thread is tangled, hang on—I just think you need some guarantee that she'll believe you. You know, about the Between and Koravia. I mean, it does seem rather far-fetched, and I've been through."

Brella had the hounded look of an animal backed into a corner. "Why are you bringing all this up now? We've been planning this for months. If you were concerned about my ability to get Keyes to Koravia, why didn't you mention something earlier?"

"To be honest, Brelly, you've gotten rather . . ." Dale drew back preemptively. "Angrier?"

Brella's nostrils flared. Apparently remembering herself, she closed her eyes and took a steadying breath. "I am not angry."

Maisie reached out a hand towards Brella's shoulder, which Brella promptly flicked away. "You rather are, Brella. For the past month, you've been particularly zealous, waving that little book around."

"Zealous?" Brella flushed, mouth pursing. "I've been doing the necessary work on the ground. I've been reaching people."

"So what's one more?" Dale winked. "Reach her."

Maisie groaned. "Again, yuck."

"Do you know why I've been angry?" Brella demanded.

Dale shrugged. "The cheese merchant is out of Stuffed Walder?"

"It's because she took the Wilds in a day. Because the king was going to knight her. That's why." She took a long, slow breath. "She was able to take Kraal nearly singlehandedly when she was just a Sergeant Major. Imagine what she'd be able to do in charge."

"She's just a person, Brella." Hill favored her with a gentle smile. "Flesh and blood."

"And we can't jeopardize this." Maisie bent low in her chair, hands clasped between her spread knees. "We've been planning for months. We need to deal with the threat she poses, and the only way is to get her to Koravia. If that means you need to, you know, open your legs for Ivinscont—"

"Yuck!" Dale cheered.

"Then I agree with Leverett on the matter."

Brella shook her head vigorously. "No, no. I can make her trust me without sleeping with her. There has to be a better . . ."

"No!" A voice slammed into Scratch's back, making her teeth shake.

"I wouldn't touch her with a . . ."

"Scratch! Wake up, please!"

"Besides, if I did plan to trick her, I could . . ."

"No, no! You need to wake up!"

The room began to fog at the edges, great clouds swallowing up the glowing, orange light, the people in their chairs. Hill and Dale grew faint, along with the threads, the spools, the colors melting into the fading warmth. Vel and Maisie evaporated into whiteness, then Mrs. Callin and Judah and Leverett until no one was left but Brella, sitting alone in her chair, ranting about how she would never, ever, as long as she lived, lay a hand on Scratch in anything other than violence.

Chapter Twenty-Four

Scratch gasped into alertness. The night was still dark, the heavy moon hanging in a warm sky. Still she shivered. Her heart pounded in her chest and her ears rang. Her whole body was filled with freezing water, sharp chips of ice cutting into her bone.

"Scratch, please. Let me explain." Brella crouched beside her, an animal at the ready. Her eyes were desperate, imploring in the dark. She shook terribly. Freckles stood dark in her ashen face, and her words sounded like choking, or drowning. "Please. It isn't what it looks like."

"It looks like you're part of a plot to abduct me." She was amazed by how level and emotionless she sounded. It made a sick sort of sense. She was beyond feeling, a hole of swallowing blankness opening up inside of her. "That you planned this whole thing. That you think I'm, what was it, a bloodthirsty imp?"

"No, Scratch. No." Brella's eyes widened even further. "That isn't what I—"

"They wanted you to seduce me." Her lips felt numb, her tongue a foreign thing. "Is that why you've been looking at me? Holding my hand?" The words sizzled on her lips like acid. "They convinced you?"

"No. I was never planning to do that. You and I, we ..."

"What were you going to do with me?"

"Nothing, I—"

Scratch held up a hand. "Not like that. I mean, in Koravia. Why did you need me to go to Koravia?"

Brella swallowed, her throat clicking. "You're too dangerous."

"Dangerous."

"Frances has been trying to stop her father from invading any other lands. We thought we had time with the Wilds. We thought we could get him to pull the troops back. And then—"

"The octagon." Victory after one day. Victory that should have been rewarded. "The king was going to knight me. I was going to be a commander."

Brella stood, breathing. Her face was twisted, pained, but she couldn't deny it. "Yes."

"Until your people got to him." She stared at Brella through a haze of stinging blur, her details fading into splotches of dimmed color. "Your group convinced him not to knight me." Suddenly, the yawning hole inside her was full of fierce, sweltering anger. "Wasn't that enough for you? Why rip me away, ruin any chance I had at a future, when you could have just—"

"Because you did it as a Sergeant Major!" Brella cried. Her voice was raspy, echoing messily off the trees. "It was only a matter of time until he changed his mind again, gave you a command. Imagine what you could have done!"

"Lived!" she cried, something cracking inside of her. "Succeeded. Did the one thing I know how to do."

"You're wrong, Scratch." Brella was openly sobbing now, bent and pleading. Pathetic, and yet Scratch and her twisted hope felt the traitorous urge to go to her. Hold her, calm her. This liar. "You c-can do so much more. You can."

"What were you going to do with me in Koravia? Kill me?" Brella shook her head ferociously. "Tell me."

"Frances is getting help from Koravia. She's been corresponding with the king when she can. We'd been planning to get her there for months. But we knew . . ." She gulped, wiping her face. "We knew they didn't trust her. Not completely. You were—"

"A gift," Scratch snarled. "A price."

"We need to win, Scratch. We'd been looking for a way to earn Koravia's trust, and then you took the Western Wilds. You're the best strategist in Ivinscont. Getting you out of there was t-twofold: an easier win for us and a w-way for Frances to prove herself. To convince the king he should back her against her father."

"And ruining my life wasn't a problem for you?"

"You've ruined lives, Scratch!" The forest was still. Barely any bugs chirped. No bats swooped. It was only the two of them standing apart in a clearing under scrambled stars. Brella's breathing was loud and ragged, but Scratch could barely hear it over the raw thump of her blood rushing through her tight and throbbing veins.

"What lives?" she demanded.

"We talked about this, Scratch." Brella's braids were disheveled, little strands coming loose from each plait. "The Western Wilds are under Ivinscont now."

"And their lives are better."

"They're not citizens. Their trees are going to be felled for the mills."

"Their trees?" It was as though a stream of ice water shot through her, turning molten anger hard and sharp-edged. "They live in trees."

"Not anymore. They live like Ivinscontians now."

She pressed down the confusion. The anger was better, crisper, brightening her vision like daytime. "They would have been annexed anyway. If I hadn't come up with a strategy, someone else would."

"Frances nearly got the king to retreat," Brella cried, wiping her eyes.

"Well, she didn't, Brella." The name was sticky hot in her mouth. "I can't apologize for being good at what I do."

"You are good." Brella pressed her lips together, inhaling a

169

steady breath through her nose. "You are. Come be good for Frances."

That knocked her back. Her knees wobbled. "What?"

"You know what he did. I told you. Kyria and the Western Wilds didn't want to be part of Ivinscont. He's going to take more and more. You know what it's like for them, now. You can't pretend you don't."

"I don't know why it should matter to me," she said, feeling the lie cauterize whatever was open and bleeding inside her until it was nothing but numbness.

Brella stumbled back. "What?"

"You're clearly not a soldier. You just gave up your whole plan. I can go back now. Sure, I'll be thrown in a dungeon, but the king will free me once I tell him that his daughter left to build an army against him. That there's a maid in his castle who is working for the resistance. That he should prepare for a Koravian invasion."

"Scratch," Brella croaked. "No."

"Pity I didn't figure out who the contact inside the castle is. But at least I can tell the king to watch out for one."

"Scratch, please. You're angry. I get it. But this isn't you."

"How the hells would you know who I am?" Brella didn't know her at all. How could she, when Scratch wasn't even sure anymore who she was? Everything she had thought before the banquet, before the princess disappeared, before she had seen the end of her life on the executioner's block—she had been right. If it hadn't been for this small, insidious resistance group, Scratch could have had everything she wanted. A command. A life. Everything.

Everything she still wanted. Didn't she?

Brella shifted, her eyes going cool. "You're right," she sneered. "I don't know who you are. Here I thought you had realized what you'd done. How many deaths you've caused. But I was right all along, wasn't I? Soldiers are cruel and mercenary and selfish. How could I have thought differently?"

Scratch could barely breathe. "I'm going back." She made

170

sure her knife was strapped in its sheath. "I won't take you in. I'll show you that mercy. But I'm going."

"What about James?"

Scratch froze. "What about him?" she snarled, bluffing away the fear. James, James, James. She saw him in her mind's eye, terrified and confused, long eyelashes wet with tears.

"He and Vel are meeting us at the blood gate tomorrow. Are you going to let him go on without you?"

"He'll know s-something is wrong." She stumbled over the words. "He'll look for me."

"Will he?" Brella's face clouded over, and Scratch was transported back to that first night, freed from the dungeons and thrown before a woman who wore her distrust as plainly as her dirtied apron. "I could tell him anything. That you've run off and died."

"He won't believe you."

"Oh won't he?" Brella replied frostily. "You believed my lies for this long, Sergeant Major."

"He knows me. He's too smart."

"Does he know you?" Brella hissed, and oh, it was a dagger dipped in poison, sharp first, and then burning, nauseating, eroding the soft bits of her that she had only just remembered, only discovered in these dangerous woods. "Does anyone?"

Scratch blinked the hot tears away and ran.

Chapter Twenty-Five

Branches scraped her arms, and roots rose up to trip her. Strange noises raked at her ears, weeping, hollow sounds that she could barely discern from her own mangled cries of pain. A bird shrieked nearby. Something chittered, low and hungry. Still she ran, her breaths ripping out of her chest, leaving iron splinters in her throat and mouth. A low branch tangled in her hair, claiming strands and scalp as she tugged herself free. The sting brought tears to her eyes.

Eventually, her body gave out. She crumpled onto the ground, reaching into the grass to steady herself. It was coarse between her fingers.

The wrenching pain she had felt since she had awakened began to dull, leaving behind a swirling mess of fear and regret. What had she done? What did fleeing help? Did she really think she could find a way out of the forest on her own?

Something skittered in the underbrush, sending the hairs on her arms to standing. When it left, she was alone.

The night was dark and thick around her. The only light came from the low-slung moon, which winked behind a canopy of pointed leaves like needles. Tall trees surrounded her, thick-trunked and thorny. She turned slowly, afraid to make a noise, afraid to disturb these empty woods. Leaves crushed under her hands and knees, too loud. She couldn't see a path back. She was lost.

There was nothing to do but weep, so she wept. She wept for her life, the one she had built from nothing, lying in shambles back at the palace. She wept for James; would she ever see him again? Was Vel lying to him, just as Brella had lied to her? Oh gods, she hoped he wouldn't find out like she had, once he had fallen too far.

Because that was the truth of it. Brella had burrowed into her skin. Into her mind. She had changed Scratch, and there would be pain in the undoing of it.

Gods, that dream. What had she seen? In that room, Brella and her co-conspirators had concocted a trap, and Scratch had walked directly into it. Pain seared her stomach like a brand. She folded over herself, clutching at the ache.

She had known Brella was a liar, but she had barely investigated beyond that. The truth was, she hadn't wanted to know. The clues had been there if she had only bothered to see them. But Brella had been there, too, dazzling and angry and more tenacious than anyone had the right to be. Brella had known who Scratch was. She had been ready to travel. She'd had too many answers, too perfect answers. She had revealed enough, just enough for Scratch to think she was getting somewhere when, in reality, she'd been walking in circles.

She was going to die out here.

"Sc-sc-scratch?"

Something emerged from the trees ahead. A woman wearing familiar muddy boots and an embroidered apron. Her hair was braided and bronze, her skin rich brown and freckled. At the sight of her, relief flooded Scratch's chest like warm water.

"Brella?" she said, the word nearly a moan. In this moment of pure relief, her body had forgotten to be angry.

"Y-yeh-yes. Scra-a-a-tch."

Instantly, the warmth of relief froze into icy horror. That was not Brella's voice. This was not Brella.

"Who are you?" She reached for her knife, pointing it at the

...something, some not-Brella, who was opening her mouth too wide, splitting her face to reveal rows and rows of teeth, yellowy stalactites hanging down from her palate.

"Scraa-aa-aatch. I have yo-o-ooou. Give to me-me-me-meeee." The thing shambled forward, feet clumsy and hands outstretched. Its head hung limply. When it walked, its ankles rolled, feet pointing impossibly inward. Its hands were long-nailed and flaky-red, and an odor rolled off it like sickly-sweet rot.

"Stay back!" Fear prickled at her skin. Her mind swam. "Get away from me. I don't have anything you want."

"Flesh or truth." It snapped up its lolling head, opening two black eyes. And then a third. And a fourth. "Flesh or tru-u-th. Give me what you wa-a-ant."

Scratch's pulse slammed in her throat, and she tasted fear, acrid and sour, on the back of her tongue.

"What does that mean?" she shrieked desperately.

The thing bent in on itself, quivering as it shifted shape. When it raised its slack head once more, its many eyes were bright green, shaded by thick brows.

"Yo-o-our truth or your flesh," croaked the not-James. "Tell me wha-at you wa-a-ant."

"I want you to go away!"

"Wrong answer." It curved down again, its hair growing long and yellow, its eyes ocean blue and too wide in a wizened face.

"She came here," it said through a grotesque replica of Purpose's mouth. "She gave me what she wa-a-a-anted. Give me that or give me fle-e-esh."

"I want to go home!"

"Wrong." It leered, black ooze dripping from the side of its wide maw. "Wro-o-ong little fetus."

It shuddered, its features shifting, worms roving under its patchy skin.

"Truth or flesh," growled not-Temperance. She looked heartbreakingly dead, and still so very young. Thankfully, the creature convulsed and morphed again, but when it rose, the form it had taken was the most frightening of all.

"Wha-a-at do you want?" rasped the Western Wilds fighter. Blood leaked down the side of his head and he held half of a broken spear in his desiccated hand. It was a soldier Scratch had killed. She had thought of it as a clean kill, just one stab under the ribs. It didn't look clean now, the ragged hole gaping from the thing's midsection, green and infected. "What do you want?"

"To do better!" she shouted, squeezing her eyes shut. It did no good; the image was burned into her eyelids. "To be better."

"Good," the thing cried. Around it, the winds shifted, pulling Scratch nearly off her feet. "More."

"To mean something. Something that actually matters."

"Yes." The winds howled, churning up dead leaves and sticks, a vortex of dust and debris. "More."

"Brella. I want Brella!" The truth of it was a cliff jump, freeing and terrifying. She could feel the wind whistling by her ears as she fell, wincing for the impact. She was honest and terrified, free and dying. Frightened, alone, falling . . .

To want was to see things clearly. All these things she had ignored, the deaths she justified to herself, the kills she claimed were necessary. The reaching for a command, the title that would change how she was seen, but not what she saw in the mirror—the skinny, hungry, lonely Lakes girl without a friend. Her insistence that she didn't want love because it would pull her away from her path. The truth, that she didn't want love because it would force her to see things clearly, force her to know herself. Force her to face the reality that all these things she wanted, she didn't want at all.

The wind died. Scratch carefully opened her eyes. Where the beast had been now stood a girl of around ten. Her skin was milk white and fresh, her hair in long, blue curls.

"Thank you," she trilled, and skipped away into the forest.

Scratch stood dumbfounded. Her hands shook. Her mouth was dry and she was impossibly thirsty. She raised her hands to her stomach, her face. She was clothed. She was whole. How? How could that be true when she could have sworn she was naked and rent?

"Well," said a voice from behind her, "I'd say that was a test well passed."

Scratch turned around and screamed.

Chapter Twenty-Six

"Generally, I expect a 'good morning,'" said the newcomer. "I shall give you another chance to provide one."

"G-good morning," Scratch stammered.

He beamed. "And a good morning to you, young traveler. I am Uncle."

Scratch did not have any uncles, but if she did, she doubted they would have shared even a passing resemblance with this new fae.

Uncle was, for lack of a better word, a bug. A very large, extremely well-dressed bug wearing wire spectacles and tails. His antennae twitched merrily above his large, oblong head. His yellow, protruding eyes peered from behind two small, round lenses, and a burgundy waistcoat stretched across his sternum, testing the resilience of the golden buttons that held it closed. His velvet tailcoat was immaculate, and what appeared to be a large leaf fluttered behind him like a cape.

"It would be my pleasure to serve as your escort this morning." He bowed low, offering a feeler for Scratch to shake. She did, despite her apprehension. The appendage was surprisingly firm, with tiny strands of something coarse on the surface. "It's a dreadful shame that we should meet like this, but, needs must." He peered around. "Shall we head back? Your Brella is rather distraught."

"Sh-she wants me back?" Scratch asked, disbelieving.

"Of course she does! Do you think Umbrella would let a friend traipse off into the forest alone, especially one with whom she has shared a blood connection?"

"What does the blood bond have to do with it?"

His yellowy eyes warmed. "She wouldn't bond with someone she didn't care for. Now, let's get a move on. I assume she told you about me." He held himself, if possible, even taller. Scratch shook her head. "She must have. I assume you've forgotten." He straightened his lapels. "Off we go then."

They walked side by side through the dark forest. Dawn began its daily crest behind them, illuminating the thorny trees in smoky cool light. Perhaps Scratch had lost her nerve, because the trees were just as terrifying as they had been in complete darkness. The bark was gnarled, the slashes and knots forming the vague shapes of leering faces, with shifting eyes that followed her as she plodded back to the glen.

Uncle didn't seem to mind being observed by the trees. He whistled a happy little tune, his spindly legs carrying him jauntily along.

"Brella called for our help as soon as you fled," he told her. "Very bad form, by the way, you scurrying off. I believe you were warned about the tests. You could have very easily been killed."

She shuddered. "What was that thing?"

"Oh that? That was Peek. We have her over for tea on occasion."

Scratch's stomach was in knots by the time they approached the familiar clearing. She wasn't sure how to feel. The dream had punctured her, and she was wounded, but running hadn't been a bandage. It was avoidance.

Uncle made a courtly bow, extending a feeler forward.

"After you."

She took a deep breath and stepped onto the grass. Brella stood, looking small and bereft, her arms twisted. She raised a sorry hand.

"Hi," Brella said.

Scratch rocked onto her toes, heart thrumming. "Hello."

"This is lovely." A woman's throaty voice floated by, so jarringly not of the two-person world she and Brella currently occupied that Scratch couldn't help but flinch. "See, Brella? You had nothing to worry about."

"Yes," Brella muttered. "Thank you, Aunt."

The woman approached, holding an arm out for Uncle. Her skin was pale white with a light violet tint. Her iridescent, sunset-pink hair fell down her slender back in thick, glossy ringlets. She peered at Scratch with slow-blinking, green-lashed eyes, and smirked with lips as soft and lovely as rose petals. From just below her chin to the tips of her toes, a thick carpet of wildflowers coated her entire body. Even her hands sported little bouquets. She stood on her tiptoes to give Uncle a kiss on the tip of his oblong head. He might have been a bug, but the fae could still blush, pink staining the green of his cheeks.

"It's a pleasure to meet you, soldier." The flower woman regarded her with cool, green eyes. "Brella didn't give me your name, but I've heard a great deal about you. Granted, it was through tears and screaming, but I reckon I've got a pretty good idea of what you're about."

"Um." She scratched the back of her head. "It's nice to meet you, too."

"Well, we'd best be off." Uncle gave another of his well-practiced bows, extending a feeler for Scratch to take. "It was a joy making your acquaintance, young traveler." He kissed the top of her hand. His lips were stiff, and Scratch had the distinct impression of being prodded by two wooden spoons.

Aunt approached slowly, rose-colored eyes narrowed and arms outstretched. As she walked, she left footprints of wildflowers in her wake: perfect, oblong flower beds of pinks and purples, yellows and reds.

Scratch accepted her tentative hug, flowers like butterfly wings caressing her skin.

As soon as their bodies touched, Aunt tensed her fingers,

181

digging in to Scratch's flesh. "Don't leave again," Aunt hissed in her ear. "You don't know what you'll bring back from out there. And I swear to you, if you hurt Brella, if you lure anything dangerous to her, I will kill you." Aunt squeezed tighter, small thorns popping from her hands, piercing the top layer of Scratch's skin. "We fair folk don't abide by the same rules as humanity, you know. I will kill you and I will enjoy it. Do not wait to see whether I am lying. Trust that I am not."

She pulled back with a beatific smile, thorns retracting into her fingers, leaving Scratch shaking.

"A treat," Aunt said, and it sounded like a warning. "Uncle, shall we go home?"

"As you wish, my lady."

Scratch watched them leave with a sense of relief, the trees parting slightly to let them through. Soon, the sound of Aunt and Uncle's footsteps faded, two lines of tiny flowerbeds the only evidence that the magical beings had been there at all.

Chapter Twenty-Seven

Silence fell. Scratch's heart thumped an insistent pattern on her ribs—go, go, go, *do* something. She couldn't move. Brella stood on the other side of the clearing, blank eyes staring out at the spot in the trees through which Aunt and Uncle had disappeared. She looked wrung out like a washrag, her clothes rumpled and her skin oddly colorless. Darkness ringed her eyes, adorned with the spidery evidence of burst capillaries. Blood lined two of the fingernails of her right hand, evidence of biting or picking, neither of which Scratch had ever seen her do before. Her slumped shoulders rose and fell with uneven breathing.

When she spoke, her voice was scratchy. "He's a katydid." Her eyes didn't leave the trees. "Uncle. Aunt is some sort of flower fae. They were both born in the forests."

Brella swayed on her feet. Scratch shot out an arm, then pulled it back just as quickly. Something told her not to touch. Not yet. Thankfully, Brella stayed upright.

"Katydids live for only a year. Sometimes a little bit more, but not much. He'll die soon." She took a ragged breath. "He's died so many times. Every year he dies, and every year Aunt cries for him. She cries so hard all of her flowers shrivel up and die. She's left naked and alone."

Brella closed her eyes and breathed, those thick eyelashes

clumped together like spikes. "The forest loves her. It needs her flowers. So when she cries, after her flowers have gone, the forest grows her a new Uncle, right from the ground. Every year, the new Uncle remembers a little more from his other lifetimes. Mostly, he forgets. So she tells him, every year, everything they've been through. They're impossibly old; well, she is. She has centuries of life to catch him up on. And she does it every time he returns. Because she loves him so, so much. She loves him so much that the loss of him wilts her, strips her."

Scratch trembled, locking her knees to keep herself standing.

"I made her a book a few years ago," Brella murmured. "It was blank. I assumed she could write. I thought maybe the fae had a written language. I was w-wrong." Her voice hitched. "I hadn't even brought a quill. I thought she would already have one. I should have asked. And she was so disappointed. That there was this thing in front of her, blank and ready for her stories, and she had no way to use it. That I hadn't asked."

Her voice broke. She brought a hand to her eyes and breathed for a few moments. "The next time I came, I brought her a quill and the primer books my siblings and I learned how to read on. She and Uncle traveled with Vel and me so I could teach her to read. I taught Uncle, too, because he was interested. We all knew he would forget. I almost said no. Teaching Aunt was hard enough. But Uncle said that dying soon didn't mean he couldn't learn to read in this lifetime, even if he forgot in the next. It turned out to be rather easy to teach him. They both picked it up quickly, and Aunt started writing their life into the book.

"What I hadn't expected was that Uncle wrote in the book, too. Aunt wrote their stories from the front and Uncle wrote from the back. Not stories, though. He wrote her notes. She let me see them once. Just a few. He wrote things like 'When I'm dead, miss me, but not too much,' and 'Hold a gold button from my waistcoat to your mouth. If it's cool, I'm thinking of you. If it's warm, I'm thinking of you.' He wrote 'If you can't get me back this time, my sweet, don't despair. Don't blame yourself. You know I never truly leave you.'"

Brella finally turned away from the trees. The red that rimmed her eyes made the amber of her irises even brighter, two gold waistcoat buttons floating in watery whiteness. She smiled, but there was something broken in the way her lower lip trembled.

"I always think I'm right, Scratch. I never ask what people want. I just give. I give wrong. I give burdens, sometimes. And I never give other people room to surprise me. I almost didn't teach Uncle how to write. I didn't think there was a point. But there was."

"Brella—"

"Scratch, if you don't let me finish, I'll never get this out." She inhaled deeply through her nose and then let loose a stream of air from her mouth. "I thought I knew who you were. I thought I hated you. I didn't." She set her jaw, though her chin wobbled. "I don't. I should have told you everything far earlier. I shouldn't have decided it was better for you not to know. I should have given you the opportunity to surprise me."

"Brella—"

"Scratch, I am almost done. I swear it." She swallowed thickly. "You're so good. So brave. I've been a coward."

"You haven't!"

"I have. Not in taking you from the palace. Not in doing everything I've done to save the country that I love. But in keeping the truth from you. I told myself it would all work out, because what I was doing was right. If I was acting justly, if my goal was true, it would all be fine, right?" Her laugh was coarse. "I always wanted a love like Aunt and Uncle have. I always thought their story was so beautiful. I never considered how awful it would be to lose someone, how horrible. Because the minute you ran off, Scratch—" She choked, tears spilling from her eyes. "The very minute, I felt like all of the flowers had died. I thought . . . I thought—"

Scratch ran, and it wasn't even a choice.

185

She kissed any skin she could reach. Hair, head, eyelids, nose, mouth, *mouth*, their lips parting, welcoming each other. Scratch found Brella's hair and dug her fingers into the strands, wanting more, needing more, because she had been granted this by whatever gods were paying attention. Because Brella, like an aching flower fae, had called her home.

She tore Brella's shirt over her head while Brella reached for her trousers, yanking them down so Scratch could step free. They threw garments here and there until, blissfully, they were naked together, warm skin on skin, tumbling into the grass and rolling, mouths on mouths, hands on thighs and waists and breasts and cheeks and lips, spit mingling with tears.

"Scratch, Scratch," Brella babbled as Scratch found her nipple and held it between her fingers, "I have so much to tell you."

"Shh." Scratch kissed her. "Not now. Just this."

"Anything, anything," Brella murmured. "What do you like?"

Scratch stiffened, suddenly aware of the cool breeze on her exposed flesh. "I've never done this before."

Brella pulled her head back, eyes wide and stunned. "What?"

Honesty. It had been an untruth that had almost separated them. She wouldn't lie, not with something as precious as this. "I was too afraid. My whole life, up until now, has been about being a good soldier. I could be distracted. It just . . . never happened for me."

"Did you not want it to happen?"

"I did." She laughed into Brella's shoulder, hiding the inevitable red flush she felt drip from her scalp to her collarbones. "But what if I'd been distracted? What if one of my superiors was old-fashioned and found out and they had a problem with it?" And what if she loved, and that love made her see . . .

"I get it." Brella left a line of smoothing kisses along Scratch's brow, which she realized then had been furrowed. "Do you not want to do this now, then? Take it slow?"

Fear gripped her. "I do not want to take it slow."

Brella laughed, and it was such a relief to hear. Better than the horns that had heralded the King's Guard's return after they had taken the Wilds, the trumpet blares that meant she was home. "Then how about I take the lead, and if you don't like anything, you can say?"

Scratch nodded mutely and let herself fall. Brella was everywhere. Her body, skin freckled and warm, her hands smooth and strong. Her eyes were inescapable, hot as a brand, burning her impression into every inch of Scratch's skin.

It felt good, better than good, but that wasn't the miracle of it. The miracle was that it was Brella: clever and keen, angry and just and protective. The woman who used her mouth and hands to destabilize a nation, now using those same bits of flesh and magic to soothe Scratch, to care for her, to lick and suck and touch. Her voice, low and resonant, calling for justice and action, now moaning and humming and speaking low, caring words of encouragement, "Just like that, Scratch. Yes. I have you." Brella, a liar and a sneak, doing something so very true.

Scratch was lost in it. She had done so much to make her name mean something and here, in this moment, none of that mattered. This was her body, small and pale and blue-veined; white skin that flushed and bruised; icy blond hair. Brella stroked and bit, bringing up redness that clearly pleased her. Brella was pleased by her. Brella, the marvel of her, dappled and nearly inhuman in her strength and confidence, brought to dazed incomprehension by Scratch, whatever Scratch was. Whatever this remade her into.

Brella spoke, and Scratch said Yes. "Can I kiss you there?" Yes. "Can I put my mouth on you?" Yes, yes, *yes*. And she was rewarded with Brella between her legs, Brella's lips and tongue on the center of her, working her while she moaned and writhed and cried out, until she came on Brella's lips—yes, yes, oh gods, yes—in a bright shower of pleasure like sparks off metal.

She drank in Brella's body, strong and tall, softness spread over gentle hills of muscle. She swallowed. "Will you show me?"

Brella obliged, leading Scratch's hand between her legs, then placing her own hand above it.

"Do you feel that, Scratch?" Her eyes were so bright, so

honey gold. "Do you?"

Scratch followed that body, those eyes, those sounds, repeating the things that made Brella's inhalations speed and hitch. She touched everything within reach, soft and hard touches, pinches and strokes, because she could, because she wanted to, because this was an honor, a privilege, being here with Brella, being able to touch the woman who had awakened her like sunrise. The woman who had made her laugh and think and come, and brought her to a place out of reality with impossible creatures and soft grasses. She touched, and she listened as Brella said "yes, Scratch," and "just like that," and "oh-oh, yes," and "please, please don't stop," and came to her climax shaking and moaning Scratch's name as if she were a god made of starlight. Like they both were brand-new gods in a scrambled night sky, renamed over and over and over.

Chapter Twenty-Eight

"I want to go over it again."

Brella groaned, dragging her feet in the dirt. "No, Scratch. We have it down."

"Not nearly. I don't want James to run. We have to be gentle."

Brella leaned against a tree. She had said they would reach the blood gate by twilight and Scratch was doing everything she could to delay them. It wasn't that she wasn't eager to see James; she was, of course. But so much had changed in the two days since they last were together. She didn't want to spook him.

"I know, sweetheart," Brella cooed. Scratch preened. Brella dropped the pet name every few moments now, like pebbles marking a trail. "But he's your best friend. He'll listen."

"But what if he doesn't?" she whined, reaching for Brella and resting her head on the other woman's chest. It was so novel, to be able to touch her like this. It felt illicit.

"Then we'll hold him down and shove him through, whether he likes it or not."

"Simple. Elegant."

"Yes, well." Brella patted her on the back. "Of the two of us, I'm the real strategist."

"I suppose, after everything, I can't disagree." The word hung unspoken in her mouth, tasting of rot: *octagon*.

189

"It was an accomplishment, Scratch. Though, as for what it accomplished . . ."

"You should have left me in the dungeons."

Brella's hands were so firm on Scratch's back. "It's not about penance. It's about doing better. Making things better for the people you've harmed."

"By fighting my own people." She mashed her face into Brella's shirt, feeling the warmth underneath. "Deposing my own king."

"I'm sorry, sweetheart."

She leaned away, peering into Brella's amber eyes. "For?"

"You're in an impossible situation. I don't envy you."

"Don't pity me. I'm a soldier, remember?" She tried for a laugh as she stepped out of Brella's grasp. "We're wasting time. Let's go over it again."

Brella rolled her eyes, but she complied. "We say, 'Hello, James. Things have changed. Please have a seat.'"

"Good." She circled the area like a royal dance master, mapping out the steps. "And he sits. And I say 'So, remember how I thought that Frances left of her own accord? I was right.'"

"And you do so love being right."

She felt herself pinking. "Hush. And at this point, I expect him to be stunned silent. So I'll say 'Yes. She left with her real lover, another sister of Brella and Vel's. Her name is Maisie.'"

"Is that really what you want to lead with?"

Scratch put her hands on her hips. "Would it be better if I opened with, 'Guess what, we're pawns in a sneaky game of royal chess, and we need to switch our national allegiance if we want to live?'"

Brella shrugged. "I don't know. I don't play chess."

"I find that extremely unlikely. Oh, hells." She groaned, lying down on the ground. "Ugh. It's rocky here."

"That means we're getting close." Brella offered a hand. "Up you get."

They didn't speak as they shuffled along toward the gate. Scratch was too nervous to talk. She couldn't guarantee words would come out; it was far likelier to be vomit. James had been as much a friend as an appendage for the past fifteen years. If he decided not to go on once he knew the truth, she wasn't sure she could, either.

She heard a rustling ahead.

"Behind me, Brella," she hissed, reaching for her knife. She crouched, readied.

"Scratch?" James burst from the foliage, his hair puffed huge and his eyes watery. "Scratch!"

She didn't have time to sheathe her knife before he came hurtling at her. She tossed it to the side instead and felt herself leap into his arms. Back in the Royal City, she never let him lift her up. Today, it didn't matter. She squished him and he squished her, and when he finally set her down, his eyes were full of tears.

"Scratch," he wailed, "I missed you so—did you get a haircut?"

"It's a long story." She self-consciously ran a hand over the exposed nape of her neck. "I have so much to tell you."

"Me first." He bit his lip. "You had better sit."

"I have, uh, things to tell you too." Her hands were clammy. "You should also sit."

"You first." He pointed to the ground. "Sit."

"No, really, James. Darling. Sit."

"Scratch. Come on. Get on the ground."

"James, please. Sit."

"Scratch."

"James."

"Scratch!"

"*James!*"

"It was a trap," he blurted, hands flapping like the desperate struggle of a plummeting chicken dropped from a height of several feet. "Please don't run, Scratch. I know you're probably angry. But you have to listen. The things we did in Kyria and the Western Wilds . . . they weren't so great. I mean, what you did was great. It was amazing. The octagon? My gods, what a mind you have. But us annexing those places? Not the wisest maneuver, I'm afraid. Did you know, darling, that Kyrians can't join guilds? And that if a mother is Kyrian and a father is Ivinscontian, the child will be considered Kyrian and still not be able to join guilds? Or work in the palace, unless they're in the Guard? Or work for any titled noble outside of a guarding capacity? And, oh gosh, forget about getting a title themselves. But, actually, speaking of titles." He gulped, going red. "Scratch, you know how you and I both thought you would become a Lady Commander? Well, it turns out that you were closer than either of us thought. It would have happened, if not for—"

"James."

"Let me get this out, Scratch." He drew in a bracing breath. "The Shaes are not who you think they are."

"James, I know."

He blinked. "You know?"

She nodded, her lips quirking up of their own volition. "I know, James. I know—well, maybe not as many details as you do, but I know. I know about Maisie and Frances, and about the Shaes and their family of rebels, and that I could have gotten a command if not for them."

"And you're not upset?" he asked, boggled.

"Oh, I am." The feeling hadn't gone entirely. But there were other feelings, bigger feelings, inching that sting out of the sunshine. "But, I'm—I'm other things, too."

"Oh, Scratch." He fell onto her, knocking them both to the ground. "This is so different."

"Is it?" She smoothed his unruly hair from his face. He was rather sunburnt, and his skin was beginning to peel. "It was always you and I figuring out how to make our lives better. It feels rather the same to me."

"I suppose." He looked up, over her head. "Though now you aren't the only one looking after me."

She swiveled around to find the Shaes murmuring together, politely giving the two reunited guards a bit of privacy. They were laughing, their mirrored mouths stretched to reveal equally white teeth, their constellations of freckles like two gods in the night sky.

"No." She swallowed. "Nor you after me."

"Do you mean . . ." He whacked her shoulder. "Really?"

She nodded, feeling her cheeks heat. "It's new."

"Everything is new, you dolt. We haven't been out here a week. Oh, Scratch, I'm so proud of you!"

"I hate to interrupt." Vel sat down beside them, scratching the patches of stubble that splotched his face. "But it's time."

She looked up. There in the wood stood a large rectangle of stone. It was like a cliff face, or the first incline of a mountain, except that there was no mountain behind it. It reminded Scratch of a shelf of quartz from a quarry, or a slab of dough. The beginning of something, be it tiling or bread. She rose slowly, drawn to the thing, her hands reaching before she could stop them.

"Ah, ah." Brella grabbed her wrist. "Together."

"Everything all right?" Vel pulled James to his side. "We're all comfortable with traitors and traps?"

"When we get through," Scratch asked tentatively, "what will we find?"

"Frances, hopefully," Brella said, eyes on the gate. Wordlessly, she handed Scratch the knife she had dropped. "We'll have to figure it out from there."

Scratch fingered the hilt, slipping the blade into her silken sheath. "Okay."

"How do we . . ."

"Both hands." Brella's voice was steady and soothing. "Both hands on the gate and close your eyes."

They lined up, all four of them, palms flat on the stone. Scratch closed her eyes and lowered her head, and—

Chapter Twenty-Nine

The stars are bright as blazes here, and they've left the sky.

"Sweets," she tells you. "They're called *Sweets*." She blows gently and one lands on your face. "They're magic." They're blue and mesmerizing, little orbs of something pulsing and warm. And they're bright, bright, bright, making constellations in three dimensions, gods forming and re-forming. Gods are everywhere here; the air tastes of them.

"Eat this," she says. It's a foxfire fungus pulled from the ground, bioluminescent and powdery, depositing shimmering spores on your fingers, your clothes, your mouth and hers—and when you kiss, it's an explosion, like a hand on your wrist and your back at once, like you've never been held before.

"Kiss me," she demands, and you do, because there could be nothing better. She tastes like, well, like a mouth, but the best one. You tell her. She laughs at you in every color.

"There will be a door," she says, and she points somewhere. "When we're ready, there will be a door." You don't worry about it right now because you're not ready, because you haven't even slipped your small and sweet bodies into the water that flows here, lapping up on a grassy shore, kiss after kiss after kiss.

You can see her how she sees you, and it's startling.

"You're wrong," you tell her.

"About?" she asks, her moonlight mouth pouting and her hot ember eyes so open.

"Me," you say. "I can see it."

And you can. It's raw, red around the edges from newness, but eager and growing. She likes things about you, these wild things. You are small. You are careful sometimes, and bold others. You're clever. Too clever. Clever enough to know how much, how often, how deeply you've been wrong. You're brave. You're cocky. You're self-serving and a little narcissistic and she likes all of it. All of it. Not some, but all.

"I'm not wrong," she says. "You are."

"Remember," you ask, "when you gave me your knife?"

"Remember," she asks in return, "when I gave you my brother's pants?"

James is here, too, and so is Vel, but you can't feel them the way you can feel her. They can feel each other, though. They haven't said, but you can see it. Vel has barely stopped crying.

"I can't believe this is what it's like," he says, over and over, spitty and bursting. "I'm going to stitch this feeling into a cloak."

"You're a baby," James says, but it's allover fond and he's twinkling.

"Come here," she says, "sit by the water with me."

She holds your hand and leads you there and it's maddening, the feel of it. That you can feel her hand and you can feel your hand and you can feel your hand in her hand and you try not to think about it because you're worried if you do, you'll go entirely insane.

"Hush," she coos, touching your temple, and the madness is gone. "Look out there."

She points. You want to look at her finger, but you force your eyes beyond. You're on an island. On the other shore, there are hills. And on those hills, there are houses. Little houses like mushrooms, smokestacks rolling clouds like foam into the warm sky. You can see figures bobbing about, ducking into buildings and out, and things that fly, hovering and swooping.

"This is an island of transport," Brella says, "in and out. But we can't go to the rest of the place."

"The rest?"

"The place that's hidden." She draws her fingers up and down, doors and windows and walls. "Some fae live in the forest. Some live here."

"How big is it?" you ask, because it looks like it could go on forever.

"It's like time." She kisses your forehead and you go warm all over. "It doesn't work the same way for them as it does for us."

You consider this. You think of hills and hills, rising and falling, and of houses on them. And maybe, if the town is full up, another hill can grow from flat ground for one more fae, in one more house, with one more smokestack to let the heat from their hearth escape into the sky.

You're crying.

"Oh, you're crying," she says.

"I am not."

"I can feel you," she reminds you, and you're hot and cold thinking about how she knows the way you see her. How she's tall and broad and sturdy, like a tree. Like a home. How she knows the words of decrees like a song, decrees she claimed through slyness, so smart, so willing to bend a rule, or break one, because she's so confident in her rightness. Her goodness. How she's brave and hot-tempered and she defends all of her people. How you are maybe her people now, and, gods, how would it feel to have her stand for you? Safe, probably. Like a roof. And how she can't abide death, or violence, because justice is living, and it's for everyone.

"It's okay to cry," she says, and it's so simple, but you believe her. So you do. You cry and cry. And you hear Vel crying, too, and James saying, "My sweet giant, my brave seamstress," and that just makes you cry more.

Maybe you sleep, or maybe you don't need to. It could be the air refreshing you, or the water, or the Sweets, little blue dots of magic in the fabric of this place. This place you never want to leave because there's a settling in your skin here. There's a restfulness. But this is a transit place, and so soon it's calling you to move.

"A door," Brella says, and there it is. "Are you ready?"

"No," you say, because it's true and you can only be true here. A lie would shrivel up and die, a sickly thing. "What if what's next is painful? What if it's hard?"

"I'm here," she says. "And so are they."

James and Vel, and James is calmer than you've ever seen him, his jutting elbows and restless legs still and serene. You're in awe of him.

"Are you ready?" he asks, or she does, and finally you can say yes because you are, you are. Because, if nothing else, this place is something to fight for.

"Through the door now," she says. "Through the gate. One, two . . ."

Chapter Thirty

Leaving the Between was like waking from deep, dreaming sleep. Scratch couldn't remember for a few moments where she was meant to be. Her vision fuzzed, colors bleeding together in the dim light of whatever room she'd entered. Her limbs felt heavy, her body sluggish. She needed a glass of water or a good stretch. Probably both.

Instead, she got shouting.

"They're here. Hold them!"

Someone grabbed her wrists with strong, calloused fingers and wrenched her arms behind her back. Her mind didn't catch up with her body quickly enough for her to scream. Instead, she blinked her vision clear. She was in a plush sitting room with paneled walls and delicate settees. There were a few soldiers about. One tugged on a rope, presumably tolling a bell that would send more their way. The soldiers wore blue tunics and leather armor, their heads bare of helmets. Across their fronts, in a darker blue thread, was a crest in the shape of a flower.

"Koravia," Scratch mumbled through dry lips. "We're here."

There came a whistle, piercing and shrill. Scratch turned to find Brella with two fingers between her lips.

"Brella?" someone asked. The voice was distantly familiar. "Are you okay?"

"I need them to stop," Brella cried, her voice strained and creaking. "Get them to stop, Maisie."

"What do you mean?" The speaker came forward. She was a woman Scratch had seen only once before in a dream. "They're not detaining you, you balloon."

"Yes, I know. Let the guards go."

"Keyes and the other?" Maisie asked, scandalized. "No way in the infinite hells, Umbrella. Good job. You've done it. They're going to the dungeons."

"The other?" James wriggled in the grip of a Koravian soldier. "My name is Sergeant James Ursus. This is Scratch. I assume you're Maisie?"

"Keyes goes by Scratch? This is—no." Maisie shook her head as if to clear it. "Stop this, Brella. Anyway, it's not my call."

"It's mine," said a figure lurking in the corner.

Between this and her surprise appearance at Scratch's thinking bench back in Ivinscont, it appeared that Princess Frances made a regular habit of dramatic entrances from dark corners. Her jewel-studded tiara twinkled in the low firelight like hot coals. She wore a red frock, roughly the Ivinscontian crimson, and her piebald hair was swept up off of her neck in some sort of elegant fashion involving pins. Scratch had never seen the princess look like this before. Not like a princess at all really. Like a queen.

"Your Highness." Scratch attempted a small bow, though her arms were bound and a soldier breathed down her neck. "Our allegiance has shifted. Brella and I discussed—"

"Yes, please tell me what Umbrella told you." Frances held her shoulders stiffly. She seemed tight and uncomfortable, like she could use a few puffs of Roselap. "This was a secret mission after all."

"Your Highness." Brella bowed clumsily, unable to keep the tension from her voice. "Yes, I did tell the Sergeant Major of your plans. But circumstances changed. She and James—"

"Stop." Frances pressed a delicate finger to her temple. She was powdered and painted, so it was impossible to tell whether she flushed or paled, but her hand shook slightly. "This is a longer conversation than we can have like this. Umbrella, Vel, you will join Maisie and me in my parlor, and we will sort this all out. Until then, I have no choice but to put Keyes and Ursus in the dungeon." She turned to Scratch, wincing slightly. "I am sorry, Sergeant Major."

Scratch gave a bare smile. "It's all right."

"All right?" James squeaked. "We're here to fight for you!"

Frances rounded on him. "You're here as a gesture, Sergeant. You are my gift to the Koravian King, much akin to a bouquet of flowers or an artisan-crafted vase. You might be of use as a fighter for me, but until I make the decision to employ you in any way other than as a bargaining chip, your chief use is to be my vase." She narrowed her eyes. "And you will refer to me as Your Highness. Is that clear?"

"Y-yes, Your Highness," James replied meekly, his face going gray.

Brella came to stand beside Scratch. She vibrated with rage. "I won't allow it."

"Brella," Scratch implored in a low murmur. "It's all right. Really."

Brella flashed her with those eyes, burning hot and fierce. "She saved my life, Your Highness."

Scratch coughed. "It was rather the other way around, actually."

Brella made a throaty noise of impatience. "A bit of both then. But she's done me a great service, and I can't just stand here and let her get thrown in a dungeon."

"Oh, Brella." Maisie covered her face with her hands. "You stupid raccoon. Not this."

"Maisie," Vel warned. "Don't."

"You've slept with her, haven't you?" Maisie hissed. "You incompetent frog. You're all frothy about her being dangerous and, 'Oh, we need to get her out of Ivinscont before she does more harm,' and now you're, what, her lover? You absolute paperweight."

"I don't think you should be lecturing me on whether it's a good idea to share my bed with someone dangerous, you daft marigold!" Brella shouted. The room went silent.

"Brella." Scratch watched Brella pale as her words sunk in. "No."

Frances drew in a sharp breath, stiffening her shoulders and clenching her jaw. "Enough. Brella and Vel, you will be shown to a room where you will stay until I decide otherwise. Is that clear?"

"Yes, Your Highness," Vel put in quickly. Brella stood stock still, her lips pressed into a pale line. Scratch tried to feel for something in the blood bond, a little shard of that connection that opened their dreams, to push a good thought Brella's way. She didn't feel anything. She tried anyway. *I have this. Don't worry. Don't make this a bigger mess than it needs to be.*

Because it could be a mess. Brella wasn't a fighter. She didn't understand what could come of this meeting. The stakes, as Scratch could see them, were too high for anything other than calm, reasoned strategy. This wasn't about her. This wasn't even about Frances. Not really. This was about Ivinscont.

"Take Keyes and Ursus to the dungeons," Frances commanded.

Scratch went willingly, not even looking back at Brella's anguished cry.

Chapter Thirty-One

"Were I a poet," James mused from the floor of his cell, "I might have something to say on this."

Scratch huddled on her straw mattress and poked at the remnants of what could charitably be referred to as her dinner. "Soldiers aren't poets."

He gestured dramatically to the wet stone walls. "Do you see any soldiers about?"

Not as such, no. The guards who had thrown them into the dungeons hadn't stayed for longer than it took to lock the bars behind them. Aside from James, the only soul Scratch had encountered in their night and day of incarceration was a meek kitchen maid who shoved a dish of lukewarm gruel under the grates and skittered away before Scratch could properly thank her.

"I'd say something about journeys," he continued, unprompted. "About ending up where we started. Cycles, and all that."

"A bit on the nose, don't you think, darling?"

"Forgive me, Scratchalina. The conditions aren't ideal for art." He sprawled along the floor like a lazy, overbred cat. "Do you think she's going to keep us in here long?"

"Not much longer."

"What makes you so sure?"

She sighed, shoving her food away. "We've been here for a full day without interrogation. Any more and she'll look thoughtless, wasting any valuable intelligence we may have on vengeance. Any less, weak. She needs us hungry enough to talk, but not so hungry that we're delirious." She shrugged. "It's fairly obvious."

"Clever." He kicked a cell bar with an outstretched foot. It clanged dully in the echoey space. He hissed at the pain, and she politely kept from mocking him. "I'm surprised she didn't send your Brella down here with us."

Your Brella. Despite the chill—which James, irritatingly, seemed entirely immune to—the words warmed her.

It wouldn't do to dwell. "Frances loves Maisie, and, for all their fighting, Maisie loves Brella. They're sisters." She stared at the drippy ceiling, hoping nothing vile decided to off itself into her eyes. "Even if you royally pissed me off I wouldn't find joy in detaining any, uh, companion of yours."

"Companion?" He beamed. "You're so cute."

"Shut up."

"Never." He chewed on his lip. "Have you planned what you'll say to her?"

"Frances?"

"No, The God of Lizards. Yes, Frances."

She thought of her last night in the castle, smoking Rose-lap with a princess she barely knew. Frances was different here. Tighter. There was a tension around her eyes that was entirely new. It made her look older.

"I might have," she replied mildly. "I don't envy her."

"I do. I'd make a fantastic prince."

"Hush." She pushed herself onto her dirt-smudged forearms. Gods, she was filthy. "No, I mean, she's in a difficult position. And to go from her secure life to living in someone else's castle . . ." She shrugged. "It can't be comfortable."

"You used to eat apple cores out of trashcans and you pity an uncomfortable princess?" He *tsked* disparagingly. "You've gone soft."

"Perhaps." She ran a hand through her shorn hair. "And you as well."

"Me? I assure you, Scratch, I'm as hard as ever." He pursed his lips. "Well, perhaps not in this exact moment . . ."

"James?" she asked, doodling a mindless squiggle in the dust. "What do you want?"

"A bath."

"And then?"

"Vel."

"If you could take this seriously for a moment."

He rolled his eyes. "How am I meant to take this seriously if I don't know what you mean?"

"If you had a choice," she explained through her teeth, patience thinning. "If the next phase of your life was open to any possibility, what would you choose?"

He eyed her narrowly. "Why are you asking me this?"

"Call it idle curiosity."

"Nothing about you is idle."

"Then call it curiosity."

"I'm calling it off."

"Cute." She rose up to a seated position, dusting herself off. "Frances will speak to me. I will set my terms. Then, we will—"

"I'm sorry, your terms?"

She rolled her eyes. "Yes, James. Did you not think I had a plan?"

"Of course you have a plan, darling. I wouldn't expect any less. I just wonder whether you're in the position to dictate terms."

"Regardless." She waved him away. "If you could decide what tomorrow looked like, what would it be?"

He opened his mouth, then closed it again. It appeared he wasn't going for the cute, quippy answer. His forehead furrowed, his thick brows drawing down.

"You know, Scratch," he said after a long moment, "I only ever cared about being with you."

"Me?"

"No, Hester." He crossed his arms over his chest. "Yes, you, you—what did Maisie call Brella? You paperweight." He grinned. "I think Maisie and I will get along very well, don't you?"

She shuddered at the thought. "Too well."

"Anyway." He sobered. With his shoulders hunched and his head lowered he looked strangely nervous. "I didn't like my family. You know that well enough. They sent me away to the Academy and then you and I met and, well, that's all there is." He swallowed thickly. "You were my family. All I wanted was to be happy, and with you."

Her heart raced. "But, the archery . . ."

He tilted his head in acknowledgment. "Sure. I liked that, too. But, Scratch, I'm only good at that because my parents spent hundreds of crowns on instructors. The only thing that I was good at of my own accord was being your friend."

Her mouth was dry, all the moisture in her body apparently taking residence in her tear ducts. It was as though a little magic of the Between was wedged into the muscle of her heart. "You want to . . . be my friend?"

"Well, of course." He squared his shoulders, bracing for another baring admission. "But I only got good at warcraft to stay with you. So you wouldn't lose use of me."

"I would never," she cried. "It has nothing to do with 'use'—"

He held up a hand. "I know that now." He smiled crookedly at her. "You wouldn't be able to get rid of me if you tried. But now I have Vel, too." He scratched self-consciously at his elbow. "He actually asked me something similar. What would I want to do next? And I thought—all right, what am I good at? Shooting arrows. Loving you. Loving him." He blushed, cheek to hairline. Scratch's ribs squeezed. "Telling stories. I thought I might . . . write them down?" He turned away, preventing Scratch from catching more than a glimpse of the fervent, eager glint in his eyes. "We're plotting an insurrection, after all. It would be a shame if no one bothered to keep a written record."

"A historian?" Scratch felt her mouth drop open. "James,

that's a fantastic idea."

"I thought so." His blush deepened. "Maybe, if I learn the trade, I could work up to being her historian."

"Her? Wha—oh." Frances, of course. "Yes, I think you could."

"I'm sure there are historians that are better trained than I am," he babbled. "I shouldn't expect to be a royal historian just because the royal in question is my lover's sister's lover. Or my best friend's lover's sister's lover. Or—"

"James." She wished they had been put in the same cell so she could clap a hand over his mouth. "I think it's a brilliant idea. And who better? There are so many good arguments for it I don't know which one I'll lead with."

"Lead with?"

"When I talk to Frances." She spread her hands, gesturing to the absolute obvious. "You have just become one of my terms. Congratulations."

His eyes widened. "Scratch, don't jeopardize your plan with my little yen."

Little yen her ass. James rarely waited—and, even more rarely, worked—for the things he wanted. It was a symptom of his coddled upbringing to strive only for the things he could easily achieve. When he wanted objects, he spent money. When he wanted men, his currencies were his well-bred looks and crystal-cut wit. He shot arrows, and the arrows always found their targets. This was the first time Scratch had seen him want something so desperately that the wanting was very nearly fear.

"I know," she said in a near whisper. "I know how terrible it is to want something, Jamie. To hope. How it feels like nothing more than self-sabotage." She swallowed. "We haven't been able to desire things. Not really. We were told to fight, and we fought. And everything we wished for was within those lines, drawn by someone else. We desired the things we were told to desire. We valued what we were told mattered. Now we really get to choose." She smiled at him. "Let's."

He met her smile, then let his fall. "If we get the opportunity. We're in a dungeon, in case you've forgotten."

She snorted. "Please. When has a dungeon ever held the likes of us?"

As if on cue, heavy, clomping footsteps alerted them to the presence of a Koravian guard lumbering into the chamber. He approached wordlessly, peering down at Scratch over a full brown beard. In Ivinscont, beards were forbidden for members of the Kings Guard. If Frances took the throne, Scratch might advise her to let her Guard keep the beards. The effect of wild hair over a proper uniform was a touch terrifying.

"Keyes," he growled. "Ursus. You'll follow me."

Scratch heaved herself to standing, shooting James a triumphant smirk before blinking away spots of dizziness. She hadn't had a proper meal since leaving Nana's, and the hunger was starting to get to her. She found an uneasy balance as the guard opened their cells and led them out of the dungeons, Scratch and James following the hulking man like a pair of dazed ducklings.

For fifteen years, Scratch had heard tales of Koravia, those black horses and wild-eyed riders wielding potion-dipped spears, trampling innocent Ivinscontians underfoot. She had imagined that Koravia's castle would be somewhat akin to a dark manor on a hill, with green, smoky plumes from alchemical chambers off-gassing through turret-y chimneys, turning perpetual night starless. The sort of place that attracted stray lightning bolts and feral black cats, wizened witches prowling the halls with phials of poison clinking under their threadbare robes.

After everything else, Scratch should have expected to be wrong about this, too.

The Koravian castle looked like the Ivinscontian castle. Eerily so. Just as in Ivinscont, paintings lined the walls here, depicting scenes of military triumph. In them, Scratch could easily spot the Ivinscontians: bloody throngs of crimson fighters, teeth bared, weapons crude but efficient. There were axes and bludgeons alongside the broadswords and lances, poking through the churning metal and horseflesh that composed the undulating Ivinscontian force. The national crimson had looked so prim in Ivinscont's pictures. Here in Koravia, it was a split vein. No, a disembowelment, visceral and gushing, offal and debris spewing forth in a wet, violent wave.

The rugs in Koravia were similar, too. And the paneling, the brass, the busts, the heavy doors lining halls wide enough to ride a chariot through. The differences were scant, the most prominent being the color: blue instead of red. Calming but impersonal, like the still surface of a sleeping lake. And speaking of lakes: there were nature scenes here. Every third painting or tapestry was meadow instead of war, or valley instead of war, or even small idyllic village instead of war. These pieces looked newer than their bloody brethren, the colors more vibrant and with fewer spots bleached pale by sunlight.

Scratch was admiring a particularly pretty tapestry of a dog resting among blue flowers when the guard stopped abruptly to rap on a shut door.

"Ursus," he growled. "You're here."

James hesitated. "Where are you taking her?"

The guard didn't answer, instead narrowing his eyes and curving his impressive body, casting a shadow over James's slighter frame.

"Th-there, you said? Good show. I'll just . . ."

The door swung open. "James!" Vel cried, ducking out into the hallway. His steps stuttered to a halt when he reached the guard. "Oh."

"I'll go in, shall I?" James swallowed, pointing toward the room. "Sorry, Scratch."

There was movement from inside. "Scratch?"

And, oh, the voice made her ache. Its low, bassoon timbre lit by the hot coals of Brella's tight, restrained anger. And the hope in it, a simple, golden thread that tugged at Scratch's soft places. Maybe it was the blood bond. Maybe it was something else, something terrifying and needy. Scratch wanted to crawl inside the voice and sleep for a few days, wrapped in the overwhelming warmth of it.

"No, Brella." Vel gripped James by the arm and dragged him into the room, James mouthing apologies until the door closed with a rug-deadened thunk.

"Well." It took locking her knees and squeezing her fist to keep her from ripping open the door and flinging herself into Brella's arms like the weak-willed idiot she felt herself becoming. Instead, she tried on a smile for the implacable guard. "Where are we off to?"

"To see the princess," he muttered gruffly, striding down the hallway without waiting for a response. Scratch dashed after him, weary and bedraggled.

"Should I change?"

He didn't slow. "Into what?"

She folded her arms over her chest. "Fair point."

The princess waited only a few paces away in another shut room. Scratch felt herself panic, her mouth dry and heart speeding. She gulped. "Are you sure I shouldn't change into something—"

The guard knocked on the door, silencing her. It creaked open and a squire popped out, primly dressed in Koravian blue, his silver hair tied in a neat knot at the nape of his neck.

"If you'll follow me," he offered, his voice low and emotionless. And, knowing that fleeing would be entirely useless, Scratch did.

Chapter Thirty-Two

The squire offered a single hand.

"Uh . . ."

"It's a hand, not a weapon," he assured her archly.

She eyed it. "I'm not used to . . . y'know. Hands." She meant being treated like a lady, but he seemed to understand. He cocked an eyebrow.

"Very well. You may follow."

He led her to a small, plush settee. She plopped onto it, bouncing against the tightly packed firmness. The whole room was done in shades of green and pink, a near-sickly spread of pastels. Large-paned windows stretched almost the entire length of the far wall, opening onto an interior courtyard. Through the evening darkness, Scratch could make out what appeared to be the tops of large topiaries.

The squire knocked on a second door within the room. Then he turned back.

"She'll be in in a moment. I'll be just outside."

Scratch felt herself tense. There was something soothing about this fussy little man, and she didn't want to see him go. Gods, she was wrecked—a lifetime trusting no one and suddenly she was leaning on absolute strangers because they offered her a hand.

"Uh, very well."

His lips twitched, and he exited without a word. The room was silent once he left, the sort of silence that one could never come by in the echoey, drippy confines of a dungeon cell. This was silence dampened by pillows and rugs, soft and unnerving. In the space Scratch's thoughts were surprisingly loud.

"Sergeant Major Keyes."

She hopped to standing, her underfed brain swirling in protest. "Your Highness."

Frances took a seat opposite the settee, smoothing her skirts over her lap. Her gown today was a deep, rich purple, like the colors of Ivinscont and Koravia blended together. Her hair was tied back, the black and white of her locks striping down either side of her head. She wore a simple golden circlet, not quite a crown but also not *not* a crown, a rather smart choice for a country-less princess taking refuge in another regent's castle.

"Sit," the pricess said. Scratch obeyed. "I suppose you're not best pleased to see me." Frances wasn't looking directly at her, instead pointing her words somewhere over Scratch's head.

"And why would that be, Highness?"

"Because I threw you in the dungeons. We don't need to dance around it."

She shifted in her seat. "I don't blame you for that."

Frances snorted, then caught herself, raising a delicate hand to her mouth. "I did it. Who else is there to blame?"

"As I see it, you didn't have much choice."

Frances met her gaze, vibrant green eyes narrowed. "Don't try to flatter me, Sergeant Major. I haven't the time."

"I'm not." She attempted a small smile, but it felt false. She let it drop away. "I'm an asset to you as either a price or a fighter. If I'm a price, I'll be in the dungeons anyway. If I'm a fighter, you'd want to see whether my loyalty would survive a trip to the dungeons. Am I right?"

Frances nodded tightly. "Yes."

"Right. Meanwhile, you only had Brella's word for my changed allegiance. Maisie, I'm sure, told you a great deal about

Brella. You know Brella bribed someone in your castle to give her written decrees. You know that she gives information to Kyrians and Westerners about how their rights have been stripped by your father's regime. All of this means that, while Brella has a great affinity for justice, she has little time for the rule of law. She'll put her nation above everything, but she'll do whatever's necessary to do it. You can trust that her motives are good, but that you might not understand them. She respects you, but it's likely she respects her methods more." She paused, pressing her lips together, watching for any change in Frances's expression. There was none. "You also know that she and Maisie fight like two penned bulls, which can't help your image of who she is."

Frances smirked. "You're wrong about that. Maisie can fight with anyone. That's part of her charm."

Scratch was momentarily struck by how young Frances looked. Despite the worry lines and layered frock, she was just a kid. "Your Highness, if I may, what day is it?"

Frances' smirk faded away. "The first of Balladeers."

"So, tomorrow—"

"It's my birthday, yes." She smoothed her hair, though it was already perfectly in place. Her shoulders rose just a touch. "I'll be eighteen."

Scratch stepped away from that potentially dangerous path. "Right, well. You only had Brella's word that I had defected. That, and your impression of who I am."

"What do you suppose my impression of you is, Sergeant Major?"

"I'm the strategist who built the octagon."

"Don't flatter yourself." Frances rose to pour herself a cup of tea. She didn't offer any to Scratch. "You may be a strong soldier, but I doubt you're the only bright mind in the Ivinscontian Guard, despite Brella's warning of your dangerousness."

"Of course." She nodded in deferential acknowledgment. "I mean to say that I wouldn't fault you for thinking that I believed in your father's cause."

"You don't?" Frances retook her seat, delicately balancing the teacup in two manicured fingers. "You've made a great deal of conquest for a nonbeliever."

"The truth is, Highness, I didn't do it for any goal aside from my own advancement," she admitted, sitting in a truth that wouldn't have bothered her only a week before.

"Hardly better. If you're not hells-bent on invasion, you're cravenly fighting for your own personal glory. How does that make you trustworthy?"

"I'm not saying you ought to find me trustworthy." Frances froze at that, but Scratch went on. "Your name, Princess Frances of Ivinscont—"

"There are a few more names in there, but go on."

"Yes, Highness. Your name has always held meaning. You are the most recent in a long line of royals. I am not." Her palms began to sweat. She carefully laid her hands flat on her thighs. "I believed I was worth nothing. That I had to achieve something great to mean anything at all."

"And now?"

"Now." She looked away, then back again. "Now I'm not quite sure, but I'm beginning to think I hold some value outside of my accomplishments."

The princess took a perfectly executed sip of tea. "Where are you going with this, Keyes?"

"I'm telling you that I understand why you put me in the dungeon." She paused for a beat, then, "What I don't understand is why you didn't have anyone advising you to do so last night."

Frances set down her cup. It rattled, just slightly. "I had Maisie."

"Your lover." She spoke quickly, because Frances was beginning to redden. "She has no military experience."

"She is a member of an organization that has effectively undermined the Ivinscontian royal family," Frances replied tartly.

Her own family, but Scratch didn't press the point. "So is Brella, but she has a blind spot where strategy is concerned. Neither Shae has spent any time in the castle. They haven't dealt with the king or his advisors, nor do they know what it's like to go to war."

"And you do." Frances leaned back, her gaze assessing. "I stand by what I said, by the way."

Scratch knit her brows, thinking back over their conversation. "When do you mean, Your Highness?"

"In Ivinscont. When we smoked Roselap in that little alcove. Nice spot, by the way. I hadn't known it was there." She crossed her legs, resting the teacup on her delicate knee. "I knew a secret passage out of the dungeons, but I didn't know about a little strip of grass on my own palace grounds. It's odd what you miss when you don't know to look."

"I found it by accident," Scratch admitted.

"I found it by following you. You know, I presume, that my father was on track to make you Lady Commander."

Scratch braced herself for the pain that wrapped around that loss. It came, but it had dulled significantly, a bruise fading to yellow and green. "I do."

"You were the exception, and you might have changed the way he looks at people with backgrounds like yours. We'll never know, of course." She tapped her teacup. *Dink, dink, dink.* "I thought that if he could see you clearly, then maybe he could be led to clarity on the invasions."

"His priority was expansion. If he saw me as anything, it was a tool toward that end."

Frances gently nodded in acknowledgment. "You're right, of course. But he was blind to anything outside of his own stubborn views. I thought that seeing you was deviation. It wasn't. You had just made yourself the perfect, undeniable option. You fit yourself into his scheme."

There was no reason to be offended. Still, it prickled. "And what could he have seen if he knew to look?"

"That the annexations were putting Ivinscont in danger," she said fiercely. "Of course Koravia knew that he was taking countries. That my father was trying to make himself a stronger opponent if Koravia decided to attack again. The Koravian king also knew that he would have to attack before my father got too strong to defeat."

Scratch swallowed. "Oh."

"The king here is different. Instead of annexations, he's formed peace treaties with neighboring nations. If Koravia decided to attack Ivinscont, five other armies would join them."

"Well." Scratch pursed her lips, thinking. "Your father wasn't worried?"

"He thought that if he just got stronger—stronger, stronger, stronger—there would be nothing to worry about." Her eyes were narrowed, the lines beside them pronounced. She shook her head. "He's a fool."

"Yes," Scratch replied. "A fool with two new additions to his country. A fool who has a rather successful army at his back."

"Of course you'd know all about that." Frances eyed her, carefully tracking Scratch from pale head to scuffed boots. "And you think that, because you know how his army works, you should be my Lady Commander?"

"I'm not trying to be your Lady Commander."

Frances stilled. "You're not?"

"No," Scratch said. "I want to be your Hand."

It had come to her the night before while she watched Frances waffle over whether to lock her and James away. Frances needed more people, people with skills she didn't have. Not that she wasn't doing well on her own. Frances was formidable at seventeen and had already enacted a plan that threatened her very existence, let alone the fate of the people over whom she reigned. She had taken a leap, either recklessly or bravely or, most likely, a combination of the two. If nothing else, Scratch wanted to see that up close.

Frances was young. She had run without a real advisor and with no guarantee of success. Scratch might not have been in possession of that level of bravery, but neither did she have that degree of recklessness. She wasn't idealistic, not yearning for a just nation like the one Brella envisioned. Her mind wasn't built for conjuring a destination, it was built for carefully laying each plank on the bridge that would lead there. Frances wanted to build; Scratch was a builder.

The princess reached absently for her teacup. She held it in her hands. She sipped. "Go on."

"Strategy is of the utmost importance to you right now," she said, feeling the momentum in her voice, the stirring in her chest. "I'm a strategist."

"All right." Frances rose and began to walk around the room, tapping her fingers against the teacup. The purple hue of her dress was so jarringly rich against the frippery of the room. "Why else?"

"I've spent the past decade in the Ivinscontian palace. I know how it operates for the most part. I've had to be observant."

"And why is that?"

"Every social grace I have, I learned," she said, remembering the sensation of moldy apple cores slipping between her skinny fingers. "I don't know if you know this, but being an outsider as I am, eyes are always on me. If I fail, it was expected. If I succeed, I'm the exception. I have had to learn how the world operates because it does not operate for me."

"Interesting." Frances moved to the sideboard to refill her teacup. She paused. "Would you like some tea, Scratch?"

Hope unfurled a tentative petal in her chest. "Thank you."

"Of course. How do you take it?"

"Milk and one sugar, please."

"Perfectly proper indeed." Frances grinned while Scratch tried not to think too hard about the reality of a princess serving her tea. "Any other professional recommendations to share?"

She received the tea with a quiet nod of thanks. "I've changed a great deal since I left the palace."

Frances retook her seat. "Yes, I've seen your haircut."

She grinned self-consciously, scratching at the back of her neck. "I'm less afraid, too."

"I wasn't aware that the architect of the Western Wilds annexation was afraid of anything."

"Mostly, I was afraid of losing the life I had built. Then I lost it." She shrugged. "There's not much left to fear when the worst has already happened."

"Scratch."

"Yes, Highness?"

Frances bit her lip, worrying it between her teeth. "What would you have done? I mean, would you have sent you to the dungeons? How would you have gotten you out if you were me?"

"Hmm." She considered for a beat, then, "I would have thrown me in the dungeons, then fed me very little. I would have kept me in there longer: another day maybe. Not too long, but long enough that I was desperate. Pliable. I wouldn't give me soft treatment because then the Koravian king might think I'm soft. I don't know how he operates, or why he's chosen to side with you."

"I do." Frances grinned. It was rakish and sly, and reminded Scratch fiercely of Maisie. "Go on."

"I would have tested the waters with the king, figured out how he viewed the situation, and then acted accordingly. The most important thing is that alliance."

"I agree."

"Good. Then I would have spoken to Brella. If I'm as dangerous as she believes, I could have deceived her, convinced her that I was an ally when I had every intention of spying for your father."

Frances chuckled mirthlessly. "Brella wasn't talking to anyone last night. I doubt even I could have gotten information from her."

"Did you give her any incentive?"

She lifted a delicate shoulder. "I gave her nice quarters."

"Nice quarters she wasn't allowed to leave," Scratch said. "They could have been the royal gardens, and she still would have seen them as a prison."

"Fair. What incentive?"

Scratch arched an eyebrow. The right one, with the scar. "Me?"

Frances laughed, louder this time. "You're saying I should have traded my prisoner, my one and only bargaining chip, for an opinion on said asset from my partner's sister?"

"Of course not. I would have lied."

"Ah, yes." The princess appeared pleased by that.

"I would have said 'if you submit to questioning, we'll treat Scratch better.' Or 'your word could be what frees her.'"

"And if she didn't believe me?" Frances wrapped her hands around her teacup. "What then?"

Scratch waved her away. "I wouldn't have pressed. Then, I would have subjected Brella to the wizards. Me as well. Get a truth serum, or some kind of spell. Find out whether I'm lying, or if I figured out how to bewitch her. Make sure I'm not a spy for your father." She gripped her teacup. "I'm not, by the way."

Frances rolled her eyes, a wordless *yes, obviously*. "And then what would you have done?"

"I would have appointed me my Hand."

Frances let out a peal of laughter, full-bellied and surprisingly deep. "You are good, I will admit." She pursed her lips. "I'll give it some thought."

"Thank you."

"Is there anything else we need to discuss?"

"Yes." Scratch took a deep, bracing breath. "Gorn."

Frances's green eyes widened, then narrowed. "What of him?"

"How long have you been planning this with him?"

The contact inside the castle. It couldn't have been anyone except the violet-eyed wizard. There had been magic in Scratch's capture, a spooled fate ball pulling her away from the feast. No apprentice of Gorn's could have been responsible. They were too low of rank to have regular contact with Frances. And the most telling bit of intelligence? She liked him.

"How did you know?" Frances demanded. "Does Brella?"

Scratch shook her head. "I figured it out on my own. Don't worry, he's safe."

The princess's shoulders dropped fractionally.

"How long?" Scratch asked.

"Years." Frances bit her lip. "He practically raised me. My

father was always . . ." She froze. "Why am I telling you this?"

Scratch tried not to appear outwardly smug. "We get along. It's an asset if you choose to appoint me."

"So it is." Frances stood, a clear dismissal. "You're free to go to Vel and Brella's chambers." She paused, smoothing down her starched skirts. "I won't apologize for the dungeons. As you say, it might have been prudent to keep you in there longer."

"One more thing, Princess. If you don't mind."

Frances flopped back down, a little gracelessly. Scratch took the looseness as a good sign. "It's about James, isn't it?"

Once again, Scratch was startled by the princess's quick mind. "Yes, actually. He's a good storyteller, and very observant. I'd like him to be your historian."

She nodded. "Fine. Yes."

Scratch nearly laughed. "That easy?"

"Truthfully . . ." Frances's voice dropped low, less conspiratorial than chagrined. "I forgot I needed one."

Scratch let herself smile. "We're building a new country, Highness. Certainly that's worthy of recording."

"Too right." Frances tensed, her hands coming together in her lap. The ghost of a wince passed across her face. "I owe you an apology, Scratch."

"Oh, no—"

"Hush, your princess is speaking," she interrupted tartly, though with none of the threat those words could have held. "That night, when I found you on the bench. I knew what would happen to you. And I still got you high and told you that you'd never achieve your life's goals."

"Highness—"

"Please be quiet. I could still have you beheaded. Anyway, I've been thinking about why I said what I said. Yes, I believed that my father had contempt for your heritage and your sex. But why should I tell you? To torture you? To see what you'd do? To have you rage at me, so that I'd feel justified in ruining your life? To see confirmation that you were really the ruthless warmonger I believed you to be?" She shook her head and sighed. "If I were

220

to tell any of my father's commanders that they had been wrong about something, they'd be polite to my face—I'm a princess, after all—but they'd rage. None of them know how to be wrong. You know how to be wrong, Scratch. And how to listen to the people who might be right."

"Thank you?"

The princess nodded brusquely. "You're welcome. I'm not sure what I'll do with you, but your ability to adapt is a mark in your favor." The princess made to stand, then stopped. "Anything else we should discuss?"

"Not at this moment."

"Very well. You may go."

"Thank you, Highness." Scratch rose. Mercifully, her legs had regained a bit of strength, and she found she could stand without getting dizzy. Frances stood before her, a young princess with Scratch's entire future in her neat little hands. It struck her then that they had both gone on the same journey. Had Frances been enchanted by the magic of the Between? Had she seen into Maisie's dreams? Had Maisie trespassed in the dreams of a princess?

Questions for another day perhaps. Scratch nodded farewell and walked carefully to the door, not stumbling once.

"You're still a prisoner, Scratch," the princess called after her, a laugh in her voice. "But I'll send you all a nice dinner, all right?"

Chapter Thirty-Three

"Her Hand." Brella lay against the rug, languorously stretching her long limbs. "When you defect, sweetheart, you do defect hard."

She was whispering, trying not to disturb the heavily sleeping Vel and James. The lads had pleaded exhaustion after mowing through the food and wine Frances had sent up for a late supper. Knowing James, the early bedtime had likely been a ploy to claim the room's only bed before Scratch and Brella had the chance.

"I never claimed to be anything other than the best." Scratch grinned over her nearly empty goblet. "You oughtn't be surprised."

"Nothing you do surprises me anymore." Brella yawned, nearly spilling her wine. She wasn't wearing her apron for once, and it hung forlornly over the side of a nearby divan. Now, Scratch could see that the inscrutable embroidered plants were from the Between, mystical little shoots and saplings dotted with blue balls of magic. "What if she says no?"

"I really don't know." Scratch downed the last bit of wine, letting it splash over the rising doubt in her throat. *What if.* "Something else. And you?"

"Me?"

"What do you want?" Scratch murmured, reaching down to push an unruly hair behind Brella's ear. Brella tracked the movement with her head, depositing a kiss on Scratch's palm that lit her up like spirits.

"My preference would be your mouth, but the lads are here." Brella's breath ghosted warmth over Scratch's fingers, and she found herself caught between a laugh and a gasp. "Have you seen the bath chamber?"

In the dark, they tiptoed across the rugs, stifling giggles. The bath chamber hid behind a door cleverly disguised as a bit of wall. Brella pressed it open and darted into the darkness. Soon, the room began to emit a yellow-gold glow.

"Gas lamp," she explained, pulling Scratch inside. "The advancements this country has made are incredible."

When Scratch's eyes adjusted to the light, she found herself in a large room lined with shining square tiles. Some were painted with flourishes of blue and white, swoops and dots forming a pattern at the intersection of flora and fauna, reminding Scratch inexorably of the Between's magical plant life and dancing Sweets. Others depicted scenes, tiny bathers soaking in identically tiled tubs, the patterns repeated in meticulous miniature. Along one wall, underneath a line of small, flickering lamps, a mirror stretched, doubling the space. Opposite, a grand window let in the night sky.

Scratch blinked at her own reflection. She looked thin, the angles of her face sharper, the hollow of her clavicle deep and shadowed. Her eyelids were puffy, her under-eyes blue-gray and cobwebbed with capillaries. Her cheeks were pink and wine flushed, her stomach a little bloated from finally having a proper meal. There was a new timbre to her expression, too. Something strange. With a jolt, she realized that the little lines had disappeared from between her brows and beside her mouth. For the first time in years, Scratch saw her own face relax.

Despite the disconcerting weight loss—she had never had much spare heft to begin with, and was loath to give any up—she looked younger than she had in years.

Additionally, she was a mess. She had dressed so carefully in Ivinscont, always trying to appear exactly as a female guard ought: much like a man, without claiming to be one. Masculine trousers with a feminine cut. A jacket that squared her shoulders in a color that turned her blue eyes piercing. Reminders to the men above her that she was a woman, yes, but not quite. Nonthreatening. Not the same as the men, nor so very different. Palatable. Respectable. Unobjectionable.

As she stared at her wilted, filthy clothes it struck her how much each day of her professional life had been shaped around absolute bullshit.

She ran her hands through her short hair, enjoying the slip of the locks as they fell through her fingers.

"Mmm." Brella came up behind her, wrapping her arms around Scratch's waist. "I adore this haircut."

"Well, it is your handiwork, after all."

"I'm an artist, then." Brella kissed her cheek. "And you owe me three crowns for the cut."

Scratch couldn't help but blush as she watched the two of them in the mirror, the low light turning Brella's brown skin into oiled oak. Brella was so tall, strong and sturdy. Scratch shivered at her own smallness, the nigh-uncomfortable, yet inexplicably exciting idea of being delicate in her lover's sure hands. She had never seen herself that way before, never wanted to. And yet . . .

"You make me want things I don't understand," Scratch breathed, feeling herself begin to tremble. In her reflection, her cheeks reddened further, and she turned her eyes away.

Brella's small laugh was warm and wet on Scratch's throat. "I feel the same way. I never thought I'd be so desperate for a soldier, of all people, that I'd want to drop to my knees on a tiled floor and have my way with her."

"*Mph*," Scratch squeaked, shocked and embarrassed and delighted all at once. "So you've changed your mind on the King's Guard, then?"

"Absolutely not." When Scratch turned back to the mirror, Brella's reflection was serious, though a little smirk played at the seam of her full lips. "They can go to the infinite hells, the lot of them. The commanders especially." Brella put a hand up Scratch's shirt, warm and confident on her tensing belly. "I don't see any soldiers here."

"I could have asked her for that, you know," Scratch mumbled, distracted by the path of Brella's clever hand. "Frances. I could have told her I wanted a command."

"Yes." Brella sighed. Her hand stilled, to Scratch's great disappointment. "I want you to be you, Scratch. I want you to have everything you want. You didn't have much choice the first time around. Selfishly, I'm relieved you chose to try something different." She buried her face in Scratch's shoulder. "I know there will be fighting. More fighting, probably for a long while. At least, this time it's fighting for something."

"I thought I was fighting for something."

"I know, sweetheart. I know." Brella squeezed her around the middle. "My opinion on the Guard hasn't changed. But my opinion on the guards themselves . . ." Scratch felt her shrug. "I understand that it can be the best of few options. It was for you, at least. But can I say that the King's Guard isn't cruel, if what they perform is cruelty? I wonder how many of them would leave if they knew the destruction they've caused. I wonder how many know, and just don't care."

"I wonder if I ever would have left," Scratch whispered, "if not for you."

Brella didn't respond. She didn't need to. They both knew the answer.

"Do you think I'm . . . absurd?" Brella asked, her voice impossibly small.

Scratch spun around. "Why the hells would I think that?"

She shrugged. "I'm a revolutionary who can't stand bloodshed. I have lofty moral principles, and they all melt away as soon as I meet a beautiful, clever—"

"Hush." Scratch kissed her on the nose. The mouth. Her flickering eyelids, so delicate and so dear. "You care so much about life. Not just that your people live, but how they live. Of course you're squeamish. Or, rather, maybe you're not squeamish at all. Maybe the rest of us are callous."

Brella waited for a long moment. "Perhaps."

They stood that way for a while, Scratch supporting Brella's weight. She thought about how desperately she had wanted that command, that knighting. She had made her life smaller to provide room for it, and she had been left with nothing but empty space. Tendrils of shame twined around her feet, and she felt like collapsing, but Brella's arms were around her, keeping her upright. She wondered whether she deserved it.

"Oh." Brella's head popped up. "There's something I want to show you." She scampered across the room to a tub that sank into the floor. The tiles were a deeper color in the tub, more blue than white, framing a bronze drain at the base. Brella crouched by the tub, turning a few knobs this way and that. For a moment nothing happened. Then, water began to gush from a hidden spigot.

"It's hot," Brella breathed, entranced. "It's steam and pipes, and they can get hot water for bathing whenever they want. It's not even hot springs. It's man-made." She beamed, eyes flickering with joyous sparks. "And it's not just the royals. Or the rich. Scratch, everyone has hot water. Either in their home or at a public bath maintained by the king."

"Busy king."

"Oh, hush."

Mesmerized, Scratch watched steam curling from the rapidly filling tub. "Everyone?"

Brella nodded fervently. "Imagine, Scratch. Taxes used to make people's lives better, and not just, y'know, for funding feasts."

"Or paying my salary."

Brella snorted. "Oh, please. You'd give up a year's pay for an indoor bath."

"Probably." She hiked up her trousers and came to sit beside Brella, soaking her feet in the warm water. It was heavenly, and she couldn't help but groan. "Oh gods, this feels amazing."

"I told you."

"I don't want to be poor again, Brella," she said, the thought crashing down on her, chilling despite the bath's calming heat. Her hands tangled together in her lap. "If Frances decides to, I don't know, throw me back into the forest as a traitor. I don't want to be poor like I was."

"You won't be." Brella wedged her fingers into the nervous ball of Scratch's hands. "Or maybe you will be, I don't know. I'm not a seer." Scratch snorted. "It broke my heart, you know." Brella's voice dropped to a low murmur. "Seeing you so desperate and hungry. So young and alone."

She bristled. "Mm, lovely. Any more words to describe how pathetic I was? Scrawny? Abandoned? Pitiful?"

"Hush. No, Scratch. I mean . . . I wish I could take that little part of you, the part that's still that girl, and feed her up. Keep her warm, you know?"

Scratch curled over herself because this was too much. "That's not me. That's before. I wasn't Scratch."

"You dream about her, though."

For a moment, she couldn't speak. When she finally opened her mouth, her voice was faint and rasping. "Well, as you've seen."

"It's not embarrassing, I think, to still have a bit of her with you. She's the one who learned how to butcher meat, after all."

"Mm. My most useful skill."

"I don't think," Brella whispered, each word carefully placed, "that we can get rid of our past so completely. The most difficult bits of us are the hardest to shake. I think the best we can do is reckon with the pain."

"And what child lives inside you?" Scratch asked, wilting under the weight of being so completely seen, desperate to look elsewhere.

Brella leaned back on her hands, the muscles in her arms standing out. "Oh, an angry one. Who shouts at her lover in the forest when she knows that lover is scared and alone. Someone who wants a just world, but wouldn't know what to do with that

228

justice if she got it. Someone with too many siblings she resents and a code of ethics that gets in her way more than it doesn't. Someone who wants to start a revolution, but can't stomach the idea of bloodshed." She shrugged. "That sort of child."

"Wow." Scratch leaned against her shoulder. "Complicated kid."

"Oh, stuff it."

"What do you want, Brella?"

"Now?" She smiled, luxuriously slow, letting her eyes flicker shut. "A bath."

They stripped themselves silently and slid into the tub. Scratch was grateful she didn't get a good look at the pair of them naked in the mirror. She expected she'd spot a scrawny, childish shrimp, literally paling in comparison to Brella's broad, womanly shape. Perhaps once she'd had a few more meals and lifted a weight or two she could stomach it.

Brella moaned salaciously in the steaming water. "Untie my hair, please?"

Scratch obliged, gently prising the curls free. She liked this act nearly as much as kissing, having Brella's trust for this. Tending to her care. It felt important somehow. Precious.

All this time searching for meaning, and she could have just plucked it from Brella's hair.

"Can you imagine, Scratch," Brella said when she was through, "what it would mean for everyone to have hot water? Like, okay." Her hands flew out of the water, sending droplets into the air. "There's a cobbler who comes into my pub a lot. Carwell. He has terrible back pain from hunching over shoes all day. So he comes into the pub, and he drinks until he can't feel the pain. And all the while his wife is going out to the pump and bringing back buckets to boil for his bath. The bath helps," she explained.

"Sure."

"The thing is, though, she's spent so many years lugging buckets that she has back pain, so now they're both drinking." Brella made a clucking sound with her tongue. "And nobody gets a bath."

"Everyone should get a bath."

Brella smiled broadly, showing every one of her teeth. "The revolution demands free access to baths."

"Public baths!" Scratch cried. "Private baths!"

"Hot baths, cold baths!"

"Ice baths!"

Brella grimaced. "Ice baths?"

"You've never had military training." Scratch flexed a muscle in her arm, inviting Brella to touch. "The ice baths almost feel good after that."

"I'll take your word for it."

"Maybe I'll train you up," Scratch mused as Brella prodded her bicep with mild curiosity. "Not to kill. No bloodshed. But I'd love to see you throw a punch."

"Good thing I couldn't when we first met."

"You wouldn't have."

Brella ceased her poking. "No," she said quietly, words heavy in the echoing, tiled space. "I wouldn't have."

Scratch drew her close. "You're so good. You see a bath and you think of everyone else who needs one."

"You needed one the most." Brella wiped an invisible smudge off of Scratch's shoulder. "Really. You look as though you've been fucked on the forest floor."

A giddy laugh burst out of her chest. "What sort of tart would allow that?"

"An insatiable tart." Brella booped her on the nose with a wet finger. "But if we're talking of goodness, sweetheart, I have to say how much I admire yours."

"Excuse me?" Scratch drew back. "Have you forgotten the bit where everything I've done up to this point has been for my own personal benefit?"

"Of course not. It's only . . ." She wiped a bit of condensation from her heat-flushed face. "That's not entirely true, is it? You always thought about James."

"Okay, fine. He was the exception to my selfishness."

"Maybe not." Brella pursed her lips. "Maybe you didn't have anyone else to care about because nobody cared about you." Brella moved closer, slow as a lazy water snake. "But I think you're dying to care; you just never learned how. I think there's so much love inside you, Scratch, that once you feel safe enough to let it go, it'll come flying out."

Scratch made the split-second decision to completely submerge herself in the water. Underneath, the world was softer. Quieter. The burning in her cheeks could fade unobserved. The pounding of her heart could settle. When she reemerged, Brella was smirking, arms folded across her chest.

"Interesting exit strategy."

"I'm from the Tangled Lakes," Scratch said, wiping water from her eyes. "We're water people."

"Sure." Brella arched an eyebrow. "Why do you think I call you sweetheart?"

"I try not to dwell on your quirks, Umbrella. Saves time."

Brella splashed her. "It's because you're sweet, you ass."

Scratch hunched down, wondering what it said about her that she was more comfortable with "ass" than "sweet." "Nah."

"How about I get to tell you that you're sweet and you get to tell me that I'm brave?"

"How about we stop talking and we do that thing you suggested with mouths?"

"One thing first." Brella held up a hand, catching Scratch before she could flop into Brella's arms. "You asked me what I wanted."

"Oh." Scratch scooted back, eager to listen. "Yes."

Brella breathed deep. Held it. Let it out. "I want to advise her. Not on how to get Ivinscont back, but what to do with it when she does. Taxes. Roads. Food stores. Gas lamps. Hot baths." She gave a demonstrative little wriggle, causing a ripple of movement in the water. "I don't know what that's called."

"Advisor." Scratch's mouth went dry, thinking of the great possibility of this. *Yes*, she thought. *You're perfect*. "Maybe Minister of Coin, when she's on the throne. Or a new title. 'Minister of People.'"

"The People's Minister." Brella's mouth stretched in a dopey smile. "I wonder if there's a precedent. If someone could give me access to the library here, I'd be unstoppable."

"I don't doubt it." Scratch ran a pale finger over Brella's nose, her eyebrow, her lips touched by stray freckles. "And us?"

"Undecided."

"Brella," Scratch hissed as Brella tugged her down for a tight, clumsy embrace.

"I'll keep you, Scratch," Brella whispered, rich voice hushed in the yellowy gas lamp glow. "That's my plan."

Scratch flushed, heat prickling at her cheeks. "That sounds fine." Her breath hitched. "I like your plan." A thought found her like a dart. "Brella, what did I leave in the Between?"

Brella blinked slowly. "What?"

"*I leave of myself when I walk through the door.* What did I leave?"

"Oh, you didn't notice?" Brella indicated her pile of clothes, languishing on the bathroom floor. "Knife."

"Wha? Oh." She looked over. Her kitchen knife, along with its trousers-crafted sheath, was nowhere to be found. "I thought it would be more ephemeral. Like, I don't know . . . springtime?"

Brella snorted. "If you want to look for meaning in it, you may feel free."

"Nah." She stretched her arms over her head, feeling the satisfying click in her spine, then dropped them over Brella's shoulders. "I'm not a poet, after all."

Brella nuzzled into her side. "Don't sell yourself short."

Outside the window, the stars were familiar once more. There was The Barber with his celestial shears. The Rider atop his sparkling steed. The Cheesemonger slicing Soft Eddard with a knife of starlight. But now Scratch knew these gods weren't alone. There were more infinite formations in the scrambled suns of the forest. Inscrutable skies that revealed gods upon gods, glowing through hidden layers of inky night. There were more than she could imagine, and there would always be more.

"Never," she said, and melted into Brella's arms.

Acknowledgments

Walk Between Worlds taught me how to write. And while writing this book has been one of my greatest joys, it was also a long and lonely process, and I only made it through because of the love and support of my people. Thank you to Alessandra Amin, Nour El-Rayes, Justine Champine, Megan Detrie, and Kati Sherril for reading what was then known as "Scratch" at various stages of unfocused word vomit, and managing, despite the chaos, to provide me with wildly helpful notes. Thank you to Anna Burke for the edits, the pep talks, and steering me towards Bywater Books. Thank you to Jenn Alexander for showing me how to find a title. Thank you to Tuck Woodstock, Kathy Tu, and T Kira Mahealani Madden for your beautiful words. *Thank you, thank you, thank you all.*

My deepest appreciation to the fine folks at Bywater Books, especially to Salem West for the initial twelve-pages of notes, followed by the months of continuous support. Thanks to Stefani Deoul, who is terrifying and wonderful and was 100% correct in saying the three consecutive sex scenes needed to be cut. Thank you to Ann McMan for the beautiful cover. It has been an honor working with you all on this book.

Thank you to my family, especially Dad and Jolean, for assuming that this book would be good before you even read it.

And thank you, Kelsey, my wife, for making all of this possible. Thank you for cooking when I was too zonked after a day of writing to even think about food. Thank you for prioritizing getting me an office. Thank you for putting up the wallpaper and the shelves and for fixing the doorknob. Thank you for saying, "Go up and write, I'll handle everything else." Thank you for liking my book, even though I thought you hated it. Thank you for forgiving me when I told my family you hated it. None of this would have been possible without you.

About the Author

Samara Breger is a writer and performer from New York. In her previous life, she was an Emmy-nominated journalist, covering sexual and reproductive health. Now, she writes books about magic and feelings. She has a crush on every character.

Follow Samara here:

Twitter | @SamaraJBreger
Instagram | @yesjbreg

Bywater
BOOKS

At Bywater, we love good books by and about women, just like you do. And we're committed to bringing the best of contemporary literature to an expanding community of readers. Our editorial team is dedicated to finding and developing outstanding writers who create books you won't want to put down.

For more information about Bywater Books, our authors, and our titles, please visit our website.

www.bywaterbooks.com